"I should have stayed in Chicago."

"Wrong!" Katherine's closest friend in the world replied. "You needed a change, a new beginning. And you needed a job. In fact, you should've moved down here five years ago."

Katherine smiled and shook her head. She'd heard variations on the same refrain ever since Suzanne had returned to Texas. "Houston's your hometown, Suze, not mine. I may have needed a change of scene but I never should've let you talk me into this job. It's going to be a very long summer."

"I think you should thank me. I got you out of the cold, harsh north and introduced you to a new way of life."

"You introduced me to highways that go around in circles, unrelenting heat and—"

Suddenly an image of Nick Martinelli flashed through Katherine's mind. The confident, outspoken, all-American male who'd sat in the second row of her classroom.

Another difference, she couldn't help thinking. *The men grow too big in Texas.*

Dear Reader,

If you've ever wondered, the answer is YES! There *is* a piece of the author in every book she writes. In my story *True-Blue Texan*, it was easy for Katherine Kirby to get lost in Houston. I did the same myself—many times—five years ago when I moved to this city of superhighways with winged exit ramps leading to the skies.

In addition to learning a new city, Katherine also faces a new job. She faces it reluctantly. After all, could a college instructor used to teaching undergraduates really help a class of adults with myriad responsibilities—adults who are high school dropouts and now want their equivalency diplomas?

I was lucky enough to find employment in my own field of adult literacy. I still cry at every GED graduation when my thirty-, forty- and fifty-year-old students march down the aisle in their caps and gowns. As I wrote the book, I held my breath, wondering when Katherine's eyes would eventually mist over.

Another difference between Katherine and me was that I arrived in my new city with a complete family. Katherine has no family, no love in her life—until Nick Martinelli walks into her classroom....

I hope you enjoy watching as these two struggle to reach goals they've set for themselves—and learn the art of compromise along the way. And I hope you, dear reader, never take the joy of reading for granted.

Linda Barrett

P.S. I'd love to hear from you! Please feel free to write me at P.O. Box 741395, Houston, Texas 77274-1395, or visit my website at www.superauthors.com.

True-Blue Texan
Linda Barrett

HARLEQUIN®

TORONTO • NEW YORK • LONDON
AMSTERDAM • PARIS • SYDNEY • HAMBURG
STOCKHOLM • ATHENS • TOKYO • MILAN • MADRID
PRAGUE • WARSAW • BUDAPEST • AUCKLAND

ISBN 0-373-71001-1

TRUE-BLUE TEXAN

This edition published by arrangement with Harlequin Books S.A.

® and TM are trademarks of the publisher. Trademarks indicated with
® are registered in the United States Patent and Trademark Office, the
Canadian Trade Marks Office and in other countries.

Visit us at www.eHarlequin.com

Printed in U.S.A.

This one's for my mom, Blanche Cohen.
A woman who knows what's important in life
and who quietly teaches by example.
I hope I learned something.

And
To all the adult learners I've been privileged to know.
Who, with their dedication to hard work,
remind me why I became a teacher in the first place.

May all your dreams come true!

PROLOGUE

KATRIN KOWALSKI DARTED between the sliding glass doors of the emergency room, barely waiting to clear the metal edges, before accosting the first pair of scrubs she saw.

"The Kowalskis? Where are they? There was a car accident." She heard the fear in her voice, tasted it, and ignored it as she'd ignored the wind and snow on this frigid Chicago night.

"You're the daughter?"

Katrin nodded.

"Let's go, honey," said the female with the stethoscope. "You might get to see your mother. The doc's with her now."

What about her father? The thought flitted in and out of Katrin's brain, but she focused only on moving quickly through the corridors of the trauma area, past the cries, the moans, the odors of alcohol, ammonia and blood. She wrinkled her nose, shoved her uncombed hair under her knit hat and wished she was back at the dorm.

"Wait right here a moment, Ms. Kowalski," said the medic as she opened a door to a separate room off the main emergency ward. "I'll tell the doc you're here."

But Katrin almost stepped on the woman's heels as she followed her into the room...and then wished she'd taken a moment to prepare.

Tubes, wires, monitors, mechanical beeps measured the pulse of her mother's life. Helen Kowalski lay beneath a labyrinth of medical devices, almost unrecognizable, her face swollen with purple bruises, the bandage around her head stained with blood. But it was her stillness that clutched at Katrin's heart. Her mom was never still. Always bustling. Always doing. Always wanting to do for her daughter.

Katrin looked at the doctor who stood at her mother's bed. "What...what...?"

"Her injuries are very bad," he began. "Come outside where we can talk." He glanced at the assistant and then at the bed next to Helen Kowalski, a bed with a sheet drawn over the person who lay there. The assistant shook her head ever so slightly.

"What?" asked Katrin as she looked from one to the other. "What's going on?" Her breath hitched in her throat as understanding broke through. And she knew she'd never see her dad again. Never hear his booming, old-world-accented voice filled with pride for his beautiful daughter. As though no other man had ever fathered a child.

"It's Papa, isn't it?" she asked, reverting to the familiar title from her childhood.

The sympathy in the eyes of the medics answered her question. She took a deep breath and willed the pain aside. There wasn't time for it now. She walked to her mother and gently stroked her hand.

"She's in critical condition, Ms. Kowalski. Her injuries are massive. She's bleeding internally; her blood pressure's dropped. We've got an IV going with whole blood, antibiotics and nutrition, and we've made her more comfortable, but that's all we can do now. She won't survive an operation at this point.''

The doctor's words twirled inside Katrin's brain, medical mumbo jumbo that she understood only superficially. Healthy nineteen-year-olds didn't often think of death.

''Mama, Mama,'' she cooed, hoping her voice wouldn't crack. She rubbed Helen's arm over and over again. ''Wake up. It's Katrin.'' She twined her fingers with her mother's and willed her young strength into the older woman. ''Please, Mama, wake up.''

She felt an answering squeeze and turned at once to the doctor. ''She knows I'm here. She knows.''

''Maybe,'' he replied. ''She's in a light coma. Her head hit that windshield straight on.''

She didn't care what the doctor was implying. Her mother was a fighter and she'd get well. She would. Katrin started talking again, the same words over and over. ''It's Katrin. I'm here. Wake up.''

''Yes, yes,'' murmured Helen, opening her eyes. ''I waited for you, my Katrin.'' Her eyes closed again and she seemed to doze.

''Please, Mama...''

''Der's insurance money for you,'' she whispered. ''Enough for college and more. Sell the house. You'll get a little money. You don't come much anyway. I like dat you call me Mama again.''

Shame washed over Katrin. She felt the heat of it

climb from her neck to her face. Since junior high school, she'd been on a campaign to Americanize her Polish-born parents. Helen had become Mom. Papa had become Dad, even Daddy at times.

"You get better, Mama. I'll be with you."

The corner of her mother's mouth lifted, but her eyes remained closed. "You're my gutt girl, Katrin," she whispered. "No time for me. You finish school. Get married. An educated man. Education is every…thing. But also a good man. A man like your papa. Listen to your mama."

Katrin gripped her mother's hand. "Yes, Mama. I know. I'll do it." She would have agreed to anything by then to ease her mother's mind. She bent closer and heard Helen's words of love trickling and fading from her lips in the old language, until the beeping of the monitor changed into an unbroken whistle and there were no more words.

"I love you, too, Mama," she sobbed, unconsciously translating and replying.

But Helen couldn't hear her, and Katrin knew it.

She raised her head and stared wildly around the room. A white blur. Nothing was real. Her mouth opened and closed, but no words emerged. She reached…she stumbled to the other bed. Please. Please. Maybe it was someone else. Anyone except her strong, adoring papa. She lifted the sheet…and howled.

CHAPTER ONE

Ten years later...

THE ELEGANT BLONDE moved through the crowd with natural grace, like warm golden honey flowing from a jar. Smooth hip action and a gently rounded derriere, with a pair of legs that didn't quit. And that was just the back view.

A beautiful feast for a man's tired eyes.

The thought surprised him. Except for his sisters, women weren't part of his personal life anymore, not since his world had come to a screeching halt two years earlier. His stomach tightened at the memory.

Nick Martinelli took a deep breath and paced himself as he followed the blonde down the busy corridor of Houston Community College. He ignored the excited chatter, the ebb and flow of fellow students searching for their rooms on this first night of the summer session. He felt his mouth twist into a wry smile. Summer session be damned. It was his first time inside a school building in eighteen years, and he felt about as comfortable as a nonswimmer tossed into the deep end of a pool.

He saw the blonde pause and tip her head back, checking the numbers on the classrooms they passed.

Her profile lived up to the promise. Creamy complexion, short straight nose and light eyes—blue or perhaps green—framed by thick lashes. With her slim, straight posture and perfectly arranged features, she exuded class with a capital C. An uptown girl.

He checked his watch again and picked up speed. The woman had intrigued him for the moment, and he'd remember her face, but he couldn't afford to miss a minute of class time. Not if he finally wanted to earn his high-school diploma.

When he looked up, the blonde was gone, and he felt himself relax. Man, he was still raw. The old Nick would have gobbled her up in a minute, but now?— now he'd stick to running the family business and studying for his GED. He'd surprise his folks with that diploma. They'd waited long enough.

He'd figured it all out. With more than full-time job responsibilities during the day, and part-time classes in the evening, his life would be brimming with real challenges. Very complete. Very busy. Just the way he wanted it.

He found the right classroom, paused on the threshold and felt his steady heartbeat accelerate into a wild tarantella, before a reluctant smile spread across his face.

There she stood in front of the room, spine straight, looking like royalty with her hair swept up in some sophisticated style. A pale cool goddess. He nodded, took a seat at a worn narrow table in the middle of the second row and studied her again.

With her fingers laced tightly at her waist, the tips were turning white. A pulse throbbed in her neck, beating as rapidly as a hummingbird's wings. His thoughts raced until there wasn't a doubt in his mind. The goddess was scared to death.

He settled back in his faded green plastic chair and stretched his long legs out in front of him. Yes, sir. Returning to school was becoming more interesting with each passing minute.

"MY NAME IS KATHERINE KIRBY and I'll be your instructor for this review class for the GED exam. If you pass it, you'll have earned your high-school equivalency diploma, which will give you the same rights and privileges a traditional high-school graduate has."

Clutching a pencil in one hand, Katherine reached for the scratched wooden desk in front of her with the other and gripped hard. Then she gulped for air. Pathetic. She was pathetic. After four years of teaching at impressive Chicago schools, she was now falling apart in this community college with a bunch of dropouts. Never before had she felt this nervous on the job. Not on the first day of her first university assignment, not while being monitored by supervisors, not when being evaluated by students and not when teaching complex and challenging literature courses. So what had pushed her over the edge today?

She studied the group assembled in front of her. Seated three to a table, they were a diverse group of all ages, dress styles and ethnic backgrounds, and they hadn't been to school since who-knew-when. No wonder she was nervous. Teaching in this unfamiliar environment was a last resort, not what she'd wanted at all. But she'd needed a job and she'd taken it. And she'd certainly do her best for the class, but...but in her heart she knew she didn't belong here. She belonged working with eager learners at a university, fresh-faced and curious, energetic readers with bright minds.

Before her sat twenty-six tired-looking people whose minds had probably shut down for the day. They needed a teacher committed to a basic-skills education, described in school catalogs as educational development. Katherine's dreams focused on the challenge of higher education.

"Class starts promptly at four o'clock and ends at seven, four nights a week, Monday through Thursday. Three absences are allowed. There's a No Lateness policy."

A low murmur traveled through the room at her announcement.

"Sorry, Ms. Kirby. That won't work."

It was the dark-haired man in the second row, with the mahogany eyes and the jaw that spelled trouble. A pair of broad shoulders didn't help. Neither did his muscular chest. Not her type at all. She preferred the academic cut. Lean and learned.

"And you are?"

"Nick Martinelli. And I'm telling you straight out, Ms. Kirby, folks are going to be late sometimes. Almost all of us are coming from work."

"You should have made arrangements with your employer before now, Mr. Martinelli," she replied. "The class schedule was listed in the bulletin."

He chuckled in response, his eyes twinkling, his

rugged features relaxed as he answered her. "I *am* the employer, Ms. Kirby. Martinelli Construction. I put in more hours than any of my crews and I'll do my best to be here on time, but that's all I can promise."

"Me, too," said another student.

"It's hard, ma'am," said a third.

She had to establish the rules at the beginning or there would be constant confusion and no progress. Students didn't understand that a lecture couldn't be made up by reading the information in a book. They'd lose the opportunity to ask questions and explore ideas with others. In her classes, the only excuse for absence was illness.

"Today is June the first. We have just ten weeks to cover an enormous amount of material before you sit for your exam in August. My job is to get you through the curriculum successfully. Your job is to be here on time." She eyeballed each student for a full second before continuing to the next one. "Every minute counts, there's no time for makeup classes. If you miss class, you'll have to work with a classmate or struggle on your own. Do I make myself clear?"

One deep voice responded. "You've made yourself so clear, Ms. Kirby, I can see right through you."

Crack! Her pencil snapped. She looked down at the pieces in her hand, then at Nick Martinelli. His gaze fastened on her and she couldn't move, could barely breathe. Those gleaming, observant eyes seemed to prove his statement. For a moment she felt totally exposed. Then the corner of his mouth lifted, a slow smile emerged, and suddenly the spell was broken.

She turned swiftly and walked to the board on trembling legs. ''Shall we begin?''

In the next hour she focused only on her work, sharing her recent knowledge of GED-testing requirements. She outlined the format of the class on the white-erase board and distributed five dog-eared soft-covered books to each student, one for every subject on the exam. For the first time in years she'd be involved with science, math and social studies. She'd need to refresh her own algebra and geometry skills. High-school chemistry and physics would be an equal challenge, so she'd be only about one step ahead of her students.

She sighed. This class would be an even bigger disaster than she'd first thought. And she had only herself to blame.

''THANK HEAVENS,'' murmured Katherine at eight-thirty that evening as she turned into the driveway of her friend's apartment complex. Finally home after an hour's effort to find the place. Getting lost at night in a strange city might be understandable, but it was also unnerving. Possessing a sense of direction would have helped. She sighed in disgust. That particular gene seemed to be missing from her DNA.

Suzanne's high-rise condo was a beautifully sculpted building on lushly landscaped grounds, with a shaded outdoor track, walking paths, an artificial lake and an indoor spa. A grand lifestyle that Suzanne could well afford, not on her university salary but because of a hefty trust fund bequeathed by her grandparents. Katherine's safety net fell far short of her friend's.

She gratefully pulled her dependable Honda into a guest parking spot and shut off the ignition. She'd have to memorize Houston's highway system if she was going to live here. She walked into the elegant lobby and took the elevator up to the third floor.

"So how'd it go?" Suzanne Baxter stood on the apartment threshold, dark eyes twinkling, curiosity written on her face.

Katherine glared at her longtime friend with whom she had shared a dorm room, clothes and tragedy. They'd never discussed the last part—Katherine's rules. But the affection she had for Suzanne remained as steady as a drumbeat. Katherine walked past her now and tossed her heavy bookbag onto the foyer table without saying a word.

"That good, huh?" prodded Suzanne.

Katherine turned and met her friend's gaze. "I should have stayed in Chicago."

"Wrong!" said Suzanne. "You needed a change, a new beginning. The fact is, you needed a job. You had no chance of getting another university position without a doctorate, no matter how good you are with the students." She walked into the kitchen and took a lasagna out of the oven—the frozen kind—then tossed over her shoulder, "You should have moved down here five years ago when I did."

Katherine smiled and shook her head. She'd heard variations of the same refrain ever since Suzanne had returned to Texas. "Houston's your hometown, Suze, not mine. Maybe I did need a change of scene, but I never should have let you talk me into this job.''

Katherine joined Suzanne in the kitchen and reached into the cabinet for plates. ''I knew a community college would be different from a university, but I was supposed to have a full-time schedule of freshman English classes. Instead I wound up with the GED prep course at night and only one English comp course during the day.'' She paused and stared at a vacant spot on the wall. ''I'm disappointed, Suze, in the work and in the loss of income.''

In a flash, Suzanne was at her side. ''It's no one's fault, Kath. Sometimes not enough students enroll and classes are canceled.''

''Oh, I know that, but—''

''And don't worry about money,'' interrupted Suzanne. ''I'll write you any size check you need.''

But Katherine shook her head, smiling at her friend's generosity. ''I know you would, Suze, just like you've offered, maybe, fifty times in the last ten years. But my own nest egg is still intact. Not to worry.''

Suzanne threw her friend a measuring glance. ''The schedule is just for the summer,'' she encouraged. ''In the fall, you'll have lots of regular English classes, literature and composition, maybe day and night. I'm glad you didn't know about this change in advance, or you'd never have taken the job and you'd never have come down here.''

Suzanne knew her too well, thought Katherine as she grabbed her heavy bookbag from the hall table and brought it into the kitchen. She'd never have been brave enough to relocate without the absolute security of a good full-time position. She'd have continued her job search in Chicago and hoped for the best.

"It's going to be a very long summer," she said, pointing to her books, now sharing the table with the lasagna. "Inside those volumes are the secrets of ionic bonding and the Pythagorean theorem, as well as prosaic fractions, percentages and decimal problems." She put her hands on her hips. "Look at me, Suzanne. Do I look like a person who remembers the Periodic Table of Elements?"

Suzanne giggled as she'd done when they'd been eighteen, and suddenly all the years in between disappeared.

"You look," she said, "like you always do when you're thrown off balance. You're scared but you come up fighting. Always. You're a wonderful teacher. You'll review the material once and you'll remember it. In fact," Suzanne continued with a smug expression, "you'll thank me for arranging the job interview in the first place."

"Is that the same as saying, 'It's for your own good?' And would you please stop laughing?" But Katherine knew the edge was gone from her voice. Suzanne was good medicine. The dark-eyed, dark-haired ball of fire could exasperate her more than anyone else, but was the sister she'd never had. If exasperation was the price for a sister, Katherine would gladly pay it.

"You really *should* thank me." Suzanne smirked, as she transferred a portion of lasagna to each plate and sat down. "I got you out of the harsh, cold north and introduced you to a new way of life."

"You introduced me to highway loops that go in circles, Houston heat that's unrelenting and…"

"…the best margaritas this side of the Rio Grande."

Katherine grinned at her friend and took her seat at the table. "True enough." She raised her hands in defeat. "Okay. You win. I'll finish this summer session, but I'll also mail résumés to every four-year college and university in Texas, and then we'll see."

Suzanne's eyes twinkled. "You don't really mean that," she said. "El Paso is almost eight hundred miles away. You'd be as close to Los Angeles as you are to Houston."

Katherine gently slapped her own forehead. "I keep forgetting how big this place is. I guess I'll start with a three-hundred-mile radius."

"Wonderful," said Suzanne. "I was starting to get worried, Kath. You push yourself too hard. You don't have any fun. Which reminds me, whatever happened to what's-his-name from the university?"

"The John Donne wannabe?"

"Yeah."

"Oh, well, um…he wished me a lot of luck."

"What a dork! Forget him and stick with me. I'll introduce you to lots of great guys. Handsome guys, brainy guys and guys with tight buns."

Like Nick Martinelli. The thought flashed through Katherine's brain and she slammed her eyes shut. She wished she could shut down her mind, but his image remained etched there, every feature clearly limned.

Damn! She didn't need this. She didn't need more complications in her already confusing life.

She looked at Suzanne, noted the determined gleam in her friend's eye and knew that she had just become one of Suzanne's infamous projects. She groaned silently. Time to find her own apartment ASAP.

"At least get the priorities right, Suze. Brainy comes first."

But Suzanne continued as though Katherine hadn't spoken. "A job and a man. That's what you need, and not necessarily in that order. I'll do what I can."

Katherine rolled her eyes, then concentrated on her food.

"Jobwise, the truth is not pretty." Suzanne said. "Without a doctorate, you'll never get hired on the tenured track anywhere. That's why I took two years off and finished the damn thing. And now students at the University of Houston call me *Dr.* Baxter."

"Unfortunately, I can't do the same." Katherine knew her voice sounded crisp, a little defensive, even a little jealous. She'd give almost anything to be able to focus only on her dissertation and get that degree. "But I've made some progress. My course work is completed. All I have left is the dissertation."

"But that's the hardest part. It could take another two years."

"Or longer," Katherine said. "But I have to get the degree. If I could get an instructor's position at a good college and write my dissertation at the same time, I'd be set."

"Maybe. But what's your plan B?" asked Suzanne. "You know what they say about the best-laid plans, don't you?"

"I know what Robert Burns said about 'the best laid schemes o' mice an' men...'" replied Katherine with a smile.

"That's the one" said Suzanne. "They often go astray. I don't give a fig for the mice, but let's talk about the men."

"Do they go astray, too?" Katherine asked, trying to keep a straight face as she cleared the dishes from the table and repacked her books.

"My man had better not. Not if he wants to retain the manly equipment he's so proud of." Suzanne joked with the confidence of someone who knew she had nothing to worry about. David Carter was topsy-turvy in love with her and didn't hide it.

Suddenly Nick Martinelli's image flashed through Katherine's mind again. A confident, outspoken, all-American male, long-legged with tight buns. "The men grow too big in Texas," she murmured while recalling the dark-haired man she'd watched moving with surefooted grace through her classroom during the ten-minute break. By the end of the evening, he'd chatted with over half the class but not with her. Which was fine. After all, she was the instructor.

"Nah," replied Suzanne, rising from her chair and stretching her arms overhead. "They only think they're bigger and better than everyone else."

"No comment."

THIRTY MINUTES LATER, Katherine stood in front of the mirror in the guest bathroom brushing her hair.

Released from confinement, her thick mane fell past her shoulders and halfway down her back with barely a wave. Totally unchic. And after she wove it into one thick braid for the night, she'd look about twelve years old. Certainly not the image of a college professor!

She should just lop it all off. Be done with it. She'd lifted the scissors so many times in the past, but faint echoes of her papa's voice always stilled her hand.

"Can we make my Katrin beautiful today?" he'd ask every morning with a twinkle in his eye. "Is there a hope for it?" And he'd take the hairbrush and perform the morning ritual, fixing her long hair into a ponytail or braids, perfect for an eight-year-old.

She closed her eyes, put the brush in her lap and massaged her temples. Maybe now was the right time to cut it. A new look. She was twenty-nine years old, at a crossroads in her life. The path behind her hadn't been easy, and ahead of her...?

She looked into the mirror once more. Ahead of her lay enormous challenge and no guarantees. Her head started to pound. She'd lost two positions already for not having the right credentials, eclipsed by individuals with higher degrees than hers. Yes, she'd known it might happen, but she'd hoped to be lucky. Lucky enough to earn her doctorate and step into the tenured-faculty track in Chicago. But her luck had run out twice.

And here she was in Houston, clinging to a less-than-wonderful job. And when she finally earned her advanced degree? There'd be no guarantees even then.

So what? Impatiently, Katherine left the bathroom and started to pace the bedroom floor. Life had no guarantees. She loved working with college students, so the only course open was to charge ahead as planned. Her hands fisted at her side. Why was she doubting herself? She could certainly handle whatever the future held.

Images of her mom flashed through her mind, as clear now as they were years ago. Mama would be so proud of her educated daughter.

Katherine closed her eyes, and for a moment became young Katrin again. "Yes, Mama," she reaffirmed softly. "Education is everything. It won't be easy, but that doesn't matter. And if I have to teach this summer course to earn a living, so be it.

"Besides, I don't have a plan B."

NICK WHISTLED a lively tune under his breath as he parked his truck in the school lot and made his way to the classroom. He'd actually looked forward to returning on this second night. He grinned outright at the thought. "Nick Martinelli" and "student" had been mutually exclusive for the thirty-four years of his life.

But now he wanted to attend class, and the reason had little to do with keeping himself busy or with surprising his parents. Maybe the truth had been simmering for a while, but it had hit him squarely in the midsection last night when he returned to his empty apartment. He needed something more, something meaningful in his life. Not the obvious; not a woman. But a personal goal to aim for. Instantly, his old dream had teased him again, a dream that required a high-school diploma to become a reality.

He chuckled wryly. He'd come a long way—from a kid who'd hated school so much he'd repeatedly run away from home, to a man who was using it as a lifeline. Now he was more than willing to put up with classes. And not because of the intriguing woman who taught them, he thought as he increased his pace toward the classroom.

Nick crossed the threshold, looked at his instructor in front of the room and froze in his tracks.

"What the heck do you think you're doing?" he roared. He sprinted from the classroom doorway in time to prevent his glamorous teacher from tumbling headfirst to the floor from the desk she stood on. Heart racing, he held her for a moment, an extra moment, shocked at his enjoyment—the fragrance of her light perfume, the soft curves of a woman in his arms— and uneasy about it, before setting her gently on her feet.

"I wanted to hang this map of Houston," she replied as she shimmied out of his hold. "How was I to know this old desk was alive? But thank you." The picture of embarrassment, her voice shook and she avoided his eyes.

He glanced at the huge city map now tilted on an angle, and then at the legs of the desk. Too bad about the embarrassment. The woman had no sense. She could have been hurt, hurt badly.

"This desk is an unstable piece of junk," he explained in a tight voice. "Look at the legs. Two are off the ground, the other two have cracks in them a mile wide. A ten-year-old would have noticed.''

He watched, fascinated, as a light pink flush stole up her pale cheek. Her cool, northern colors seemed strange to him. Donna had been warm Sicilian, filled with fire and fun. His heart squeezed. What was he doing, yelling at this woman who meant nothing to him?

''Maybe a ten-year-old would've noticed, but I'm not ten years old.''

''I noticed.''

Now she blushed a deep, dusky rose, and he couldn't tear his gaze from her. She was such an easy target. He should be arrested for teasing her.

''What you should be noticing,'' she said tartly, ''is that class is about to start.''

He looked around at the others in the room. All three of them. He turned back to the dangling map.

''I think we can afford a few minutes' deferment while my new assistant and I fix your map. Hey, Jeremy,'' he called to a sloppily dressed teen. ''Ms. Kirby needs a little help up here.''

He chuckled as Jeremy shot out of the chair so hard it toppled over. The sixteen-year-old—a juvenile on probation who was living in a group home—had been moonstruck ever since he'd laid eyes on Katherine Kirby yesterday. Nick almost felt sorry for the kid and his raging hormones.

''Let's get this piece of cra...garbage out of the way, before you climb up on that solid, strong, four-legs-on-the-floor table and attach this impressive map to the wall.''

"No problem, Nick."

"Thanks, sport. Sometimes teachers just have to learn from their students." He winked at Katherine and had the pleasure of watching her laugh. And relax for a moment. And look so damn lovely, he wondered how it would feel to stroke her cheek. His fingers twitched and he refocused his eyes on Jeremy's progress.

"Ms. Kirby," said Jeremy, "I've never seen a street map this big. How'd you make it?"

"I enlarged it piece by piece with a photocopy machine," she told him. "I'm new to Houston, and need all the help I can get. But you'll see that *this map* is going to help everyone in the class, even folks who've lived here all their lives. Thanks for hanging it."

Jeremy blushed redder than the teacher. Nick's eyes narrowed. The kid was in love, or in lust. Painful, either way. "I think you can start class now, Teach," Nick said. "The seats are full, it's ten past four, and the world didn't come to an end."

"Stick with construction, Mr. Martinelli, where projects rarely come in on time. I'll stick to our schedule and produce a lot of graduates."

"I hope you do. Myself included."

"And one more thing…"

Nick raised his eyebrow in expectation.

"Don't call me Teach."

He grinned. "Katherine's a lovely name."

KATHERINE WAITED for Nick to take his seat, and then looked out at her class. Teaching such low achievers scared her. Some hadn't been to school in many years. Some had dropped out only last year. Each one had a unique history, and she had no real idea how to reach any of them or where to begin, but she had to try. The standard college lecture was out. But the map could be a tool.

"Fifteen percent of the GED exam is based on interpreting graphics such as maps, political cartoons, illustrations and charts. I've highlighted our campus on this map. I'd like each of you to find your street and highlight it. Then we'll work on using directions."

She stepped aside as students found and marked their own streets; then listened as they discovered new neighbors, and winced as the noise level escalated from the excited voices. No, these students were nothing like her old ones.

"How about you, Jeremy?" asked Katherine as she handed him a marker. "Can't forget about the fellow who hung the map."

The boy shook his head.

"Can't find it? I'll try to help. We'll all help."

"No."

"No?" she questioned.

"I...I...don't live near here. It's not on the map."

"But it's a map of the whole city, Jeremy."

His hands gripped the desktop. He glanced at the door, poised to bolt.

Now what? Katherine looked at the map, then back at the youngster. "Okay, let's say you had a cousin on West Alabama that you were visiting after school. How would you get there from here?"

She saw him visibly relax, loosen his grip on the

desktop and finally walk toward the map. He studied it for twenty seconds and then explained precisely how to get to the designated street.

"Excellent, Jeremy."

"Just one problem, sport."

Katherine twirled toward Nick. "There's no problem. He found it perfectly."

"It's a one-way street, and too far to walk to from here. So if you were driving, Jeremy, how would you get there?"

The boy looked from one to the other, but his gaze came to rest on Nick. His eyes sparkled, his face came alive. He stared at the map and rattled off two alternatives with a third possibility in case the second choice was blocked by construction.

Katherine shook her head. What was a sixteen-year-old boy, an obviously bright teenager, doing in this class for adults? And how about the women in the back? Fifty years old if they were a day. And why was a man like Nick here? Okay, he wasn't her type. But she couldn't fault his obvious intelligence. And why was he taking an interest in Jeremy?

Undercurrents swirled through the class. Stories. Twenty-six of them—each unique and yet each looking for the same ending. Suddenly she longed to know more about her students. Maybe she could assign autobiographies. An idea began to take hold. Maybe she could gather enough stories for a book. She felt a smile start. Maybe this was one way she could impress the academic community. The tips of her fingers tingled. Yes, she could execute such a project and do a darn good job with it. She'd get permission from the students, of course. She liked the whole concept. She liked it very much.

As long as she didn't get too involved with her subjects.

CHAPTER TWO

"CITY IN THE WOODS? On Lake Ave? Lady, you're so close, you could spit."

Katherine smiled wanly at the gas station operator and prayed he wouldn't demonstrate. With pencil clutched tightly in her fingers, she wrote his directions exactly. She was around the corner from her target.

Saturday morning had flown by and she still hadn't accomplished her mission. How hard could it be to find a decent apartment in a growing city that sprouted new construction all over town? Certainly harder than she'd thought. Or maybe her requirements were unreasonable.

Location: As close to the college as possible. Size: Large enough for everything to have a place including her scores of books and her computer. Price: The sticking point. Some of the nicer apartments were condos, but until she had a secure full-time position, she wouldn't consider investing. Too bad the affordable rental units were so small. Her bedroom at Suzanne's was as large as some entire apartments.

Katherine got behind the wheel again. Everywhere she went, she met other people also looking for new housing. A growing city fostered competition among home-hunters. Well, she couldn't afford to be too fussy. So what if all the apartments looked alike with their white paint and white carpeting? Cool in the southern heat for sure, but as sterile as a dentist's office. She shrugged. Compromise was old news.

Following her new directions, she left the busy shopping area and drove slowly around the corner. In a quarter mile, stores gave way to vacant land. Lake Avenue narrowed as it meandered along.

"Wow. Would you look at that," Katherine whispered as she tapped her brakes to feast on a hidden oasis. Along each side of the road palm trees marched one behind the other, sentinels to another world. On the left, small stands of live oak and pines provided shade near a pretty lake. A woman and child shared a sandwich on one of the several benches beneath the trees. Katherine felt the corners of her lips inch up into a smile. Lovely. Different. She craned her neck to the right, and her approval turned to excitement.

Small clusters of terraced apartments were scattered among mature trees. Built of rose-colored brick, the buildings were accented by gray wood, cast stone, and on the terraces black wrought iron. While the materials wove the common thread, the facades and rooflines were individual to each building. She followed the street around when she realized that the development continued...in fact, was still under construction. It was as large an acreage as some of the other places she'd seen, but so much more wonderfully presented.

She'd never be able to afford it.

Reversing direction, she pulled into the complex,

into a spot in front of the management office. Then she crossed her fingers for luck.

Thirty seconds later, she stared into the rugged face of Nick Martinelli and would have gladly rented an apartment in any other development she'd seen that day.

HE'D NEVER GET TIRED of watching her blush, and wondered if he was the cause or if she was just shy in general.

"Good morning, Katherine." What had happened to the formidable professor? With a thick ponytail hanging down her back and the wispy bangs on her forehead, she looked more like a Kathy than a Katherine. Did she have any idea how beautiful she was?

"Good morning." She coughed and half turned toward the door, looking ready to dash through it.

"Condo shopping?" he asked quickly.

She glanced back, then turned to face him, and just as in class, stood taller than her five and a half feet before she attacked. "Not today. But tell me, why isn't your name outside where people can see it?"

He was glad it wasn't or she never would have ventured inside. "Don't like surprises much, do you?" He felt himself start to smile. The day promised to get a lot more interesting. "Martinelli signs are displayed around the corner where the buildings are under construction. This section is finished and almost all sold."

"Then I won't waste your time," she retorted. "I'm in the market to rent." She flashed him a gen-

uine smile. "Sorry. No one told me these were condos. They look very beautiful from the road."

Not nearly as beautiful as her smile, not even close.
He shouldn't care about the uptight professor, but he
wanted to see more of those smiles. He looked at her
waiting patiently for his reply, and words flew unbid-
den from his lips.

"This is the prettiest place in Houston, built solid
as a rock. Not every unit has to be sold from the get-
go. We can work out a rental with option to buy if
you like what you see. Or," he added in a stage whisper, "you can spend the rest of the day in your car
getting lost...again and again."

Her lips twitched then. A giggle emerged. Then a
laugh, then a belly laugh, and she was holding her
sides as the laughter turned into whoops. "Oh my
God," she spluttered as a tear rolled down her cheek.
"Oh, my. How did you know? I've been getting lost
all morning."

He grinned hard, enjoying her honesty. For some
reason, he could read her as easily as he read the
Houston Chronicle. He must have absorbed every
clue she'd given about herself in school.

More tears streamed down her face as she collapsed
into a chair. She pointed at him with a shaky arm.
"And the map! My gigantic map. The one from class.
It's been with me the whole day on the front seat and
I still got lost."

Her visible beauty had captured his interest; her
laughter tugged at his heart. But only a small tug, he
reassured himself. There was something very appeal-
ing about a woman who could laugh at herself. As he

watched, she made no effort to control her giggles or the hiccups that followed. The proud sophisticate of the classroom who barely cracked a smile. How many facets of her would he discover if he stuck around? Tempting, very tempting, but... A frisson of fear ran through him. The water was getting deep, and he hadn't gone swimming in a long time. Shrugging slightly, he walked toward the door. Right now he'd stick to showing her what Martinelli Construction had to offer.

"MY DAD AND I BOUGHT the tract of land and preserved the best of the trees. Then we planted more. Treed lots for new construction are a rarity around town, but fortunately, with a ten-month growing season, these babies shoot up faster than a teenage boy."

Katherine watched Nick pause beside a crepe myrtle boasting dark pink flowers, and rub his hand along the trunk. A strong, capable hand. "I bet you planted these particular babies," she said.

"You'd win."

"And I bet you invested more heavily than normal in this parcel of land."

"Double bingo. But we'll get a hefty return on investment."

That remark squelched her eagerness. Even rent would be out of her league. She halted and turned toward him. "Nick, I know you're busy and I don't want to waste your time. I'll probably rent one of the little apartments I saw today."

He put his hands on his hips and shook his head from side to side. "You do that all the time."

All the time? He'd known her for less than a week, too brief a period to comment on her habits. She raised her eyes to his. "What are you talking about?"

"You worry and then make false assumptions. You worried about an exact start time in class. For what? Now you're worrying about the cost of rent before you've gotten the facts. Worrying is not going to change anything."

"I'm not a worrier. I'm a planner. I believe in establishing rules, in having a safety net, in being prepared."

He met her glance as he replied. "There is no safety net, Katherine. Golden rules are broken every day, and bad things happen to good people. As for the rest of the rules, well, they're meant to be broken. You're old enough to have learned that by now."

His warm gaze belied the intensity of his words, but held her immobile before he continued. "And as far as being prepared goes, you always seem prepared for the worst."

Too many truths to contend with at once. "Darn right I am," she finally retorted.

"It's no way to live."

"It's my way, Mr. Martinelli." If her voice was sharp, she didn't care. She owed him no explanations. She had good reason to be cautious, and if she wasn't as carefree and lighthearted as other people, so be it. "Now, shall we look at the apartment?" She walked forward again, but stopped when she realized she was alone. She looked back. Nick stood where they had spoken.

"I've upset you and I'm sorry," he said as he approached her. "That wasn't my intention."

The tough construction worker was apologizing? And doing it sincerely? She studied his face—forehead, eyes, mouth—and all she saw was regret. And concern. And warmth.

"Apology accepted," she whispered. No man's face had shown such careful regard for her since the first few months after her parents died. Every psychiatrist she'd dealt with then showed the same concern. So had her parents' friends and neighbors. And Father Brezinski had, too. But they'd known her all her life, or in the case of the physicians, learned about her whole life.

Nick Martinelli had known her for four days.

He extended his hand and she took it. "I'm sorry I've upset you," he repeated, "but my belief stands. The rules don't work."

A flash of pain crossed his face so quickly she almost missed it. Almost, but not quite. She recognized pain.

"Then we'll have to agree to disagree," she said softly.

"That'll do for now."

Silence descended for a moment. "Want to show me that apartment?" asked Katherine.

"It's the next building, right past that live oak. I'm glad I didn't scare you away."

She smiled and raised her chin. "I'm a lot tougher than that." And she was. She'd trained herself to be. No more tears at sad movies or real life tragedies in the newspaper. No more volunteering in soup kitchens or after-school centers as she had in college. She needed to survive, herself, not be dragged down.

"Uh-huh," replied Nick. "The professor looks real tough."

He seemed serious, his voice didn't quaver, so why did she get the feeling he was laughing at her?

She forgot about her doubts as soon as she walked into the second-floor apartment. Spaciousness. Everywhere. A combination living and dining area to the left with sliding glass doors to the terrace. On the right, an open study with built-in bookshelves from floor to ceiling, and—oh my God—a loft, an actual loft with a spiral staircase leading to it. She could live her life in this one room.

The walls were painted a toasted almond to blend with the oatmeal-colored carpet and the shaded off-white ceramic-tile floor in the kitchen area. She pictured floor plants strategically placed...

She spun around to her host. "It's wonderful, Nick. Really lovely. So warm and homey but so generous with space."

His eyes twinkled, and a slow grin meandered across his face. "That's exactly what we were trying to do. Look up. See the vaulted-ceiling design? There's where your space comes from."

She looked up then turned around. She walked the length and width of the rooms. They were comparable to other dimensions she'd seen.

"I can't believe the spaciousness is just an illusion."

"This is a second-floor unit. I was able to play with the blueprints, with the ceiling schematics. No big deal.'' He started looking uncomfortable. ''Want to see the rest of it?''

''Wait a minute. The ceiling schematics? Blueprints? Did you design all this, Nick?'' She was impressed. Anyone would have been.

''What do you think, Professor?'' His voice sharpened suddenly. ''Can a guy without a high-school education design a house or not?''

Confused by his attack, she stared into his dark eyes, hot eyes brimming with challenge. Yesterday, she would have said no. How could a high-school dropout do this kind of work? Not the labor, but the creation, the planning, the computations. Whoa!

''Don't sweat it, Katherine. It wasn't a test.''

She heard his normal good humor return. ''You didn't answer my question, Nick. Did you design it?''

His gaze drifted over her face for the longest few seconds in history. His expression gave nothing away. ''Nah. I just threw some ideas at our architect, and he ran with them. Are you ready to see the bedroom?''

She followed his lead now, but determined to continue their conversation in the future. ''I'm almost afraid to look at the rest. I'm going to love it too much.''

''You're at it again.''

This time she knew what he meant. ''We agreed to disagree. Remember?''

''Touché. Let's go.''

Of course, she loved it. She wanted it. And when Nick quoted a monthly rent in her range—the top end—she almost kissed him. Almost.

"It's too good to be true. I know what the others were charging…"

"Martinelli Construction is a family business. We take a fair profit and charge a fair price. That's our reputation." He crossed his arms in front of his chest. "End of discussion. The apartment's yours."

Pride. It stood out all over him. In his flashing eyes, the set of his mouth, the ghost of a smile. But she wasn't going to argue when he'd offered her the best of all possible choices. "Well, thank you. A six-month lease?"

"With option to buy."

"But I'm not sure I'll be here…"

"No strings, Katherine. Relax. You might learn to like this town and want to stay." His eyes twinkled now and his mouth curled into a smile. A warm, welcoming, dazzling smile.

And her heart jolted.

It must have been the heat. Katherine started the engine of her Honda and impatiently waited for the air-conditioning to cool her down. She still felt the effects of Nick's smile. A killer smile. Her response was totally out of character, a result of the heat and the excitement of a new home.

She'd written him a check and he'd seen the Chicago address. "But I'm staying with a friend here," she explained. When she gave him Suzanne's address, his eyebrows rose.

"River Oaks?" He emitted a long low whistle that spoke volumes. "Your friend must be a very accomplished woman."

Curious, she'd looked him full in the face. "And how did you know my friend was a woman?"

A mischievous glint entered his eyes. "If the questions on the GED exam are as easy as that one, I'll get the highest marks in the class." He paused and gently tapped her chin. "Your friend had to be female, because no sensible male would let you get away."

She'd stared, tongue-tied, unable to form a coherent response.

In the car, she thought back to that moment. If he was flirting, he'd done a damn fine job of it. If he was simply exuding inherent Southern charm, she could live without it. Whichever it was, the man had planted himself firmly in her mind.

Well she'd have to get him out of there. They might both be over twenty-one, but he was her student, for heaven's sake!

NICK SAT at the wheel of his long-bed pickup, on his way to Martinelli Construction's headquarters, eager to wrap up the week. Tonight he had a date with his books. When Katherine had left an hour ago, he'd informed the sales manager at the City in the Woods property about the rental agreement with her. His close-the-sale-oriented sister wasn't too happy. He grinned at the memory of Tina's reaction.

"Rented? You rented a unit that we could have sold outright in five more minutes? You must be ill." With a catlike spring, she'd jumped on a chair, raising her five-foot-nothing stature to a height where she could put her hand on his forehead and check for a fever.

"I'm fine, munchkin. Let it go. Katherine will be renting for six months, then we'll see."

"Katherine?" Her eyes narrowed then relaxed. "Katherine who? Nicky, did you meet someone?"

Nick swore he could smell the burn as Tina's brain cells went into overdrive. He could also hear the hope in her voice.

"Just a nice woman who needs somewhere to live for a little while. Let it go," he repeated.

In the truck, Nick shook his head. He'd made a tactical error. Tina the terrier could never let anything go. She'd be at him again later if he wasn't careful. He'd either have to play the heavy and shut her up or avoid her altogether.

Who was he kidding? He'd never hurt her intentionally, but sometimes it was tough having three sisters who loved him to the point of regularly sticking their noses where they didn't belong. No matter. He had set them straight in the past, and he'd do it again. With or without kid gloves. He'd developed a variety of techniques through the years.

He exited I-10 at Eldridge, drove a half mile and pulled into the Martinelli Construction parking lot, absently noting which cars were there. The place was almost never devoid of family and today was no exception. He loped up the three wide steps leading to the front of the marble and glass building.

They had built their own offices ten years ago when the city was coming out of a recession, then added a wing five years later when they purchased a large general-contracting firm whose childless owner wanted to retire. Now they operated both a commercial and a residential division. Excellent decisions to grow a business, and the family had never looked back.

The office was busy for a Saturday. He waved at the part-time receptionist in the spacious entry foyer, ignored the awards and letters of achievement displayed throughout the visitors' area and headed to his sister Josie's sanctuary down the center corridor. Josie sat at her usual place in front of the computer, handling the financial records. With big round eyes the color of rich chocolate and a wavy mane of blue-black hair reaching down her back, she seemed much too young to almost be a certified public accountant. But once she passed her final test, that's what she would be.

Nick couldn't wait for it to happen. He wanted her with the company full-time. Now she worked for one of the prestigious CPA firms in town, and the family was lucky to have her on weekends. He watched as she cradled her swollen belly and patted it lightly.

"Everything okay, sweetheart?" he asked as he hugged her gently. "Or is Junior giving you a hard time in there?"

She smiled up at him. "Junior is doing what he or she does best. Kicking Mother. So, now tell me, bro, who's Katherine?"

Which proved that telephones were faster than pickup trucks. "Don't push it, Josephina. And tell Christina Marie that she's too old to be such a motor mouth. Where's the big boss?"

"I'm looking right at him."

He sighed. This sweet, most softhearted gal was no pushover. "C'mon, Josephina. Where's Dad?"

She nodded toward their father's office, but as he began to walk toward it, Josie reached for his arm.

"Josephina? Christina Marie? Please don't be angry, Nicky. It's just that we...we want you to be happy again." A tear rolled down her cheek.

Damn. He'd forgotten how easily pregnant women cry. He sat on his heels and looked into her tear-stained face. "Hell, Josie, if you don't want your husband to murder your brother, you'd better stop crying now." He looked around as though he was frightened. "Is Mike watching, or can I live another day?"

She wiped her eyes and smiled, and his muscles relaxed one by one. He took her hand. This gentle sister deserved a little honesty. "It used to tear me up inside whenever Donna cried. I know Mike would feel the same way about you. So yell or scream or do anything else you want, but don't cry. Deal?"

Her smile wobbled, but she was a trooper. "Sure. But the problem is, Nicky, that we miss you. We miss the old you, we miss seeing you happy. All you do is work and sleep and have a meal with the family on Sunday."

"And that's enough."

She shook her head and patted her belly. "Deep inside, you know it's not. You've known the real thing."

She had him there. "And isn't that more than some people have? Chill out, Josie-girl. I'm doing the best I can." It would have to be enough.

He tugged her hair gently and walked toward his father's office located right next to his own. He prayed fervently that his mother wasn't in today. His sisters' phone lines could easily stretch to include their mom. He was in luck. His eyes rested only on his dad, leaning over some blueprints at the drafting table.

"I've been waiting for you, Nick," said the founder of the Martinelli Construction Company. "Come around here and look at these." He motioned to the thick stack of papers next to the prints.

"The specs came out?" Nick walked toward the older man, still sturdy and active at sixty-two, with a leonine head of salt-and-pepper hair. Enough to make a man vain, according to his mom.

"Yesterday. I signed them out myself as soon as they were available from the city's engineering department. No couriers, no messengers. Myself."

Nick met Joseph Martinelli's meaningful gaze. "Good. That means we have all the necessary materials to submit a reasonable bid."

"Yep. Now close the door and take a look. This is one big contract, and there's no reason why we can't have a real chance to win it. Three elementary schools and all going to one contractor."

"An unusual move," Nick replied.

"They're trying something new, to save time, I guess. The school population is growing fast, faster than the city anticipated." The lines around his father's eyes deepened as the older man looked at him in concern. "No wagging tongues this time, Nicky. It may be public knowledge that we picked up the specs and are interested in bidding, but only the family will work on this project. Design work, costs and material needs stay among us. Not even Sally should be involved. She may be a top-notch secretary, but she's not family."

"I agree, Tina, Josie and Mike, Joanna, you, me, and how about Danny?" asked Nick, referring to the youngest of his siblings. "Let's make him work for a living before he goes back to school." He grinned at his own joke—Danny had worked construction every summer of his life—but this time they'd need his quick brain as well as brawn.

His father returned an identical grin. "You bet. Danny's ready, and maybe Mama could help keep us organized, but your big sister's working part-time at the hospital, and with those three beautiful babies, Joanna's not available too much."

There should have been four babies in the family. The thought haunted for a moment, but Nick inhaled deeply and clapped his father on the shoulder. "Nothing will leak out this time, Dad. If we don't win the contract, it will be because another firm underbid us fair and square."

His mind raced back three years to another city project they had bid on. And lost by a hair to a competitor. It had been too close. Some parts of Martinelli's estimates were identical—down to the penny—to the winner's, but they couldn't prove anything, and couldn't imagine who in their organization would divulge figures. Their key employees had been with them for years.

"Since the deadline is September 15," Nick said,

''we'll need help with computing material needs. But that shouldn't breach security since none of our employees will have knowledge about the total project.''

''In this business, we're always on a deadline,'' said his father.

Katherine's words suddenly popped into Nick's head. Something about how in the construction industry, projects never came in on time. He'd like to teach that woman a thing or two about doing things right.

''...so we need to get started right away. I made you a copy of the specs to take home. Look them over tonight and we'll talk tomorrow.''

Nick shifted mental gears. History and science were on the agenda for tonight. Okay, he'd move science to the morning, follow that with the required writing sample and study the specs tonight after history. Math was his strong suit, ran in the family. As for literature, he didn't want to think about it.

He knew himself well enough to know that he'd have to set a schedule if he wanted to succeed. If only he could read books as quickly as he read blueprints. Ah, well. A guy couldn't have everything. Fortunately, he did read a lot faster now than he had in high school, when all the real trouble had begun.

''I'll be over after dinner.''

''After dinner?'' asked Joe. ''You want to worry your mama? She'll think you're sick and boom!— she'll go to your place to check on you. No good, Nicholas. You better eat with us.'' Curiosity kindled in Joe's eyes for a moment. ''Unless, maybe you have some special plans?''

And then there was the downside to a big family. Nick sighed in resignation. He was thirty-four years old, had lived on his own for years, had been a husband and a father, ran a thriving business with his dad, and still had no privacy.

Hell, he'd just have to power-read through all his material and show up for dinner. He wished himself luck.

"YOU GOT AN APARTMENT where?" shrieked Suzanne as she stood in the doorway of Katherine's bedroom. "That's one of the hottest properties in town. You can't afford it." Suzanne almost raced toward Katherine, forehead creased, lips thinned. "Katherine Kirby, tell me you didn't sell your mutual funds. Didn't we decide that was your untouchable money?"

Always in high gear, her friend resembled a mini-tornado, with a wind that could be felt five states over. Their different styles, one so animated and one so reserved, complemented each other, Katherine thought, and were critical to cementing a friendship.

"Relax. My little nest egg is still intact." She shook her head. "I can't imagine any circumstance that would tempt me to use that money."

"Then how'd you buy that condo?"

"I didn't. I'm renting."

That stopped the tornado in her tracks. "Renting? I don't get it," said Suzanne. "Come with me."

She led the way into the kitchen and reached for the newspaper still open on the table. She flipped the pages over until she found what she wanted. "Look at this spread in the real estate section. City in the

Woods. These units are selling for more than your nest egg, kiddo. It's prime property, convenient to everything and gorgeous besides. So how did you do it?''

Katherine leaned over the table and studied the ad. The depiction looked very much like the reality, and there was much more to come. When Nick said his company was developing the property, he wasn't joking. She hadn't noticed the pool club and playground. And he hadn't mentioned it.

''Well, Mr. Martinelli said they sometimes rent, so I did.''

''Martinelli? As in Nick Martinelli?''

''Hmm…yes. Why?''

''Because he's all business and doesn't give anything away.'' Suzanne held up her hand in a policeman's stop motion. ''Now don't get me wrong. He and his family are generous with charity. I've met him a few times at university fund-raisers because his sister, Josie, is active in the alumni association.'' Suzanne paced the floor now, impatience in every step. ''But when it comes to business, they're all business! So what's the catch? You didn't agree to pay thousands a month for rent, did you?''

''Of course I didn't. Nick's price was competitive with the other apartments I'd seen. But, Suzanne, none of them could compare. I guess I was at the right place at the right time.''

Suzanne stared at her blankly for a moment, and then started to grin. ''Nick Martinelli. Offering you a fair rent for a glamorous condo. Good work, Katherine. Well done! A real looker, rich and smart. And now one of the most eligible bachelors in Houston. Hardly dates though, and never the same woman twice. Just read the society column in the *Chronicle,* and you'll see his name from time to time.''

Nick? Society? Katherine wrinkled her nose. ''I don't think we're talking about the same person.''

''Sure we are.'' Suzanne's voice lowered. ''The paper ran a whole spread on him a couple of years ago when his wife and daughter were killed.''

''What did you say?'' Katherine gasped. ''Killed? How awful! He's too young to be a widower.'' The sharp image of a strong and agile Nick sprinting to her rescue in the classroom flashed through her mind.

''Awful doesn't begin to describe it. A drunk driver during the Christmas holidays. A head-on collision. Nobody walked away.''

Suddenly dizzy, Katherine fumbled for the back of the kitchen chair and collapsed into it. She smelled the blood and imagined the sound of impact. Hospital corridors swept through her mind's eye, one after another, as a decade disappeared and she was caught up in the aftermath of another horror. A snowy Chicago night. She'd eventually seen her parents' demolished car. No one had walked away from that collision either.

Her heart ached as she thought of Nick. Her high-energy student, always with a smile in class, had suffered excruciating loss. A wife. A child. And had managed to survive it somehow. She clutched her stomach and moaned with his pain.

''Suzanne to Katherine. Suzanne to Katherine. Come in, Katherine. Wake up.''

Suzanne's voice nagged at her, like a pesky mosquito. She turned her head slowly, feeling like a sleepwalker. "I'm okay, Suze," she said, one word carefully following the other. "I haven't zoned out like that in years." She inhaled deeply, recaptured her energy and patted her friend's hand. "Don't worry."

Suzanne's attempt to smile fell short, but her manner was as irrepressible as usual. "What? Me, worry? Not in my vocabulary."

"Good," Katherine replied. And she meant it. She felt strong again. She and Nick had both toughed it out. They were both survivors.

"So tell me more, Kath," continued Suzanne, obviously curious. "You walked into the management office and Nick Martinelli gives you this terrific deal? Out of the blue? Just like that?" She snapped her fingers for emphasis.

Suzanne's summary made Katherine squirm. A nagging doubt that she'd managed to smother earlier crystallized in her mind, but she answered her friend's question honestly. "Yes…sort of. Well, not exactly. I've met him before, Suzanne. I know him."

Katherine appreciated the incredulous expression on her friend's face.

"You've been in town less than two weeks. How can you know him?"

"He's a student in my GED class."

Never once in all the years she'd known her, had Katherine seen Suzanne at a loss for words. She did now.

"But, but…are you telling me that Nick Martinelli, the brains and power behind a successful and prominent business, never graduated from high school? I don't believe it.''

Now that she knew him better, Katherine could hardly believe it either. ''Maybe he had to drop out to help his family's business.''

''Not that family. His older sister's a nurse, Josie's an accountant, there's another sister I don't know about, but the young brother is premed at the University of Texas in Austin. No way his father made him drop out. Those parents believe in education.''

''Well, I don't know about his family, and it's none of my business. But while he's my student, he'll be treated like everyone else.''

Suzanne grinned. ''Good try, Kath, especially when he's not treating you like everyone else.'' A heartbeat passed. ''I, Suzanne of the glib tongue, am actually stunned. Your student's education, or lack of it, must be the best-kept secret in town.''

Startled at this revelation and at the plethora of feelings assaulting her, Katherine thought back to the meetings with her department chair before classes had begun. At no time had a secrecy issue been mentioned.

Now disbelief, wonder, fear and something unfamiliar—the need to protect—filled her. She straightened her spine and held Suzanne's eyes with her own. ''Then forget I said anything. Everyone deserves privacy, even those mentioned in society columns.''

Suzanne nodded slowly. ''You don't have to convince me. As a teenager, I shuddered every time 'successful businessman Thomas Baxter and socialite wife Wendy's' marital problems provided copy for the paper. Now that they have their 'arrangement,' I laugh.''

Laughter through tears, maybe, thought Katherine as she looked at the forced grin on her friend's face, but certainly not laughter with joy.

''I've learned something about secrets in my time,'' Suzanne continued. ''They can often take on a life of their own.''

Katherine's lips tightened. ''I don't like gossip,'' she said with a shiver. ''Not even harmless gossip. Nick's secret will be safe with me, and that's a promise.''

CHAPTER THREE

NICK ENTERED the classroom, waved at a few other early birds and took his now-regular seat in the second row. Somehow he'd managed to arrive early for the past two weeks. He couldn't afford to miss a minute of lecture, he told himself. His promptness had nothing to do with the attractive, interesting woman who taught the class.

And who was he kidding? He shook his head in disgust. Lying to himself had never been his practice and he wouldn't start now, even though her allure was coupled with the metallic taste of fear.

He took a deep breath...then exhaled. Okay. She was new to the city. Maybe she needed a friend. He could surely offer that much to a woman who needed to be shaken up a little, who needed to learn to break some rules. A simple friendship. Some Houston hospitality. Nothing dangerous in that, he told himself.

He glanced at his watch. Katherine hadn't arrived yet, but that was all right. He needed time to reread the poems she'd assigned yesterday. Right now, finding time was the key to his life.

He felt, rather than saw, his young buddy plop down in the next seat. "Hey, Jeremy," he said as he turned toward the youngster. "How's it—"

Stormy blue eyes met his inquiring gaze. A thrust jaw, clenched fists on the desk. An explosion waiting to happen. "You wanna know how it's going, Mr. Rich Builder? Well, it sucks, man. Everything sucks."

Eighteen years rolled away, and Nick could have been looking at a blond version of himself. The anger, the passion and the impotence of youth. The confusion and the need to break out of his own skin.

"So what are you going to do about it?"

The kid leaned forward. "Yeah. Like I could really stop my old man from drinking. He'd drink friggin' turpentine if that's all he could get. He's in the friggin' hospital right now, probably dying. The stupid son of a bi..." He choked and suddenly the blue eyes filled with tears.

Nick jumped to his feet. "Come on, Jeremy. Let's blow this class and figure out some stuff."

The silence hit him just then, right in the back of his brain before heat infused the back of his neck. The silence, the heat and the light fragrance that was Katherine's. Without turning, he knew she stood right behind him before she spoke in that calm teaching voice she had.

"I'm sorry you're upset, Jeremy, but if you leave the class, you'll lose three hours of test preparation. Now *you* may be able to afford that, but your friend here can't." She avoided Nick's eyes as she walked to the front of the room, but her words seemed to stop Jeremy in his tracks.

The little devil! Did Katherine know what she was

doing, or was this just her typical "follow the rules" approach to life?

His tears sucked back inside, Jeremy looked at Katherine's retreating back and then at Nick. He didn't say a word.

Nick helped him out. "There are times when real life is more important than school. Come on, I'll buy you a soda and we'll talk."

The boy was silent for a minute, his forehead creased in concentration as he stared at Nick. "How about if we talk during the break?"

Nick emitted a long, low whistle. "You should go into politics, Jeremy. Think about it. You've already mastered the art of compromise, so you're halfway there."

The boy almost smiled before he shrugged, a typical teenage shrug, and Nick breathed a little easier. Shrugging was familiar territory.

KATHERINE WALKED to the front of the room, wondering what she had interrupted but thankful that the two "men" seemed to be settling down. She bit her lip. Maybe she shouldn't have made that crack about Nick needing every minute of class time. In fact, no one could afford to miss class, but the words had just fallen out of her mouth. Well, she'd had to do something! Jeremy had looked ready to burst, and Katherine had no clue how to handle teenagers on a rampage. She shouldn't have to. She was here to teach, not get involved with personal problems.

It was two weeks into the term and time seemed to

be rushing by. Before she knew it, her students would be sitting for their exams.

She wanted all twenty-six of them to pass. Not only because it would reflect well on her but because *they* wanted it so much. And worked for it. Her eye fell on Dorothy, a forty-one-year-old African-American single mom who had told Katherine she wanted to set a good example for her teenage daughters. Yesterday, Dorothy had confided that her kids had taken over dinner preparation every night and waited for her to get home before eating. The happiness shining in the woman's eyes had made Katherine blink her own.

Then there were the three young Hispanic cousins, all working, but who wanted better jobs. They needed a high-school diploma to reach their goals. She smiled at Maria, Rosa and Elvia in their front-row-center seats. They sat taller and beamed back at her.

And then she looked at Jeremy again. Smart as a whip, but couldn't seem to focus on his work. Where were his parents? Why wasn't he in regular high school?

And Nick? What was the story behind his education, or lack of it? She couldn't figure him out at all.

There were more questions than answers, but individual profiles were starting to develop. Her fingers itched for her keyboard. She'd set up her computer immediately when she moved into her apartment this weekend, and then she'd plan the autobiographical writing assignment for her students. Maybe they could title the collection, *Changing Lives*.

She faced the class, leaned back against her desk and felt her pulse quicken. How would this class react to the poems she'd assigned them, those old high-school friends of hers whom she hadn't visited in so long?

"So why," she asked, as she made eye contact with each of the students, "did Richard Cory 'one calm summer night, go home and put a bullet through his head'?"

"That was weird, man, how the poem ended. I was surprised," responded Jorge.

"Obviously, he was depressed," said another.

"But he had nothing to be depressed about! He was rich, respected. Lot's of *dinero* in the bank," said Gloria, the bank teller.

"So what? The money didn't matter. He was sad. Why else do people commit suicide?"

"He shoulda taken Prozac."

Katherine joined in the laughter. "Comic relief is great, Rosa," she said, "but the only direct answer I've gotten so far is depression. Why should he be depressed? Doesn't he have everything? What does the poem say?"

"Well," said Dorothy, "it *infers* he's like royalty in that town. It says 'He glittered when he walked.'"

"He had everything. He was a fool," commented an impatient voice.

"You're wrong," said Nick. He spoke quietly and with conviction. "He didn't have everything. He had nothing. His work, his money—they were on the out-side. He killed himself because he was empty *inside,* so empty that he got lost, couldn't even find his soul. And Richard Cory, without his soul, couldn't find a reason to live, couldn't even find God."

No one spoke. Katherine looked at Nick, saw grief flare briefly in his eyes, and knew his eloquence came from painful experience. Her heart constricted. How could she have ever assumed this man was only a simple laborer?

"So," she said quietly, "the poet doesn't tell us why. We have to draw conclusions." She leaned forward into her students' space. "Why was he so empty inside? Had he lost all his money in the stock market? What could have been missing from Richard Cory's life?"

"Love."

"A family. A wife and children."

Bang! Jeremy's fists hit the desk and he rocketed to his feet. He glared at Katherine, at Nick, at the door. "The poem stinks, the guy's a jerk and my old man's an asshole, too. Don't these grown-ups know you're not supposed to kill yourself when you *do* have kids. *Adiós, amigos.* I'm outta here." He pivoted and dashed toward the exit.

With barely a second's delay, Katherine started after him, but was no match for a well-muscled six-footer with terrific reflexes. Nick waved her off. "I'll handle this. See you later." And he was gone.

She turned toward the class. "You've just witnessed, firsthand, the power of the written word." Her lips trembled as she spoke. "I must admit, it was an eye-opener for me, too."

HE THOUGHT he was in good shape, but racing after an agile teenager gave Nick second thoughts. Pride spurred him on as he vowed to visit the gym more often.

Anger lent him an extra dose of energy. Anger with himself for waiting too long to talk to Jeremy. Angry, hurting boys needed someone to listen immediately. He could testify to that.

They were almost neck and neck at the end of the empty corridor. Then Jeremy plunged through an exit door and flew across the lawn, veering left in the direction of the parking lot.

Nick gauged the angle and distance between them. The play called for an offensive tackle, but he had to intercept before the kid reached the concrete walkways and paved lot. A grass mattress held much more appeal than concrete. Head down, wings on his feet, he flew toward Jeremy and snagged him around the waist. The kid didn't have a prayer.

"Oof, ahh, let me go. You're crazy, man."

On the ground now, Nick wrapped his arms around the boy, not an easy task. Jeremy seemed to have as many limbs as an octopus, and fought with the determination of a cornered one. He fought dirty, but he wasn't a fighter. Didn't know any real moves, defensive or offensive. But that wasn't why Nick prevailed. He had to admit his weight and size carried the day. The kid's anger and frenzy would have easily stopped someone of his own stature.

"I'm not letting go, Jeremy, not until you're calm." The kid lay facedown in the grass, Nick's knee in the small of his back. And still he wiggled and surged like a hooked bass. His labored breathing resounded in the warm summer evening.

"You can keep on fighting me, or you can give it up," said Nick softly. "Your choice. But remember, I not only outweigh you, I can also outwait you. You're at the top of my agenda tonight. There's no competition." He paused a moment. "So, Jeremy, what's it going to be?"

The answer came two heartbeats later with the total relaxation of the youngster's body. Nick felt the boy's back muscles slacken under his knee. The wriggling stopped. Jeremy's head stilled and he turned it until his cheek rested in the grass. Gradually, his breathing returned to normal.

"Will you get your heavy-ass leg off me now?"

"As soon as I have your word you won't get up and run."

The boy grunted.

"Couldn't hear you," replied Nick mildly while maintaining his position.

"Yes, sir. I won't run."

So, the kid had some manners tucked away inside. Nick backed off, stood poised, and watched Jeremy get slowly to his feet. Watched him plant those feet wide apart, tilt his chin up and glare at him with suspicious eyes.

A female's gravelly voice invaded their arena. "I wondered how long you were going to eat dirt, Mr. Tucker. As for you, Mr. Martinelli, I see you still rush in where angels fear to go. And praise the Lord for that."

"Aw, shit," mumbled Jeremy under his breath.

The kid needed to clean up his mouth, thought Nick as he pivoted toward that familiar voice, a big grin on his face. "Estelle King! My favorite social worker! I'd ask how you are, but I see you're as beautiful and busy as ever." He embraced the older woman, affection for her filling his heart, a kaleidoscope of memories tumbling through his mind.

"As long as boys get themselves into trouble, I'll be busy."

Nick looked from the woman's brown eyes shining from her dark face, to the skinny kid who stood watching them both.

"I should've guessed," Nick said. "Jeremy is one of yours, huh?"

"Yep," she replied. "Same as you were."

Nick had kept his attention on the boy as he talked and noted his reaction to Estelle's statement immediately. Wide-eyed interest coupled with a smirk.

"So Mr. Perfect isn't so perfect after all," he said.

Nick locked eyes with the youngster. "I'm far from perfect, but I'm also not the one in a heap of trouble today."

Jeremy looked away, but Nick saw the misery on his face as he was jolted back to his reality.

"You tried to do me a favor today, Jeremy," Nick said in a quiet voice, "by staying in class because you thought that's where I needed to be."

"So? No big deal."

"But it was, son. Ms. Kirby's poem hit a nerve so tender, you jumped out of your skin. You wanted out of there."

"Damn right, but it wasn't her fault," Jeremy replied quickly.

Nick smiled. Personal pain hadn't wiped out Jeremy's crush. "True. But now I'm going to return the favor. The three of us—you, Miss Estelle and I—are going to sit at a table in the shade right back there," he said, nodding at the school's terrace, "and you'll be able to talk, or sit quietly, or ask questions.

"I'll listen and I'll answer your questions as honestly as I can. And maybe, when things get bad again—and they will—you'll know there are folks you can talk to besides the counselors at Richmond House."

Nick stood relaxed, arms dangling at his side, but met the boy's eyes squarely, this time feeling he was the catch on the fisherman's line, staring into the face of his determined captor.

Jeremy barely blinked. *Can I trust you?* he seemed to ask.

Try me.

Why?

Because I care about you.

You hardly know me.

Trust me because I've walked in your shoes. Because we are both human beings. Because Estelle can't do it alone. Because I need you.

The last thought almost knocked Nick to the ground. *Why did I stop volunteering with the boys at Richmond House after Donna and my little sugarplum were gone? I related well to the kids, and they respected me. I should have kept it up.*

"Okay, man. Let's go."

Nick snapped back to the present. "My friends call me Nick."

The kid's cocky grin said it all. And Nick realized

that although the timing was bad—couldn't have been worse for him with all the other demands in his life—a promise had been made. A promise he would never break.

CLASS WAS OVER and neither Nick nor Jeremy had returned. In her four years of teaching, she'd never run into anything like this. She wasn't qualified to be a psychologist or handle behavioral problems.

She stood behind her desk, gathering her books, markers and the other ever-present paraphernalia teachers seemed to accumulate, crammed them into her too-small tote and hoped that Dr. Goldman would be in her office. It was time for her department chair to clarify the rules.

She grabbed her purse and bag then stepped around her desk, prepared to leave. Until she looked up.

Nick lounged in the doorway, one muscular shoulder leaning against the frame, arms crossed casually in front of him. A man comfortable in his own body. His own sexy body. Strength emanated from him. She saw it in his quiet stance, his confidence, as he stood quietly waiting for her.

The usual lock of hair curled down his forehead, and Katherine couldn't suppress a grin at its persistence. Her eyes met his twinkling ones and locked. With pulse points throbbing, a curious shiver ran deeply through her and heat rose up her body until her cheeks burned.

A knowing smile inched across Nick's face, and Katherine blushed harder. Darn her fair skin! Weren't there lessons she could take to control the blushing? She took a deep breath, then a second.

"You, ah, scared me, Nick. I didn't hear you return."

"I know," he replied, satisfaction in his voice. "I *could* say you were so focused on what you were doing, I didn't want to disturb you. But the truth is, I enjoyed watching you work. Did you know the tip of your tongue sticks out when you're concentrating?"

She did, as a matter of fact.

"And that you wrinkle your nose sometimes, too?"

He didn't seem to expect an answer to either question, so she said nothing.

Nick straightened up from the door frame and started walking toward her. Twinkling brown eyes, sexy smile and all.

She wanted to back up, to run...and she wanted to stay planted at the same time. She gripped the edge of the desk behind her and waited for sanity to return.

What was wrong with her? Katherine Kirby did not fool around with students. Katherine Kirby did not fool around, period. She had serious relationships. Make that one serious relationship. And she'd never before had to tighten her thigh muscles to control the unexpected throbbing she was experiencing right then. She needed time to think about this!

Nick halted a foot in front of her. "Have dinner with me, Katherine..."

Hmm...maybe Suzanne was right, and for some reason, Nick was treating her differently.

"...and I'll fill you in on Jeremy's situation."

Her imagination had gone into overdrive. Seemed his interest rested on the boy. But Jeremy's name refocused her thoughts, reminded her of her prior intent. She sidestepped away from the desk, away from Nick, and started to pace.

"I'm uncomfortable about Jeremy. I was on my way to discuss him with Dr. Goldman before I allow him to continue the class."

His twinkle disappeared, but Nick's manner remained calm. "You're not thinking about dropping him?"

"I'm a teacher, Nick. I'm supposed to impart knowledge into the minds of students. I have twenty-five other students that need attention, including you. You can't keep leaving class whenever Jeremy needs you, and the others can't be distracted with excess emotion in the room. It doesn't belong here. I'm sorry, Nick, but I think he needs more than I can give him. He's got more problems than just needing a GED."

Nick walked toward her, put his hands on her shoulders and turned her until she faced him. She had to look up, a good way up to meet his gaze.

"It's not all on you, Katherine. He lives in a place now where he works with counselors every day. He and the other boys who live in Richmond House are on probation and get lots of counseling."

She startled. "Probation? For God's sake, Nick, he'll need counseling forever. And besides, they don't seem to be doing a great job. At least not recently."

"They told him yesterday evening that his father—an alcoholic—is dying from liver failure in the county hospital. This morning they took him to visit. Can you blame the boy for being a mess today?''

Katherine sank into one of the student's chairs. ''There's obviously no mother?''

Nick shook his head then crouched in front of her. ''Died when Jeremy was born. His social worker, Estelle King, filled me in. Want to hear more?''

She nodded.

''His measured IQ is over 140 and he has a crush on you that's higher than that.''

She threw her hands in the air. ''And that's supposed to make me happy? No wonder he's offered to carry my books to the parking lot every night this week.''

Nick chuckled without humor. ''It also explains why his attitude toward me alternates between hot and cold. He sometimes hangs on to my every word, but then he thinks I'm his competition.''

''Oh, Lord,'' she replied. ''What a situation.''

Nick nodded. ''Regardless, he needs his high-school diploma, Katherine, a worthy goal on his way to becoming a man. A man, when he was never a boy. I think there's something wrong with that. Don't you?''

Of course there was, but she couldn't take on everyone's problems. She'd worked hard to stay whole and happy. Ten long years of effort. Of being strong. If she weakened, she'd get sucked right back into a vortex of pain.

''We all have skeletons, Nick. I walked his walk, too, some years ago. And I toughed it out. Yes, I had counseling. With professionals. Just like him. But I didn't bring it to class with me. I went to class, concentrated on my work, and I was able to overcome.'' Her heart lurched, but her voice held strong. She would not get involved!

"Lucky for you, your instructor didn't assign *Richard Cory* on your most vulnerable day. You weren't blindsided by pithy language striking your heart when your heart was already bleeding.''

Gotcha. She bowed her head and felt tears gather. Totally out of character. She shielded her eyes from him because in a minute she'd be sobbing. Not allowed. She'd outlawed crying long ago.

"Please, Nick,'' she whispered hoarsely, "just go away and leave me alone.''

She felt her fingers being taken, then her palms caressed and held. His hands were sure and strong. And gentle. She wasn't alone, and she was glad. She almost squeezed his fingers in return.

"I'm sorry, Katherine, for shaking you up,'' said Nick.

She shook her head. "I'm fine.''

"And I'm a ballet dancer.''

The corners of her lips twitched at the image.

"You won't be alone, Katherine, working with the boy. You'll be part of Team Jeremy, and I'll be with you every step of the way…and then some.''

"Even though Jeremy resents you half the time?''

"Of course,'' Nick replied. "I'd resent me, too, if I were him. He's a normal adolescent male feeling his oats, and he's got his eye on you. It won't last forever, only until a pretty girl his own age smiles at him.''

Katherine felt a tear run down her face. "I hope

you're right,'' she replied, ''but I need to think about all this before I make a decision about Jeremy.''

''Don't take too long.''

HE'D THOUGHT his own heart would break when he'd seen that solitary tear. Katherine was a proud woman. Proud in her posture, professionalism and intellect. She wore them like protective armor, but he didn't understand why. Why did she hide? And why did he care?

He carried her bookbag as they walked in the warm evening air toward the parking lot. They walked in silence until they reached her car.

She turned toward him then. ''Okay. Maybe you're right. I won't talk to Dr. Goldman about removing Jeremy from class yet. Are you happy now?''

Her eyes glowed blue fire, and like a firecracker, energy sparked from every inch of her. Magnificent. She might have been upset, but she was so alive!

There was only one answer he could possibly give her. Something he'd been fighting since the first night he saw her standing so bravely in front of the class. He put the bookbag on the car, caressed her cheek and tilted her face toward him.

He leaned in for a taste.

KATHERINE DIDN'T SEE IT coming, had no warning at all, until his lips were on hers and she was in his arms, enjoying every second of the experience. A new experience, like nothing she'd ever felt before. But Nick was like no man she'd ever known before, either.

His tongue traced her lips. Teased them. Gently,

encouragingly. She closed her eyes and allowed herself to feel. And when he invaded her mouth, those shivers she'd experienced earlier returned tenfold. Her pulses throbbed everywhere. Her head started to spin, and she sank into his embrace.

All this from one little kiss? Breathless, she pushed at Nick's chest, glad to note that when he stood straight again, he looked almost as unfocused as she felt.

She watched him inhale deeply, watched his blue shirt expand along with that broad chest.

"Yes," he exhaled. "In answer to your question, I'm happy. And it has almost nothing to do with Jeremy."

Truth shone in his eyes, a smile lightened his face. A strong, handsome face, full of character. He must have dozens of women falling at his feet all the time. But not her, she vowed as she tried to pull herself together. She wasn't the falling type. And he wasn't her type. Despite the kiss. Despite her reaction. She'd bring this all to an end right now.

"Nick," she began, "I'm not looking—"

"Hush," he interrupted, placing a gentle finger on her still sensitive lips. "I know you're going to come up with a load of reasons why we should forget this happened. I can see every expression on your beautiful face even in the fading light. My answer this time is no. No, I'm not going to forget. You can try, of course, but Katherine, I don't think you're going to forget, either."

"So sure of yourself?"

"No," he replied slowly. "Just too old to play

games, and too experienced to ignore a kiss when it's special. They don't come along often. In fact," he continued, "twice in a lifetime seems lucky to me."

She instantly remembered what Suzanne had said about his family. Twice in a lifetime? Whoa! He was going too fast for her. A dose of reality would put the brakes on both of them. "Even though I'm searching for another one, I can't afford to lose this job," she said.

"Huh?" His honest confusion was evident. He normally had no problem articulating his thoughts clearly. Now he was reduced to a huh?

"You may be right in what you said earlier," she admitted. "I may not forget...uh...tonight so fast, but the bottom line is you're a student in my class."

"So?"

"So teachers and students do not...do not... ah...socialize privately."

"Socialize privately?" He started to laugh, and she wanted to throw her purse at him, but didn't because he'd probably catch it and laugh some more.

"Do you consider my job a joke?" she asked. "I assure you it's not. And if you want to collect your rent from me, you'd better make sure I keep it." She heard the indignation and the hurt in her own voice.

"It was your choice of words," he said with a final chuckle, "not your job. You're a professional. You've gone to school for years to acquire all that knowledge." All traces of laughter were gone now. "I'd be the last person to belittle it. But, Katherine, what can you be worried about? We're two adults meeting as equals outside the classroom. Furthermore, you don't even give me a grade in this course. I take the statewide exam in the testing center. You have absolutely no power over whether I pass or fail. So what's the problem?''

He did have a point or two.

"Maybe next time," Nick continued with a mock leer, "I'll take a traditional course with you and earn my grade the old-fashioned, fun way. If I wanted to guarantee an A, how many times—"

Whump! Now she did swing her purse—hard—and caught him just above his vitals.

He curled forward for a second and then straightened. "Fast and sneaky, girl. You'd be a great addition to the touch-football games we play at home.''

She didn't know a wide receiver from a tight end, and she wasn't going home with him. End of story.

"Good night, Nick," she said, slipping her key in the car door and opening it. She turned toward him. "You missed the entire session today. Study when you get home.''

"Yes, ma'am," he drawled. "And you study on this.'' He leaned forward and claimed her lips in a slow, gentle kiss.

CHAPTER FOUR

SHE SURE "studied on" that kiss, Katherine admitted to herself on the way home, and for the rest of the week as well. On Saturday, after three weeks of teaching, she stood in her new apartment wearing running shorts and a cropped T-shirt, with boxes piled in every room, glad to have the massive unpacking job ahead of her. A humongous distraction was just what she needed.

The memory of Nick's kiss floated in and out of her mind at all hours no matter what she was doing, and her heartbeat accelerated every time. That kiss shouldn't have happened. She shouldn't have enjoyed it. Not with Nick Martinelli, construction boss and designer. He wasn't her type, never had been, never would be.

Sure, he was a nice guy, with a great body and a good brain, but he wasn't for her. Too big and broad, too confident, too...too...much man! Too little education. He read material so slowly he might not pass the darn exam. A timed exam. She worried her bottom lip as her fears became nightmares. The huge clock in the testing center would tick the minutes away. One by one, other students would turn in their answer sheets and leave. But Nick would still be scrambling to complete his work. Perspiration would bead his lip. He'd try hard, but he wouldn't beat the clock. He'd have to guess at the last questions.

Katherine pressed her stomach to calm the butterflies, and made a mental note to coach Nick in proper guessing techniques.

He'd never admit it, but he had to be worried, too. For no reason other than his pride. After all, he didn't need the diploma to get a better job. But what adult, in this day and age, didn't at least want to be a high-school graduate?

No, indeed, he wasn't the right one for her. In fact, he made her nervous. A decisive man, he took action quickly and apologized to no one for it, like the time he ran after Jeremy. His opinions didn't concur with hers, either.

Definitely a mismatch. Despite the memorable kisses, the caring heart and the positive attitude.

She kneeled on the floor to line the kitchen cabinets. So what kind of man was she looking for? She pictured quiet intellectual discussions with references to great literature, someone well respected in his field and on campus, someone who would take pride in her accomplishments, someone with twinkling brown eyes and a curl of dark hair on his forehead...

She closed her eyes in frustration as the image of a certain construction boss filled her mind. Stop thinking about him! Surely other men could kiss as well as Nick Martinelli.

The doorbell rang and Katherine breathed a sigh of relief. She'd have to focus on someone else now.

But there stood Nick, pizza in one hand, a stack of

papers in the other, and bottle of cola under his arm. Her stomach rumbled loudly enough for both to hear it.

"I always did have a good sense of timing," he joked as his admiring eyes took in every inch of her from bare feet, legs and stretch shorts, all the way to a face bare of makeup.

She felt the heat climb to her cheeks but ignored it. "I won't argue with that," she said as she led him into the kitchen. "But what are you doing here in this neighborhood? Are you working in the sales office again today?"

He slid the pizza onto the counter along with the soda and his stack of papers.

"Not quite. I'm working at home for the rest of the day, where it's quieter. I've got a load of reading and computing to do. Most of the family is back at the office, but they can reach me at any time." He patted his pocket. "Cell phone."

"I see." And she did. In a crunch, they all called Nick and robbed him of personal time. She grabbed for some paper towels. "If you can take those boxes off the chairs—careful, my mom's good dishes are in that one—we can sit down and eat."

"Done."

She found some glasses and poured the cola. "So is City in the Woods on your way home?"

A killer smile and a nod accompanied his short answer. "Yup. We're neighbors."

"Really?" She felt her eyebrows raise in inquiry.

He nodded. "I've been a rolling stone for the last couple of years. Just kept on moving into every residential project we built, and now I'm here." His eyes fixed on the view out the window. "Can't seem to settle down," he said softly, "but it works, business-wise. Who better to be on hand if something comes up?"

"Where, exactly, is here?"

"Two buildings over."

Confusion and sympathy were replaced by a slow burn. He should have revealed that when he rented her the apartment. "I don't appreciate being manip-ulated," she said. "Why didn't you tell me?"

"Tell you what? You came looking for a place to live. I didn't bring you here."

"You made me a deal I couldn't refuse," she re-plied, all thoughts of pizza forgotten. "And you knew full well you were right next door."

He shrugged as he drank a half glass of cola, look-ing relaxed and comfortable as he leaned back in his chair. "Why should that make a difference? I would have done the same for any friend."

"Friend? You hardly knew me when I rented the apartment, and you still don't know me."

"I know enough. And we're getting better ac-quainted every day." He leaned over and put his fin-ger under her chin. "Relax and eat your pizza," he whispered before kissing her.

She swore the sauce sizzled from his kiss. Every kiss he gave her sizzled. Strange! But maybe he was right. Maybe she did worry too much about every-thing. According to Suzanne, Nick had gone through a lot, too, yet somehow managed not to get as uptight as she did.

But he didn't have it all together yet, she thought with a flash of insight. A rolling stone who couldn't settle in one place. No home since his wife died. She'd bet her last dollar on that.

She licked her lips when the kiss ended. "So what's the big stack of papers you're working on, and when are you going to practice the reading passages for your exam?"

"I need a forty-eight-hour day," he admitted. "The company's going after a big job, building several elementary schools for the city. "It's a big contract that we need to win, not just for the money, but to continue building the reputation of our industrial division." He paused and took her hand. "It's top priority. A company is only as good as the people who run it. Our reputation is everything. We've got only five years' industrial construction experience, and every project counts toward developing credibility and trust."

"Maybe," she began slowly, "this isn't such a good time to prepare for the GED exam. Maybe you should wait."

He shot out of his chair and paced. "No, Katherine, no. If not now, when? There will always be big projects, other concerns. It's too easy to procrastinate. God knows I've done it my whole adult life. But not anymore. I want that damn diploma!"

So she'd been right. He wanted it for his own self-esteem. To know he could stand shoulder to shoulder with everyone else.

"I understand, Nick. You're a very bright, astute man. Why shouldn't you have affirmation of it?"

His forehead creased. He shook his head. "It's not that." He sat on his heels in front of her chair and spoke quietly. "I don't need to prove anything to anyone else. And I don't need to prove anything to myself. I know who I am, diploma or not. I need that piece of paper because it's my passport to the next step before I'm too damn old."

She swallowed. Almost afraid to know more. Determination showed in every line, every contour of his expression. "Next step, Nick? What do you mean?"

He stood up and started pacing again. "Most people would laugh, and maybe they'd be right. And I've never mentioned it to my family, but I want you to understand." He sat back in his chair and reached for her hand.

She waited again.

"It's about dreams," he finally said. "About my career at the company. I want to do more. I don't have the right words to explain, but that poem we read in class scared me."

What was he talking about? What poem? Before she could ask, he spoke again—quickly—as though he was slightly embarrassed.

"The one about postponing your dreams again and again, until you either dry up or explode inside." He squeezed her hand. "I liked it because it's how I've felt for a long time, but especially in the last couple of years when...when I've had too much time to think. And that's why I registered for your class."

She blinked back the tears, her heart and mind crashing together like brass cymbals in a marching band. He'd just reminded her—more forcefully than the most brilliantly written textbook—of why she'd become a teacher. That's what teaching used to be about for her, but lately she'd forgotten. "You and millions of other people take that poem to heart...and Nick, I'm not laughing."

He looked directly into her eyes, searching, questioning...

She held his gaze.

"Somehow I didn't think you would," he finally said, the corner of his mouth lifting.

She released the breath she hadn't known she'd been holding. His trust humbled her, and she couldn't let him down. She leaned toward him and took his hand in both of hers. "So you want to go to college," she said, continuing their eye contact. "You want to design buildings, and structures, and play with space. You want to be a licensed architect."

"You just hit a home run with bases loaded." His eyes gleamed with appreciation. "Very astute, Katherine. How did you guess?"

For once she was a step ahead of him. "I've got a good memory, and I'm getting to know you very well, too."

"I'm glad," he said.

Their eyes locked. She glimpsed his soul and couldn't have looked away if the condo had caught fire. He took her hand, stood up and brought her alongside him. She read his intent before his mouth touched hers and didn't object at all.

But he took it slowly this time, and she wanted the sizzle. She raked her fingers through his hair, both arms around his neck, her breasts tight against his chest. She traced his lips with her tongue and he welcomed her inside. He crushed her to him, his arms around her, his hand on the small of her back, on her bare skin. The fluttering in the pit of her stomach spiraled instantly. She could barely breathe. Her legs locked and then she felt it.

Sizzle!

CONSCIOUS THOUGHT barely pierced Nick's sensual haze, but in the back of his mind, he realized someone special rested in his arms. She might not know it yet, but Katherine was made for him.

"Easy, baby, easy," he crooned as he began to stroke her back. Long strokes from shoulder to waist and up again.

"Hmm?" She regarded him with unfocused eyes, beautiful eyes filled with the same sensual haze engulfing him.

"What do you want, sweetheart? If we continue the way we're heading, we won't stop."

He felt her come to awareness. Saw the blush suffuse her neck and face. Saw her eyes clear and widen with realization of her involvement. And saw her retreat, the usual furrow marking her forehead.

"Nick, what are we doing?" She pointed to the cartons in the unkempt room. "In the middle of a kitchen...this isn't me. I don't do these things...I mean...kiss strange men. Have affairs. I don't have affairs. Oh my God. What am I saying? What am I thinking? I'm a babbling idiot." She raised her hand to her eyes and looked about to cry. "What have I done?"

He took a deep breath. "Maybe shared a bit of your heart with me?"

She couldn't have looked more stricken if he had slapped her. "I'm so sorry," she whispered. "I can't…"

"Is it your job?"

She paused, but shook her head. "I tried to tell you earlier…I'm not looking for a relationship, Nick, especially not right now. Not in my plans. I'm doing fine the way I am. I can't exactly explain what just happened, but I'm sorry, it's not the real me."

She glanced at him quickly, apologetically, then away. But he saw the true regret and confusion in her blue eyes, now almost violet with emotion.

His muscles relaxed. Honesty he could deal with, but he'd have to clear the air with a thunderstorm first. "Slumming with the bad boy?" he asked quietly. "Ever make love to a dropout before?"

She twirled faster than a tornado to face him, hands on her hips, eyes now flashing fire, as furious as his Donna had ever been. "I hadn't even thought of that. Don't you dare demean me and don't demean yourself. You can get those ugly thoughts right out of your mind, and you can leave my home right now." Her voice was quiet and deadly.

"Nope," he said, sitting back down on her kitchen chair, arms behind his head, as relaxed as he could make himself while keeping an eye on a steaming woman. "I didn't think you were the type, either. So my theory is that—"

"I don't care about your theory. How could you have even suggested that horrible idea?"

She was going the whole nine yards, and he deserved it because Katherine truly didn't know how to play those games.

"And don't you ever, ever talk that way about me or yourself," she continued to rave. "And you know what else, you're condemning everyone in the class when you speak like that...of all people, I never would have thought it of you."

More than nine yards. Maybe the goalpost. He waited, trying hard to hide his grin. "Are you finished yet?"

She glared and nodded.

"You're absolutely right, Katherine. I'll never say anything like that again."

Her glare changed to confusion. Maybe he was laying it on too thick, but it was hard to concentrate when all he wanted to do was take her in his arms and pick up where they'd left off.

"And I'm very sorry if I hurt your feelings...." Thicker and thicker.

She walked closer to him now, her confusion turning to suspicion, her beautiful face still so easy to read.

"What is going on here, Nicholas Martinelli?" she asked, staring down at him in the chair. "Give me one reason why I shouldn't throw you out right now."

He snagged her around the waist and onto his lap. "Easy question," he replied before nuzzling her behind the ear, and feeling her quiver in response. "You like kissing me. And we'll be doing it again in the future, many times.''

''Really?''

''Absolutely.''

''You have it all figured out?''

He nodded. ''It's a proven theory. Sometimes, sweetheart, when you least expect it, a relationship can just sneak up on you. Whether it's in your plans or not.''

WHY NOT HAVE AN AFFAIR? Katherine bolted upright in her bed early the next morning, exhausted from a sleepless night but excited by her idea. It might be the perfect solution. She liked Nick, evidently was attracted to him, although she couldn't quite figure out why. Most women would have swooned over his rugged good looks and matching physique, but that description had never turned her on before.

And now she had the chance to explore. Be flexible. Change plans! And who would they be harming? She and Nick were two consenting adults, so there should be no conflict. She had nothing to do with grading him. In fact, she was more a facilitator than his teacher. She plopped down on her pillow again and fell asleep immediately.

Two hours later, she groped for the ringing phone with vague notions of pulling it out of the wall. Her eyes refused to open, she barely muttered a greeting.

''Rise and shine, Kath.'' Suzanne's cheerful voice came through loud and clear. ''David and I are on our way over to take you to brunch. And his brother is meeting us at the restaurant. After eating, we'll all go back to your place and help you unpack whatever else you've got.''

Two generous offers she couldn't refuse. ''Give me an hour, Suze, that's all I ask.''

''You would have had more notice if your phone wasn't busy all last night. Who were you talking to?''

''Oops. Sorry. I was online, checking out college web sites. Even filled out employment applications and e-mailed résumés to a few. But I'll be ready in an hour. I promise.''

''You've got it.''

And she needed every minute of it. Shower, shampoo, blow-dry, light makeup, fold up empty cartons from kitchen, unpack linens. She glanced at her watch just as the bell rang, and with a smile opened the door.

Three people stood on the threshold, the two men shaking hands, and Suzanne looking as if she'd won the Texas lottery.

''Mornin', sugar,'' she gushed as she stepped into the condo. ''Look who was walking over to visit just as we were getting out of the car.'' She glanced back at Nick as though clarifying who she meant. ''I always say the more the merrier, so we invited him to join us, and he kindly accepted.''

Katherine bit her lip to keep from laughing. Suzanne's Southern roots always became more pronounced when she was happy.

Nick looked as delicious this morning as he had last night. In a navy-blue sports shirt and a pair of tush-hugging beige chinos, temptation was written all over him. Katherine's palms tingled. The open V of his shirt drew her like a magnet. She longed to dip her fingers in and feel the heat of his skin, the curly hair on his chest. She wanted to feel his strong hands exploring her. She blinked hard. Good Lord! It was eleven in the morning, her closest friend and her friend's fiancé were standing in the doorway waiting for her response, and all she could think about was Nick's strong hands.

"Good," she mumbled, feeling a blush hit her cheeks and knowing eagle-eyed Suzanne wouldn't miss seeing it.

"Seems like we all wanted to feed this hardworking girl today," said Nick as he stepped inside behind Suzanne and David.

"And what a delightful idea it's turning out to be," said Suzanne, looking from Nick to Katherine. "Yes, indeed, just splendid...and soon to be even more interesting."

Katherine watched Suzanne lean confidently against her bespectacled David, a lanky and good-humored geology professor, watched as David's arm gently circled her waist and pulled her against him. So natural. So comfortable. So simpatico. Yes, that's what long-lasting love should be like. Two people who fit with each other.

And that's why she and Nick were destined for an affair, a raving-hot affair with no strings attached.

She stared at him now, at his smiling mouth, his warm dark eyes twinkling at her as he stepped closer.

"Morning, sunshine," he said before casually kissing her on the lips. "Sleep well?"

She could have fallen into his kiss. That simple, off-the-cuff kiss. Her grand idea was starting to make her nervous. "Like a baby," she finally answered.

"Liar," he whispered.

She quickly turned toward the others. "Is everyone ready?"

A SIXTY-FOOT champagne brunch buffet offered everything from smoked salmon and boiled shrimp, to omelettes and waffles made to order, to fajitas and pasta, chicken, fish and a dozen breads, a virtual culinary potpourri.

"There's no dearth of food in Houston," joked Nick as the group was seated in a long booth for six. "With so many restaurants in the city, you could eat out every night for a year and not hit the same place twice."

"That's the truth," said Suzanne with laughter in her voice. "And with my cooking, it's a good thing, too."

Katherine looked at David. "She's not kidding, you know. Prepare for frozen dinners or restaurants."

"I can always whip something up in the lab if things get desperate," David replied with a grin, "or she might have to settle for fast food."

"What a dilemma," said Suzanne. "Learning to cook or eating junk." She wrinkled her nose. "I might have to think about buying some pans."

Katherine laughed with the rest of them, but found the conversation touching. Suzanne had never offered to learn to cook for any other man, even as a joke. She looked at David with new eyes. She saw a nice-looking fellow, tall and sinewy rather than broad, with big gray eyes behind his rimless glasses. Throw in a dry sense of humor, a high intelligence and a quiet confidence. Suzanne had found herself quite a guy.

But he didn't make Katherine's heart pound. Even when she removed Suzanne from the equation. She peeked at Nick. Her heart pounded. Interesting. She'd have to think about it.

Glancing across the room just then, she caught sight of a tall, lean figure with familiar gray eyes walking toward them. "Would that be your brother?" she asked David as she watched the man approach.

David turned his head. "Sure would," he replied, standing up and waving the man over. "This is my brother, Jonathan, folks. On the English faculty of the University of Texas in Austin. He's attending a conference in town this weekend."

"Good morning, everyone."

Katherine watched as Jonathan shook hands with Nick and kissed Suzanne on the cheek. *UT-Austin. Fabulous school; fabulous library.* Maybe Suzanne had done her a *real* favor this time.

Jonathan turned to her and took her hand. Held it. "I've looked forward to meeting you, Katherine. Suzanne sings your praises almost every time we speak."

She felt herself blush and once again cursed her fair complexion before darting a killing glance at her friend. "Suzanne sees the best in everyone," she replied evenly. "She's a good friend."

"I definitely agree," Jonathan said, holding her gaze as he sat down across the table from her. "She tells me you're looking for a university position. How can I help?"

Wow! He came to the point quickly. Next to her, she heard Nick inhale and felt him shift position on the bench. When she glanced at him, however, he seemed as relaxed as usual, a smile in place...but in his eyes...nothing. No twinkle, no warmth. Just a very thoughtful expression as he glanced back and forth between David's brother and her.

"But...but...you haven't even seen my credentials...you haven't seen me in front of a class," Katherine protested.

"But *I* have," said Nick quietly before Jonathan could respond.

"Nick!" She reached for his hand. "You don't have to..." What was he thinking? He'd never exactly said to keep his presence in her GED class a secret, with the exception of his parents, but she'd never heard him broadcast it either.

He pressed her fingers gently. "If you won't brag about yourself, somebody else needs to do it." He turned to the professor again. "I've seen her teach many times and I'd be honored to provide a reference."

"What course?"

Katherine saw the twinkle return to Nick's eyes as he leaned forward to make his points. What on earth was he going to say?

"It's an interdisciplinary curriculum unique to the community college, combining popular and classical literature—a lot of poetry and nonfiction as well—in an historical context."

Clever, clever, Nick! True, he'd omitted the math, but still... She glanced at Suzanne, and saw her friend grab a napkin and industriously wipe her smiling mouth. But Nick wasn't finished yet.

"I know for a fact that her classes are so interesting there's a very low rate of absenteeism." He paused.

"What more do you need to know? The students love her."

Katherine had never seen eyebrows raise as high as Jonathan Carter's. "Nick, I think you should quit while you're ahead. Any more, and you'll undo everything you've accomplished."

She looked at Jonathan then. "My résumé and application were electronically sent to Austin. I'll send my transcripts this week. Take a look. If you're comfortable, I'd appreciate a good word."

"I'd be happy to follow up," he replied. "If you're really as good as he says you are, there should be no problem if an opening arises. In fact, if you'll also submit writing samples, there might be an outstanding opportunity for you."

Although he'd snagged her interest, to Katherine's relief the conversation revolved around her companions' lives after that. The talk never lagged. David and Nick exchanged stories as if they'd known each other for years.

"I was always fascinated by the oil rigs down here in Texas, especially out in the gulf," said David. "And when they hit a strike and the black gold gushed to the sky, I thought it was the coolest thing. I didn't think of it as money when I was a kid, but as the earth's secret, like a secret code I had to break."

"And did you?" asked Katherine, intrigued by how a young boy's mind could work.

He grinned. "A time or two or three. My phone rings now when the big oil boys need another opinion. But I prefer working with my students, just like Jonathan. Maybe because our dad was a teacher. I don't know. Maybe it's genetic.''

''I won't argue against genetics,'' said Nick. ''My family says I was born with a hammer in my hand. When I was a kid, my dad and I used to have nail-driving contests to see who could drive a straighter nail. It paid off. My phone rings when people want to invest in quality.''

Katherine watched the two men grin at each other as though sharing the secrets of the universe.

Suzanne tapped her on the arm. ''They're bonding.''

Katherine nodded. Male bonding. A phenomenon she'd never witnessed before in real life. Interesting for sure. But what stood out in her mind was how Nick could hold his own with anyone. His general knowledge made him part of every conversation, and his personal confidence earned people's respect.

She'd seen it happen in her own classroom, but hadn't thought much about it. But now she saw a pattern. Nick liked people and people liked him. He took an interest in them. He was an extrovert, while she was just as happy with a book.

She and Nick were not really well matched at all, so why did she feel so comfortable with him? So excited by him? So many questions to ponder.

''JUST HOW MANY BOOKS do you own, Kathy?'' asked Nick an hour later as he shelved another box.

''Even I'm impressed,'' admitted Suzanne.

''No,'' said Jonathan, ''it's about what I'd expect of an English teacher.''

Katherine stood in the middle of her study, surrounded by boxes, books and incredulous friends. "Wait a minute, Nick. That's Shakespeare, under the S's, please. Put it on that far shelf near the window wall."

With hands on hips, she surveyed her domain. She loved the three walls of built-in shelves. She loved the picture window and the loft. Her computer and desk would fit in just fine against the long wall. "I never counted," she finally answered. "I just keep buying and I guess I never throw any out."

She stroked a green bound volume. "Here's an old friend. Whitman, *Leaves of Grass*." She sighed. "The poets know how to get to the heart of the matter with language that can make you cry, or laugh, or startle." She looked at Nick and smiled. "We've already seen that in cl—"

She clapped her hand over her mouth in an effort to recall her words. After the clever reference he gave her that morning, how could she have almost given his secret away?

"They're all your friends, aren't they?" Nick asked without a pause, seemingly unaware of her gaff.

"What? Who are?"

"Your books," he said. "The writers, their stories, you think of all of them as your friends."

"They are my friends, longtime comfortable friends. Some have been with me my whole life, longer than I've known Suzanne. They don't change. They don't disappear. I can count on them no matter what."

"But they can't keep you warm at night, Katherine," he replied in a soft voice so that only she could hear. ''When the light goes out, a book disappears, and the bed is awfully lonely.''

She winced at the truth of his words.

Nick studied her expression, relieved that she looked more thoughtful than resentful at his last remark, and he didn't want to push his luck. He glanced at his watch, trying to shift items on his megaschedule, but the schedule wasn't too flexible. He led Katherine into the semiprivacy of the kitchen.

''I'm due at a big business powwow in fifteen minutes. I'll call you when I get back.'' He wasn't going to allow Jonathan's presence to change his plans.

''A meeting on Sunday? I thought bosses hired other people to do the work.''

He grinned. ''Not at Martinelli Construction. Remember the school project I told you about?''

She nodded.

''It's a family-only, hands-on effort. We lost a big job for the city three years ago to a much weaker competitor, and we don't want any mishaps this time. We have to work up costs, develop schedules, meet with subcontractors and so on.''

His mind raced to the myriad tasks ahead of him. He sighed. ''It's a big job. Huge. What's more, my secretary's nose is going to be out of joint when she realizes she's being excluded. I'll have to buy her a big gift when it's all over, but in the meantime, I'll ask my sister, Tina, to be extra sweet to her.''

''Why Tina?''

''Because Tina's the office manager, and she'll also be handling the administrative end of this project with some help from my mom. Sally will have to pick up the slack on Tina's regular work.''

''So Sally's good enough to take on a lot of extra work but not good enough to work on the special project?''

He felt his blood heat at Katherine's challenge. A new experience. He'd always taken the lead with Donna, and she'd been content with that. They'd teased each other and had fun, but they'd rarely disagreed.

Katherine was different. She'd defend her views without hesitation, but she also listened to reasonable arguments. ''It's business, Katherine. Nothing personal. It's also a form of protection for her. If, by chance, our figures somehow appear on a competitor's bid, she won't be implicated at all. In essence, I'm doing her a favor.''

''A favor that she doesn't know about.''

He nodded. ''I can't explain a situation that we couldn't prove three years ago. That's mudslinging. Only the family knows about it.''

She looked straight at him, her blue eyes serious, her eyebrows drawn toward each other. ''That's not quite true.''

''What do you mean?''

''I know about it. And I'm not family.''

HE THOUGHT ABOUT her remark all the way to his parents' home in west Houston. The home he grew up in, the home that had kept expanding as more children were born, until there were more bedrooms than children. But his mom was happy. Plenty of room for the grandchildren to sleep overnight.

Katherine. Katherine. Conflicted by all her own rules. Torn between her head and her heart.

She resided in the back of his mind almost constantly, and for the first time since he lost his girls, he felt lighter. Maybe almost happy, although it was hard to remember that particular emotion.

He chose not to examine his feelings too closely, and instead chuckled at the memory of his leave-taking from Katherine's apartment a few minutes earlier.

He'd promised to call her later, take her out for dinner. She'd hesitated, nodding toward her other guests. She'd offered to cook something simple for everyone, but when he viewed all the work still waiting for her, he'd said no, they'd all go out.

And that's when Suzanne had said quite audibly, "This one's a keeper." At that remark, Katherine's face had matched the red blouse she wore. And that's the only reason he remembered the color of the blouse. Most of the time his eyes had been glued to her beautiful face or her long shapely legs.

And he had to give Suzanne a hell of a lot of credit. She'd essentially told her soon-to-be brother-in-law to buzz off. Perceptive woman! He'd have to thank her when he saw her next time.

He focused on the road ahead. Life was getting interesting again. Full of possibilities.

CHAPTER FIVE

JEREMY KNEW his old man was going to die, had known it for a week, but it still jabbed him in the gut when it happened.

"So what do we do now?" he asked Estelle King later that day in the bedroom he shared with five other boys at Richmond House. He was proud of himself; his voice sounded strong. No crying, no fear. He'd handled it at the hospital and he'd handle the rest of it, too.

The boss lady stood next to him, kindness in her smile, watchfulness in her eyes. "He'll be buried tomorrow morning in the county cemetery. We'll both go. Your friends are welcome also." She shook her head slowly and patted his shoulder. "I'm sorry, Jeremy. It's tough to lose a dad, even if he didn't know how to be a good one."

He stood taller and looked out the window to the back lawn. That's what he liked about Ms. Estelle. She talked straight, even if it hurt.

"He wasn't any father at all. Not really." Angry words came from his mouth as the tears pushed against his eyes. He blinked them back. "Doesn't matter now. Fact is, he killed himself. Yes, ma'am. That's what he did. And it didn't take just a week. It took sixteen years, ever since I was born.'' He turned and leaned toward her until their foreheads almost touched. ''Truth is, Ms. Estelle, I killed both of them. She died having me, and he died not having her.''

He'd never seen the boss lady get angry so fast. Before he blinked twice, her hands were on his shoulders holding him in place.

''You listen to me, Jeremy Tucker,'' she said, ''and you listen good. Nothing at all is your fault. Bad things happen to everyone. Your parents wanted you. Your mom died. That was a tragedy. But you deserved a stronger father.''

He shrugged out of her hold. ''Too late now.''

''It's never too late for friends. You've got friends here, and…well, if you're still sixteen by the time you finish your community service and get your diploma, you'll be eligible for foster care. Maybe you'll find a family, Jeremy. There are good people out there.''

She was delusional. ''I don't need a hand-me-down family who's in it for the money.''

''The state doesn't pay what a teenage boy eats, son.''

He grunted at her joke. ''No, that's not for me. No way am I going into someone else's family. What's that you always tell us, Ms. Estelle? You have to play the hand you're dealt.''

''That's right.''

''Well, my hand is so empty I don't even have a pair of deuces in it. Let's count. I've got a rap sheet for shoplifting a mile long—''

''But when you finally landed in court, you were

tried as a juvenile,'' Estelle interrupted. ''You were lucky.''

''Right,'' Jeremy mumbled. He'd appeared in a real court last time because his father couldn't sober up enough to stand with his son in front of a probation officer instead. Jeremy couldn't leave the detention center where the police had brought him, and that's how he'd ended up at Richmond House. Hell, he'd *had* to steal stuff. How else could he get clothes and food for him and his dad?

He could've peddled drugs. Easily. The demand for the white powder was so great it was pitiful. Users were everywhere, and there was fast money to be made on almost any corner of the city, even for kids younger than him. But he'd chosen not to. Alcohol was a drug, too, and he'd seen enough of that. Stealing was better.

He continued his list. ''No high-school diploma...''

''You'll have it in six weeks.''

''No job,'' he continued.

''You'll get one.''

This woman always had an answer for everything. ''Who hires kids on probation?''

''Plenty of folks. And when you turn seventeen and are finished with everything you're required to do, you'll have a clean record. You won't be on probation anymore and you can be declared an emancipated juvenile. In other words, you'll be a legal adult.''

He knew all that. He'd read everything he could get his hands on regarding the juvenile justice system. Ms. Estelle was a good person, but she didn't understand. He lived in a place for kids who didn't fit anywhere. People on the outside didn't want to be bothered with them. He couldn't leave soon enough. As soon as he got that diploma, he'd split. The hell with waiting until he was seventeen.

With that diploma, he'd get a good-paying job. He'd get his own apartment. Maybe a girlfriend. And a computer. Definitely a computer. Nobody would tell him what to do. What time to get up, what time to go to bed.

Or maybe he'd be like that guy Ms. Kirby talked about in school, the famous one who lived by himself at that place in Massachusetts. Walden. That's what she called it. And Henry David Thoreau was the guy's name. Yeah. He just lived with nature. All peaceful like. Jeremy could do that, live in the woods, on a lake. He could figure things out, write down all his ideas.

He had the rest of the summer to think about it. Then he'd choose.

KATHERINE PICKED UP the kitchen phone on the second ring, just as she prepared her usual cantaloupe and cottage cheese brunch. Student essays took up half the table, and she made room for her plate while she reached for the receiver.

"This is Rose Goldman, Katherine."

"Good morning, Dr. Goldman," said Katherine, quickly trying to figure out why her supervisor was contacting her at home. She didn't have to wait long.

"I'm afraid I have some bad news about one of your students—a boy named Jeremy Tucker."

Katherine closed her eyes, mental snapshots of Jer-

emy in all his moods fueling her imagination. *Please.
Let him be all right.* She gripped the phone so tightly
her fingers hurt as she waited for Rose to continue.

"His father passed away, and he won't be in school
today, but he wanted you to know about the funeral
tomorrow in case you can make it. An Estelle King
called with the information and she also gave me the
directions to the cemetery."

So the end had finally come for the senior Tucker,
but her thoughts were for the boy. *The poor kid. Poor
Jeremy.* Her breath came in gasps as remembered
grief enveloped her. *Don't go there, Katherine. Take
a deep breath. Jeremy is strong. He'll handle it.*

"It's a little unusual to become so close to a student in such a short time," Dr. Goldman continued.
"I'm surmising that Jeremy is one of your younger
ones."

It should have been a relief finally to discuss Jeremy with Rose. But Katherine hesitated, surprised by
an unfamiliar need to protect him even from as lovely
and professional a woman as Rose Goldman. Dis-
cussing Jeremy's behavior now seemed like a betrayal
to the youngster.

"He *is* my youngest student. A boy with unlimited
promise. And now he's—" her voice quivered "—a
boy with unlimited pain…just a boy…alone." She
swallowed hard, and despite her best efforts her memories twirled through time faster than a Texas tornado.
*Poor thing. She's so young. So alone. No brothers or
sisters. No family.*

"I'll be happy to cover your class while you attend

the funeral,'' said Rose gently, ''if there's a scheduling conflict.''

At the sound of her supervisor's voice, Katherine
focused on the present again. ''I'll take the directions,
but...but I don't know if I can make it.'' *Coward!*
She closed her eyelids tight to shut out the truth. ''I'll
probably visit him later on at home.'' The boys'
home, she thought. Richmond House.

''You're going beyond the call of duty, Katherine,
and I'm delighted. Our GED students have had so
many setbacks already that it makes a world of difference when a teacher reaches out. If I haven't already said so, I'm very happy to have you on staff. I
hear good things about you when I chat with students
in the hall.''

High praise that shifted Katherine's thoughts to her
professional life and left her tripping on her own
tongue. While she thanked her supervisor and made
appropriate closing remarks, all that ran through her
brain was, ''She chats with students in the halls?''

The thought lightened her heart. Dr. Goldman
quoted student opinion, and it was good. High opinion meant students were apt to try harder and learn.
Although it hadn't been her choice to teach this class,
she'd do her best while it was her responsibility.
She'd have wonderful memories when she finally
moved on to the position she really wanted, wherever
it might be.

The phone rang again a minute later.

''Hi, baby.''

Her body tingled at the sound of Nick's deep voice.
''Hi, yourself.''

"Did you get a call about Jeremy's dad?"

"Yes, I did. Poor kid's got a tough row to hoe."

"I knew you'd feel that way, so I told Estelle we'd both be at the funeral tomorrow morning. I can pick you up."

He assumed too much. Beads of sweat prickled her skin. A slight nausea settled into her stomach. She'd have an emotional meltdown if she attended the funeral. She just couldn't go. Nick would think the worst of her, but she'd have to take that chance. "You shouldn't have made a commitment for me, Nick. I…I don't go to funerals."

A five-second pause, then "Excuse me?"

She couldn't blame him for being confused. "I'll visit Jeremy afterward."

"Afterward? When the hard part's over?" he asked slowly, a note of incredulity in his voice. "After the kid watches his father being lowered into the ground? After he realizes he's alone in the world?"

"I'm doing the best I can," she retorted with vigor.

Silence met her remark for a moment before Nick's calm tone reassured her. "All right, Kath. I believe you. I don't quite understand, but it's okay. I do believe you."

Tears gathered as she replaced the receiver and held her head in her hands. She didn't deserve such understanding. How much longer could she play this game? How much longer could she lie to herself? She'd just lied to Nick, too. She *wasn't* doing the best she could. Deep inside, she knew it.

Ignoring the past wasn't working anymore. It used to be easy when, except for Suzanne, her circle was limited only to acquaintances. She was known as a private person; it was accepted. Maintaining that persona should have gotten easier as time went by. Sometimes, it was. But now, it was harder. Harder to make excuses to those she cared about, harder to make excuses to herself. For God's sake, she had to grow up and act like an adult. Join the human race.

She hadn't told Nick about her parents yet. That's why he didn't understand. She could have told him the night he'd brought the pizza and carried her mom's dishes to a safer place. An opportunity had presented itself, but she hadn't taken advantage of it. No, still too afraid of reopening the wounds.

She slammed her palm on the table. There was a young boy out there tonight who was facing an abyss. Pain or no pain, she'd be with him. He wouldn't face it alone.

SHE HADN'T TOLD NICK she'd be going. Just in case. But now, as her fingers clenched the wheel and she forced herself to take deep breaths, she would have appreciated a ride. Too bad. She'd have to handle it. She turned into the entrance of the cemetery and slowly followed the directions to the grave site. She pulled behind Nick's truck, gathered her mental resources and got out of the car.

Three adults and two boys stood near Jeremy. A fourth adult, Nick, stood next to him, his arm resting casually on the youngster's shoulders. They looked so natural together, as though they'd been companions for years.

Her jitters forgotten, Katherine watched quietly in

the clear morning air, savoring the picture they made, these two men who had touched her life, and who seemed connected by some invisible force. She saw Nick turn Jeremy to face him, watched his expression as he spoke to the teenager.

She couldn't hear the words, but could witness their delivery. Intensity, concern and strong affection for this lost boy were displayed with every phrase. Jeremy nodded a few times, his head tilted back to see Nick better.

Katherine smiled as she approached them. She was used to that position herself. Then Jeremy took a step closer to Nick, looking almost…hopeful? And received a bear hug, which he returned in full measure.

Nick glanced up then, must have heard her footsteps on the concrete path, and the smile he sent her could have warmed the coldest winter day. She stared at the hardworking, caring, generous man, with his arms still around the boy, and her heart opened like a flower to the sun. Heat warmed her skin, and a bubble of joy filled her, shocked her, as she realized what it all meant.

She was falling in love with Nick Martinelli—as incredible as that seemed. Suddenly, she knew no matter what followed, her life would never be the same.

She took a deep breath, met Nick's glance and returned his smile with a wide one of her own.

NICK'S PULSE SHOT into orbit when he saw that smile, his blood racing like a Thoroughbred crossing the finish line. He wanted to throw her onto the ground and make passionate love to her. Right there in the cemetery. Fortunately, Jeremy's solid presence prevented him from making a total fool of himself.

"Look who just arrived," Nick said, turning the youngster toward Katherine. The boy's eyes shone as though the *Baywatch* beauties had bestowed their presence on him. They both had it bad, Nick thought. No question about it. And it didn't look as if Jeremy would be over his crush any time soon.

The youngster shrugged out of his clasp and walked slowly toward Katherine. Then stopped within five feet of her. Didn't say a word. But Katherine stepped closer and extended her hand.

Jeremy took it.

Good boy, Nick thought as he joined them.

"I'm very sorry for your loss," said Katherine.

"That's okay."

She looked thoughtful for a moment, then shook her head. "No, my friend. It's not okay, but we can't undo it."

She glanced up at Nick then, with such warmth he nearly stumbled. And then she turned back to the boy.

"You're not the only young person ever to face this, Jeremy. I promise you that." She rubbed her hands nervously down the simple dress she wore, and Nick wondered what would come next.

"I lost my parents, too," she said, her voice starting to crack. "And that's how I know it's not okay. It stinks." She closed her eyes and a single tear fell. She brushed it with her fingers and looked surprised at the wetness on her skin. "I was just a little older than you—nineteen—and I haven't cried in years until today.''

"Then you're probably due," Nick replied. She looked so fragile, his breath caught in his throat and his own voice sounded gravelly. He squeezed her gently around the waist, then took her right arm and Jeremy's left. ''The chaplain's going to start the service now,'' he said. "Let's go.''

He led them back to where Estelle and the others stood around the plain coffin next to the open grave. Katherine nodded at them, but didn't speak. Nick glanced at her pale face and Jeremy's still form, and hoped they'd all get through this…himself included.

He bowed his head but kept one arm around each of his companions. His senses remained alert while his thoughts wandered.

They each had their unique memories, ghosts of lost loves who visited now only in their dreams. He missed his laughing Donna, his first love, and he grieved for his baby, his Jenny who'd squeal with delight each time he walked through the door at the end of the day. He'd never forget them. Never.

But Katherine drew him like a lodestone, nestled into the back of his mind, always in his thoughts. Yes, she was certainly attractive, and bright, too. But more important than that, real heart lurked beneath the bravado she'd adopted to hide her fears. The bravado she'd adopted to survive.

He looked at her clenched hands with knuckles as white as parchment, but she remained beside him— toughing it out—she called it, and glancing at Jeremy from time to time, as though checking up on his well-being. For a woman who had once wanted to throw the boy out of class, Katherine certainly showed some personal concern now.

Where would all this lead? He shrugged his shoulders. All he knew at the moment was that three separate lives were now intertwined.

KATHERINE RETURNED with the rest of their group to Richmond House, where a simple buffet lunch had been set up at one end of the dining room. Very few boys were at the facility at this time of the day; most attended mandated activities.

She glanced at her watch, happy to note she still had some time to spend with Jeremy after the stress of the burial. He had tried to be so brave, but when the casket was lowered, she and Nick had both heard his gasp, had heard him whisper, ''Damn you, damn you,'' had seen him lurch forward. Nick had held him tightly then. But Katherine had seen the desolation in the youngster's eyes. A streetwise sixteen-year-old had no weapon against the ultimate reality.

''How're you holding up, Kathy?'' asked Nick as he made a beeline for her and studied her face.

''Better than he is,'' she replied, nodding toward Jeremy, who was standing with his two friends, hands in his pockets, looking a little dazed. ''It's going to hit him tonight when he goes to bed, or maybe tomorrow when the familiar routines seem distorted. Or it might not sink in for a couple of weeks. But whenever it hits, he'll be overwhelmed. He's going to feel totally alone.'' She turned to him. ''And the truth is,

Nick, he is. He belongs to no one. There's not a soul standing between him and heaven.''

Nick's eyes widened and a whistle—long and low—preceded his response. "Is that how it was for you?''

She nodded. "You'd better believe it." She heard her own words and was amazed at how freely she shared her feelings with Nick.

They walked toward the boys who were now building triple-decker cold-cut sandwiches.

"Hey, Mr. Martinelli," said one of Jeremy's friends in greeting. "Are you and Jer really in the same class?''

"Yup.''

"How come you don't got your high-school diploma yet? Man, you're too old to be in school.''

Nick started to chuckle, then laugh. "So make sure you graduate on time, Trevor, before you're in my shoes. You might want to start working on your grammar.''

"Nick's not too old," defended Jeremy. "You should see all the different people in our class. Some of them are almost as old as Ms. Estelle! And Nick's about the smartest one there. He understands everything. Right, Ms. Kirby?''

Jeremy's expression told its own story. Despite some obvious resentment at times, it seemed the boy had developed a case of hero worship that anyone in the room could diagnose.

"Right," replied Katherine. "And you're not so bad yourself, kiddo. I'm expecting high marks from you.''

He didn't reply, but his ears turned bright red at her compliment.

"He's that good, is he?" asked Nick with a raised eyebrow and a wink at Katherine. "How's his math?"

"Almost as good as yours." Nick's math skills surpassed her own. And Jeremy caught on quickly. He just needed more exposure to it.

Nick turned toward Jeremy. "I'm looking for someone to work part-time with my brother. He needs someone who learns fast, who can calculate materials and costs, and who will sometimes work on-site as a carpenter's helper. Ms. Estelle said you could work in the mornings, keep going to class in the afternoons and do your community service on Saturdays."

Jeremy's face became alert, but again he didn't say anything.

"And what kind of salary are you offering one of my top students, Mr. Martinelli?" Katherine asked with a twinkle as she moved closer to the youngster. "He may eat like an elephant but he doesn't work for peanuts."

Everyone groaned.

"Oh, Ms. Kirby. That was really bad."

She looked at Jeremy and winked. For the first time that awful day, he looked like a kid. For the first time that awful day, she started to relax. The boy would make it. She was glad to have a few more weeks with him just to be sure.

She slipped an envelope out of her purse and gave it to Jeremy. "Tonight, if you're feeling bad, take this out and read it. Especially the last two lines. And remember that you know at least one other person who's walked in your shoes. You're not alone, honey." Impulsively, she leaned toward him and kissed his cheek. "I'll see you in school tomorrow."

She turned toward Nick. "And I'll see you in class later today."

"And beyond."

His eyes captured her gaze and held it. She couldn't blink, couldn't move, couldn't breathe. One look from that man entranced her. He wanted her, was staking his claim.

"I'll walk you out."

She smiled. "I can find my way to the door, even with a lousy sense of direction." She waved to the others and turned to leave. Nick remained by her side.

The door closed behind them, and she was in his arms, his mouth on hers for a lingering kiss.

"I've wanted to do that since I first saw you at the cemetery, with your chin jutting high and your body so carefully still."

On this sad and crazy day, when painful memories could have easily overcome her, she felt so alive. And this man had everything to do with it. As did the boy.

"I like your ideas." She put her arms around his neck and returned the favor.

"Katie, Katie," he groaned between kisses.

She stiffened. A nickname from the past. She pulled herself away and patted Nick's shoulder. "See you later."

It had been a trying day with Jeremy's loss and the recognition of her own. Memories. And now more reminders. So far, so good, but she needed time to decompress. She didn't want to push her luck.

NICK SPRINTED into the Martinelli building, collar button opened, shirtsleeves rolled up, tie and jacket left in the truck. He glanced at his watch. Right on time.

Tina met him at the door. "Why didn't you answer your cell phone, Nick? Mom and Dad were frantic. Mike's out at a site, and they took Josie to the hospital."

"Josie?" he asked sharply. "What's wrong? The baby's not due yet, is it? I thought Josie had a couple months to go."

"She did, but now all bets are off. All I know is that she left work, drove herself here and called the doctor. Then everyone went to the hospital. I'm alone now."

Nick looked around. A dozen people were in view. Tina seemed to have her own definition of alone. Sally, his secretary, walked over.

"Everything in the office is under control, Nick. But Josie gave us a scare."

"So I hear."

"I've got a pile of messages for you. Want me to check your e-mail as well?"

He paused, then smiled. "Thanks, but I'll get to it myself."

"You'll need more hours than a day holds. Seems that every subcontractor you called wants to meet with you about the school project. They want to know your time frame. I've set up tentative meeting dates."

An excellent assistant, but not for this project. "I haven't solidified the time frame yet. And I'll probably have to reschedule some of those meetings."

He glanced meaningfully at his sister's astonished expression. She knew darn well that every aspect of the scheduling had been completed. She nodded imperceptibly and smiled at Sally.

"We need you to learn some of my stuff, Sally, so I can carry Josie's work, and you can carry on for me after the wedding. September will be here before we know it and I'll be away for two weeks."

And the city's bid was due on September 15. Nick sighed in resignation. He hadn't forgotten about Tina and Richie's wedding, but it just wasn't on the forefront of his mind.

"I would appreciate that, Sally," he said. "I'm sorry for not speaking with you earlier. For reasons that don't concern you, the school project is separate. Please refer any calls about it to Dad or me. And if we're not around, give them to Tina. The rest of the business has to go on as usual. And that's where you come in."

She looked genuinely puzzled. "I don't get it," she said. "You want me to do Tina's job, and Tina to do my job?"

Nick smiled. "Sort of, but not exactly. Only with the school project."

"Sounds weird to me, but you're the boss." She looked at Tina. "Show me what I need to know."

Nick watched the two women walk away together and vowed that after the project was submitted, he'd explain it all to Sally. And when other government jobs came down the pike, she'd be part of the action.

He closed the door of his office, picked up the pink message slips and got on the phone. Construction in Houston was booming; a labor shortage was threatening. He'd be meeting with potential subcontractors from dawn to dusk—concrete companies, plumbing companies, electricians, air-conditioning and heating people, drywall carpenters, masons, painters. He needed his architects' and engineers' input. He needed quotes, he needed guarantees about availability. He needed to get his bid in order.

Tina poked her head in the door sometime later to say Josie was okay but being kept in the hospital overnight. The doctors had stopped the premature labor, but she was ordered off her feet for the duration, approximately two months.

Nick nodded, concern for his sister temporarily alleviated, but concern for Martinelli Construction cranked up a notch. Josie's condition meant his mother would be available only part-time, if at all. Anna Martinelli had always made it perfectly clear that for her, children came before business. Even a thirty-year-old child would fall under that rule. Mike would be distracted, too. He'd come to work all right, but his ear would be attuned to the phone.

Nick couldn't pull Danny in from the field either. Not yet. Their other jobs had to keep going just as always. And his dad was already working full-time. Joseph Martinelli would work a twenty-four-hour day if he could; he loved the business he'd founded. But Anna would have something to say about that. She wanted him to slow down, retire. No, Nick couldn't allow his dad to do more.

The bottom line was that he would have to pick up the slack. He rolled his shoulders and stretched. Man, he felt stiff. He glanced at the clock on the wall and blinked with incredulity.

His GED class was more than half over. Damn! This was the third one he'd missed. Katherine was probably ready to throw him out, and who could blame her.

His thoughts stopped right there and he inhaled deeply. Who was he kidding? He'd never be able to finish the class at this rate. He slapped his hand on the desk in frustration. He had the energy to do all the work, but he could not physically be in two places at once. He pushed himself out of his chair and heard it hit the wall behind him.

Not again. He would not postpone his dream again, or he really would explode. Somehow, he had to find a way to make everything work.

KATHERINE CLOSED the classroom door behind her, her thoughts focused on the absent Nick. It was unlike him not to leave a message. Before she took three steps, however, she saw a young woman down the hall waving madly at her, a piece of paper in her hand. Her muscles relaxed fractionally, then completely, when she took the pink memo sheet from the work/study student and read Nick's name on it.

Caring about someone ignited a whole new set of nerve endings. Normally, she'd notice an absentee only as a statistic in her roll book. Nick's absence, however, had weighed heavily on her the entire evening.

But according to his message, she'd be seeing him soon. At her place. With the table set for take-out Chinese that he'd bring from Kim Son, on Westheimer, his favorite Asian restaurant.

Hmm...no reason she couldn't light a candle or two. No reason she couldn't slip into something very comfortable. It sounded as if his day had only gotten tougher since this morning with Jeremy. No reason she couldn't help him relax. She'd be a good listener if he wanted to unwind.

Her pulse raced at her blossoming thoughts. Intimacy of any type still scared her. It loomed in her mind like the blank pages of a novel waiting to be written, not an activity for the faint of heart. Connecting to another person required a whole heart.

Now it required *her* heart.

CHAPTER SIX

NICK STOOD in front of Katherine's apartment, a bag of aromatic food in each arm, and pressed her bell with the tip of his finger. Too much dinner for two people, he acknowledged silently, then smiled. He didn't know her preferences, so he'd bought a little of everything. He heard her turn the lock, and when she opened her door, all thoughts of food were obliterated.

Black silky material swayed against her, first revealing, then concealing her feminine curves as she stepped back to let him in. This Katherine was better than any dream, he thought, eyes glued to the nightgown-like dress she'd chosen to wear. Her blond hair hung down her back, unconfined, and she was barefoot, with red-painted toenails peeking from beneath her gown when she walked. It didn't get much better than this...until she smiled.

His libido roared, and the bags of food almost hit the floor. She outshone the *Mona Lisa*. Easily. Every day she revealed another part of herself. Before him stood not the professional teacher, not the feisty debater who challenged him, not the caring friend she'd been to Jeremy. No. Before him stood the epitome of woman—a siren—beautiful, intelligent, sexy, caring, and smiling at him with her lips and her eyes.

He forgot to say hello.

"Are you coming in?" Katherine asked. "Or are you going to stand in the doorway all night?"

He wanted to bolt the lock and keep her captive for a week. Instead, he shoved the food onto a nearby table and walked toward her. Her eyes widened, and he knew she read his intention before he covered her mouth with his own.

He tasted her sweetness, his tongue tracing her lips, softening them, until they parted for him. She explored his mouth, too, returned his thrusts, and when she moaned softly, her arms tightening around him, holding him close, he felt he'd come home.

He closed his eyes and breathed deeply, wanting to memorize her natural woman's fragrance, wanting to memorize how she felt in his embrace. From the first time he saw her sashaying down the school corridor, he'd wanted this golden girl. Warm honey, he'd thought. And now he wanted to taste the sweetness over and over again.

As soon as Katherine saw Nick standing in the doorway earlier, she knew tonight would be different. His brown eyes, hot with wanting, told their own story, and her own rapid pulse rate revealed her response. One touch of his lips and she'd melted against his broad chest, against the length of his strong body.

Katherine had never felt drugged from a kiss before. Not even with her poet in Chicago. No, not once in all her adult years. Until now. How could she have been afraid of this? She'd been waiting for him all these years. For Nick.

He nibbled her lips, her jaw, her neck, and she shivered down to her toes.

"Delicious," he whispered as he swung her into his arms. "Let's get comfortable."

She didn't protest. Didn't want to. Just held him close as he carried her to the sofa and kept her on his lap. "I like your brand of kisses, Nicholas Martinelli. Let's do it again."

"And I like teaching the teacher," he replied as his lips descended to capture hers, warm and sweet as vintage wine. And just as heady.

She purred deep in her throat, then felt Nick's hands stroking her back, her sides, her breast. The silky gown provided no protection, and his every touch sent fire through her veins. She quivered as he lightly feathered her nipple, and almost burst as he did it again. Incendiary touch!

She opened her eyes, wanting to see his face. She saw the tenderness in his expression as he studied her. "You're beautiful, Katie," he whispered. "So beautiful and smart. Soft in all the right places." He tightened his embrace. "You feel just like a woman should feel in a man's arms. And you fit perfectly in mine."

Her eyes filled. No man had ever made her feel as special as Nick did. She knew people considered her attractive. She credited her genes and rarely thought about it. But until now, she'd never felt anything but ordinary. A tear fell as she raised her head to kiss him.

"You're crying!" His voice held horror. "Did I hurt you? Where?"

She shook her head, and stroked his cheek. "No, you touched me." She patted the left side of her chest. "In here."

"Oh, Katie, baby..." He kissed her again, crushing her to him, then bestowed light butterfly kisses all over her face and neck.

She wrapped her arms around him and rested her head against his chest. "I'm just not used to this."

"It's been a very long time for me also," he admitted quietly. No light twinkled in his eyes now.

"You must have loved her very much." She hadn't planned them, the words popped out of her mouth, but she knew they were true.

"I did, and still do," he replied. "Love doesn't end because a life ends."

She waited a moment, suddenly uneasy, then left the comfort of his lap. "How about that dinner you brought?"

He grinned ruefully. "Is playtime over?"

"Playtime is over," she repeated with a forced grin as she led him into the kitchen. "How can I play with someone who doesn't know my name?" she teased. "Katherine, Kathy, Katie. Before you know it, I'll be Katrin again."

As quickly as she spoke the words, she covered her mouth with her hand to pull them back.

His eyebrows lifted. "Katrin? Nice. I like it."

"I don't believe I said it," she replied. "It's been so many years, I'd forgotten the sound of it." The corners of her mouth curled into a slight smile. "I'm Katherine now."

His dark eyes searched her face. "You are who you are. By any name. Tell me more. I'm interested in the whole package."

She leaned against the refrigerator and looked into the dark eyes studying her with patience and expectation. He spoke the truth; he wanted her. And she wanted him, but he still loved his wife. A truly romantic love that had survived the ultimate tragedy.

She couldn't compete with the memory of a perfect love. If she tried, she'd lose.

She swallowed hard. How had she allowed him to break down her barriers? The first man who had. The first man who could! But she needed to be first in his heart, too.

So selfish of her. Unlike the rational, logical person she was. And she didn't care. Almost.

Was she expecting too much? He'd been a strong, quiet presence in her new life, always managing to be there when she needed him. He did strange things to her heart, wonderful things, scary things.

And she trusted him. That was a major discovery. Something new. Different. Darn! She knew life would get complicated once she let herself love someone. Tangled emotions. An overused phrase that fit her confused thoughts exactly.

He said he was interested in the whole package. The package included the bad as well as the good. Now they'd see if he really meant it.

She took a deep breath. "I was born Katrin Elena Kowalski in Chicago." She reached for a framed portrait, temporarily stored on an empty shelf in a kitchen cabinet, and gently stroked the glass. "And these are my parents, Helen and Peter Kowalski, born in Poland, orphaned there during the war and resettled with cousins in the United States when they were youngsters."

She avoided his eyes. "I've been hiding from them for ten long years."

So now he knew what a coward she was. She turned her head and stared blindly out the window where darkness prevailed, waiting for his exclamation of disbelief. Ten years! How could you?

She felt him take the picture from her hands. "You're the image of your mother," he said softly with approval. "She looks happy, and your dad has a twinkle in his eye, like he's got a little secret. I wish I could have known them, sweetheart. Both such handsome people." He gently pulled her against him. "You were so young. You must miss them terribly."

He blindsided her with words and thoughts. Her breath caught, tears fell, silently at first, then quickly turning to quivering, painful sobs. A dam opened that had been locked for too long.

With one glance, Nick had seen her dad's humor, her mom's serenity, while she had spent years trying not to see anything. Trying not to miss them. Keeping herself too busy to think at all. Forging a new life where there were no memories. Selling the old house as quickly as possible. Changing her name to Kirby. Avoiding the old neighborhood and the neighbors.

She leaned over the countertop, reached for some tissues, and poured out her grief and her guilt. Strong arms carefully turned her around, and she was in Nick's embrace, crying all over his shirt.

"Their funeral didn't seem real," she gulped. "It was like watching a play. So I pretended…"

"Shh…Katie. It's okay. It's a survival technique. You were a kid, and you were trying to survive. Period. Now you're somewhere else. Now you can handle it differently."

She hiccuped and blew her nose. Survival. Broken lives. First her parents. Then her. They had survived a European Armageddon in their youth. She would survive, too. She was their daughter and couldn't do anything less. In fact, maybe she could do more. Maybe her own life story should be included in the anthology of her students' autobiographies.

She took a deep breath and looked around her. Looked at her bare feet, touched her swollen nose and searched the face of the man who still held her securely in his arms. The caring man who now leaned over to kiss the top of her head, who had started making love to her a short while ago and was now loving her as she needed to be loved. With tenderness and strength. The caring man who had no idea she'd been stupidly jealous of his poor wife. What an idiot she'd been! About so many things.

Her glance captured the two bags of food Nick had brought in, and suddenly she was hungry. From the sublime to the ridiculous. The situation seemed surreal.

"Hmm…the evening didn't turn out quite as…as…cozy as I had envisioned," she said.

His eyes lit up. "Honey, it's never too late for cozy."

He sure knew how to pick up her spirits. "I'm sorry about all the crying," she added. "I'm stunned, actually. It came out of nowhere."

"And it'll probably come again, Katie. It's called grieving. And there are no rules." He paused. "I happen to be very familiar with the process."

She looked into his face and saw the pain still visible in his eyes. "I know," she said, squeezing his hand gently.

"So," he said a moment later. "Can a guy get a hot meal around here, especially when he supplies the dinner?"

She felt herself grin. Nothing like hunger to bring the world back to basics.

She bustled with the food, grateful for the chance to absorb what had happened. After all these years, she had just broken down. She, who prided herself on living life unemotionally, on making sensible decisions, on maintaining control. Only with Suzanne had she ever fallen apart since the funeral. And now Nick.

It all came down to trust, a most rational conclusion.

Sitting across the table from Nick, sharing an intimate meal, Katherine suddenly felt shy. She'd just unloaded a decade of feelings, unplanned though it had been. Weren't most men uncomfortable with emotion? Nick seemed to take it in stride, but what was he really thinking behind the smile he wore?

WHAT WAS SHE really thinking behind her smile? Nick looked at Katherine across the table, watched her deliberately place each forkful of food into her mouth, chew and swallow. He'd bet she didn't taste a thing.

Knowing Katherine, she probably wished she could undo the past fifteen minutes. She hadn't had enough time to understand that they were the healthiest fifteen minutes she could have spent.

"So, how's the hamburger?" He raised innocent eyes to her.

"Fine."

He put his fork down and reached for her hand. "Hey, girl. You just insulted the best orange chicken in Houston."

She looked at her plate, looked at him and inhaled deeply. "Oh, brother. I'm a mess."

But she didn't pull her hand away from his. "I did the same thing in the beginning," he said as he pressed her palm. "We had a beautiful home, and when Donna and Jenny were killed, I moved out. Just couldn't stay there. And didn't want to stay with my folks. Checked into a hotel for three months. And one day I went back. Didn't plan to. I just found myself there.

"The grass was trimmed, the house clean. Dad had seen to that. But it wasn't home anymore. Not when the people I loved the most were gone."

She nodded and he didn't speak for a while. He couldn't. In his mind's eye, he was back in that house, back with the echoes of happy laughter before the silence came. He squeezed his eyes shut for a moment. "I just walked through it and left. Could barely breathe. I went back a second time and saved what I wanted, mostly pictures, her baby shoes...I don't know. Just some things. But I couldn't bring myself to sell the darn house for almost a year.''

Her eyes hadn't left his face, had barely blinked while he spoke. He kept her hand in his, brought it to his mouth and kissed her fingers.

''Ah, Nick,'' she murmured, as she squeezed his hand in reply, ''we're quite a pair.''

He liked the sound of the ''we'' when she said it. He liked the word *pair* even better. ''We're doing just fine, Katrin, just fine.''

She laughed wryly. ''Is that right? You're a rolling stone without a home yet, Nick. Your words, remember? And I keep chasing after jobs, looking for something I don't have. Something permanent, where I can grow some roots.''

''Don't you get it, Katrin?'' How could she not see it? ''We're both looking for the same thing.''

OF COURSE she got it. Maybe a heartbeat after Nick did because her brain had stopped working when she heard him use her given name as if he'd used it a million times before. Katrin. It fit naturally into his sentence. In fact, it felt right. And her heart felt lighter than it had in a long while.

Cool it. Slow down. Don't imagine things. Nick was one of the romantics of the world. He had a way with people, great instincts. He could talk to anyone and everyone liked talking to him. He knew Katherine pretty well, too. Liked her, if his kisses could be used as a yardstick. They had some common experiences, so he'd know how to reassure her; he'd know how to be a friend.

He'd concluded they were looking for the same thing. But that didn't mean they'd find it with each other. He'd never actually said anything about love or commitment or the future. A shadow colored her thoughts, but practiced in hiding her feelings, she changed the subject.

"I was concerned when you didn't show up for class today, Nick. I thought you might have been with Jeremy again."

Nick shook his head. "I did call him right after I called the college with the message for you."

"How's he doing?" she asked, anxiety tingeing her voice.

"As well as he can, I suppose. Didn't want to hang up the phone, so I guess he was glad to hear from me. I talked about his new job, wanted to give him something else to think about."

She winced. "I knew the first night would be hard."

"He said something about an envelope you gave him. Said he's saving it for later. Want to share the mystery?"

She busied herself clearing the table, not meeting his eyes. "It's just a poem. My usual way of saying something important. It's by William Henley and it's called 'Invictus.' Each stanza is powerful, but I want him to believe the last two lines of the whole work…if he can."

She turned from the sink to see Nick waiting with eyebrows raised.

She cleared her throat. "The lines are about being master of your own fate. The captain of your own soul."

A long, low whistle was Nick's response. "That's about as far away as he's feeling right now."

"I know," she replied. "I just wanted to give him hope, a goal. And I wanted him to know that I was thinking about him so he wouldn't feel so alone."

"Yeah," said Nick softly as he slowly approached her. "That's really the worst part."

She nodded, a lump in her throat, as a kaleidoscope of memories accosted her. Then she focused on the man beside her once again. "But Jeremy has other problems. Estelle filled me in earlier. Shoplifting, fighting, refusing to follow rules, and a few court cases thrown in. He's got a lot to overcome and that's why we've been having some problems at school."

He held out his hand. "You're a beautiful lady, Katrin, inside and out." He paused. "Don't be discouraged about Jeremy. There are plenty of kids with problems that turn out all right. Believe me. I know."

She put her hand in his and looked up at him. "Thanks for the compliment," she whispered. "And thanks for the support."

He kissed her on the forehead first, then lightly on the mouth. "Good night, Katrin. Let's hope we each find what we're looking for."

She felt the difference in his kiss, the distance. And she felt her smile wobble. Happiness was such a fragile thing. With no guarantees. It seemed they all had a long way to go.

TOTALLY EXHAUSTED, Nick fell asleep as soon as he
hit the pillow. And two hours later, was wide awake.
Something in Katherine's behavior nagged at him. He
reviewed the evening in his mind, piece by piece,
until he zeroed in on the moment she'd pulled away
emotionally. When he'd said they were both looking
for the same thing, she'd changed the subject to Jeremy.

She always threw up fences when she was scared.
But why this time? She'd certainly greeted him with
open arms. And he'd ended the evening by kissing
her on the forehead after their discussion about the
boy. How stupid! A genial uncle could kiss her on
the forehead, and Nick certainly didn't feel like her
uncle.

In his bed, Nick swore in frustration. He should
have swept her off her feet with a good-night kiss
she'd remember for a lifetime. Katrin needed the reassurance. He knew her well enough to know that.
She could hold her own with anyone professionally,
but in private life she needed what every woman
wanted. To know she was the one. The special one.

The thought stopped him cold. Was she really the
one, or just conveniently there for a man waking up
from a long sleep? He walked to the kitchen for a
drink of water. Hell, life was getting too complicated.
Memories were getting too complicated.

His history had been in that kitchen tonight, up
close with him and Katrin. Donna, the baby, their
home. Was he feeling guilty? Too afraid to try again?
Had Katrin sensed his confusion and provided him
with an easy out?

He stood at the sink, glass of water in hand, slowly raising it to his mouth. His thoughts whirled and he searched for the truth. Sexual need? There were dozens of Houston beauties who'd oblige. He'd had no interest. Guilt? No, not really. It was time to go on with his life.

Fear? Ah...that struck a chord. To love again required courage. Surviving one tragedy had taken a heavy toll. If anything happened to Katrin—no, he squeezed his eyes shut—he couldn't even contemplate it.

He'd answered his own questions. Tragedy had a way of making a person more introspective, of cutting through the excuses and getting to the heart of the matter.

He wouldn't run away. Not his style. Especially when he pictured her in his life, as part of the future. Katrin wasn't his second choice. She was his second chance.

KATHERINE TOSSED and turned in her air-conditioned bedroom, kicking her covers to the floor. The room wasn't warm. It was her. Thinking about Nick.

She glanced at her clock radio. One in the morning. Darn! She needed to get up early and find the University of Houston's central campus. Soon the library would be her closest friend as she made headway on her dissertation. Maybe she'd call Richmond House to see how Jeremy got through the night. Estelle would tell her.

A myriad of thoughts hammered at her mind, but her brain kept revolving back to Nick. He still loved his dead wife. He'd made that clear. So where did that leave them? Was he glad to have gone home with only a casual kiss? Was he looking for an easy way to end their relationship?

No. Nick never took the easy way with anything. She knew that much about him. If he wanted out, he'd say so. Gently, but honestly.

Shoot! She had the least experience with men of anyone she knew. How was she supposed to figure out what was in his brain?

Words were her business. She could figure out meanings to just about anything. But so far, Nick hadn't said the simple words any woman could understand.

Maybe he never would.

JEREMY TUCKER PUNCHED his pillow for the tenth time and turned over on his back. From his bed in the far corner of the room he could see the other boys' shapes illuminated by the night-light in the hall. There was no door to block the light. None of the bedrooms had doors. That's the way it was in this place. It didn't make much of a difference anyway. With six boys in a room, privacy didn't exist.

He had two drawers in the dresser to call his own. Inside were five shirts, three shorts, two pants, socks and underwear, identical in number and almost identical in style to everyone else's. Hell, he lived in an institution, put there by the County Probation Department for a Class C misdemeanor—theft. They also got him for truancy.

How could he have gone to school when he'd had

to take care of his dad? Without warning, tears dripped from the outside corners of his eyes all the way to his pillow. He turned over again, this time punching the mattress. Why waste tears? His dad had been a loser. Sweet at times, but weak and useless. Funny and loving at times, and sometimes downright mean. Damn useless as a father. Not like a father should be. But at least he was family.

And now what?

Waves of terror almost suffocated him, like a boa constrictor wrapping itself around its prey. He had no one. Not one relative. Nobody. At sixteen years old, he was totally alone.

He slammed a brake on his fear. So what if he was alone? He'd been dealing with the adult world for years by himself. Courts, judges, police, landlords, storekeepers, doctors. There hadn't been many facets of the world he hadn't dealt with already. So he'd deal a little longer. It wouldn't be much different.

Nature called and he got out of bed. Maybe he'd chat with the counselor on duty. He couldn't sleep anyway.

"Hey, Jer," came a whispered hail from the next bed.

"What?" he replied to Trevor. The fourteen-year-old had run away from home three times before a caseworker finally proved he was being abused.

"Are you gonna split now?"

"Why would I do that?" Jeremy replied.

"Why not? You're kinda free, aren't you? You can't get back with your father, so why stick around?"

He hadn't quite thought of it that way. "I've got plans, Trev. But not yet."

"You gonna hang with Nick, huh? And the babe?"

Anger boiled his blood. Instantly. He walked to the other boy's bed and glared down. "Ms. Katherine's not a babe, man. She's a lady. Get it?"

The kid avoided his eyes. "I get it. But she looks so good, man. That's one hot lady."

"Stop looking so hard! Go drool over a *Playboy* the next time we're at the mall, and leave Ms. Katherine alone."

"Sure, Jeremy. Sure."

Jeremy looked at Trevor's big dark eyes, now troubled and a little frightened, and was sorry he'd snapped at the kid. Trevor never did well with anger or tension in a room.

"Go to sleep, Trev. Everything's okay."

The boy inhaled deeply. "But in case you decide to run, take me with you."

Jeremy smiled. "I'll think about it," he lied. He wouldn't take anyone with him when he left. All the kids talked about running away. Half of them had tried it. That's why almost as many counselors went on an outing as boys did. Trevor wouldn't run, though. Not even with Jeremy. Trevor thought Richmond House was heaven and, despite reassurance, was terrified of being sent back to his family.

And Jeremy wasn't ready to go anywhere yet. The kid didn't have it wrong. If Nick turned out to be a dud, there'd be plenty of time to split. Besides, he'd given him a job. A chance to earn some money. And Ms. Katherine...she was special. That poem she gave him. He'd had to look up some of the words and phrases, but he definitely got the drift.

She believed in him. She thought he was strong. He was down, but not out. That's what it meant. And she'd told him she'd gone through the same thing. If she could make it, he could, too. He just didn't quite know how. Yet.

He climbed back into bed and reached under his pillow for the poem. She liked him a lot. Had taken the time to find this poem and come to the funeral and everything. Maybe she *really* liked him. Maybe she thought he was a special guy. His heart raced at the thought.

He should get her a gift. Jewelry. Women liked jewelry. He'd palm some the next time he went to the mall. A great idea. He had golden fingers, and shoplifting was his specialty. He smiled with satisfaction, fingered the poem again, and finally fell asleep.

SALLY JENSEN LEFT Martinelli Construction after six the night of the funeral. She didn't mind working late; she never minded earning extra money. At times she had to pinch herself to believe that she, Sally Jensen, had escaped the poverty, drugs and gangs of her old neighborhood.

She patted the roof of her Ford Escort—almost new when she'd bought it—and slipped behind the wheel. Owning a good car meant something. She'd never take it for granted.

Just as she never took for granted the computer training program she'd completed several years ago. Ironically, her local social service agencies had provided a way out of the neighborhood for her. She'd grabbed the opportunity and ran right into a reception position with Martinelli Construction, and then a year later became Nick's secretary.

And now, at twenty-three years old, life held sweet promise. A great job, an excellent car and her own apartment in a decent neighborhood. Not much in the savings account yet, but that would come.

She covered her mouth as she yawned three times. The last few weeks had been busy and somewhat strange with this family-only project. A big mystery. Suddenly, she had to learn Tina's job, while Tina worked with her brother. A temporary arrangement, Nick had said, but…what was that old saying? Something about blood being thicker than water. And Sally wasn't family. As long as her job remained safe and secure, however, she wouldn't complain.

She unlocked her apartment door and saw her older brother, all two hundred fifty pounds of him, lying on her couch, watching television, eating her food and finishing the entire pitcher of iced tea she'd brewed the night before.

"Good chicken, Sal," he greeted her, waving a drumstick in the air.

Sweet and lazy, and trying to get around her. "You said that yesterday, Eddie. And three days ago, you liked my meat loaf. Why don't you learn to cook?"

His frequent surprise visits were getting out of hand. She didn't earn enough to feed him constantly, and more important, she wanted her privacy at the end of the day. A nice, quiet life. Memories of a noisy, crowded housing complex with too many single mothers, too many children and not enough of anything to go around were easy to recall. She silently vowed to change her locks the next day.

She kicked off her pumps, picked them up and walked to the bedroom to change out of her work clothes. "Why are you here again, Eddie?" she called over her shoulder. "Is it just for a meal or is something else going on?" She knew her words would sound sharp to an outsider, but she also knew her brother and all his weaknesses. She loved him, but she didn't trust him.

"Can't a guy visit with his little sister once in a while?"

She blinked twice and returned to the living room. Every hair on her neck seemed to stand on end. Goose bumps covered her skin. He wanted something. And he'd try sweet-talk first.

"Not when he's supposed to be at work," she replied before the truth hit her. "Oh, no, Eddie. You lost your job, didn't you? Second shift is working now..."

"So what?" he snarled. "It was a crap job. Couldn't stand it, anyway."

Her stomach churned. She didn't need this. "But you earned a paycheck every week. I can't afford to support you. You need to get another job."

He waved his hand at her. "Everything's under control. I've got something going for me. For us. Something big." He stood up and held his hands far apart. "Real big."

She wanted no part of his plans. Delusions, really. Eddie only put his mind to two things: get-rich schemes and card games. Gambling. "I can take care of myself," she replied. "Don't include me."

"Too late," he said. "You're part of the deal."

Her hands fisted at her side. "Then deal me out. Whatever it is, just deal me out."

"You don't understand, Sal. I can't. You're key to it all." Suddenly, he avoided her eyes and pressed his lips together hard. "If you don't help me, Sal," he whispered in a choked voice, "I'm a dead man."

CHAPTER SEVEN

"OF COURSE JOSIE can't go to the fund-raiser!" Nick bellowed at his dad. "She'd be on her feet all night." He leaned over his desk until he was eye to eye with his father. "Mike isn't making a big deal about it, is he? Who cares if their alma mater is the beneficiary of the event? Josie can't go."

"Mike? Are you kidding?" responded Joe Martinelli. "He's watching over her like a hawk."

Nick's blood pressure dropped instantly and he sank back into his chair. Two hours' sleep didn't cut it, but he had only himself to blame. Fear had struck him for a moment last night and his parting kiss to Katherine had been a mere peck on her lips. Fool! Now he wished he could crawl into her bed and never leave. "So what's the problem?" he asked his father.

"No problem if you go instead," replied Joe. "Martinelli Construction is donating materials and labor for the new library. We're in the program book. We need to be there."

Nick closed his eyes. He understood the value of publicity and goodwill as well as anyone, but at that moment all he understood was that another chunk of his time was being eaten away.

"How about you and Mama going?" he suggested

with vain hope. "You love crowds. You love brag-
ging about the business."

"Nah. Your mama wants to visit with Josie. She
said you should bring a date with you, Nicky. Have
a nice evening."

Nick opened one eye, saw the unusual flush on his
father's face and knew he was being set up. Hell, they
both were. His mother had no scruples.

"Did she also tell you the name of the woman I
should bring?" he asked quietly.

"Yeah. You want to hear it?" Joe sounded defensive, belligerent, and looked uncomfortable. He
seemed to find the view over Nick's shoulder fasci-
nating.

In a word, his dad felt cornered. Nick knew the
signs; he'd been there more than a few times himself.

"I'm not sure." He looked at Joe, and his dad
looked back at him. They both started laughing at the
same time.

"You know your mother," said Joe with a shrug.
"She likes to keep up with her kids."

An understatement if he ever heard one. "And, of
course, Pop, you're not interested at all." Nick strug-
gled to keep a straight face.

"You're my son, for God's sake," Joe blustered.
"You got something to tell me, I'm listening."

Nick loved his old man. They'd traveled a lot of
roads together through the years. Lots of rough ones
in the early days, and then again in recent times, and
some beautiful smooth ones along the way. No matter
what he faced, his dad was there. Quieter than his
mother, surely, but rock solid and steady.

"Just tell Mama...I'll be taking a wonderful woman to the party. No names. That'll drive her crazy for a while."

"Son, that's enough to make her show up for ten minutes!"

Terrific.

KATHERINE SAT at her desk in the empty classroom, trying to concentrate on lesson plans, but found herself glancing from her watch to the door every five minutes. Jeremy had planted himself in the back of her mind, and she expected him today. Nick, however, had carved a home in the forefront of her mind, and she had no idea whether she'd see him or not. His attendance had been the most irregular in the class.

With gritty, lack-of-sleep eyes and determination, she'd stuck to her plan and visited the university library that morning. *The Role of Family in the Works of Early Nineteenth-Century English Female Novelists* wouldn't write itself! And she itched to tackle it. Then she'd come directly to the community college. Sheer willpower would get her through the rest of the day.

She smiled as students started filing in, and blinked unshed tears as many placed cards and small gifts on Jeremy's desk. He'd become a personality in the class, perhaps because of his tender age, perhaps because he voiced his opinions so readily, or perhaps because every adult there knew he'd come from a hard place, possibly harder than their own. Whether he realized it or not, he'd made an impression.

Jeremy walked in just then and his eyes sought her out. She smiled and extended her hand.

"Welcome back. How're you holding up today?"

"Okay, I guess. I did my community service this morning. And I...I wanted to tell you, I liked the poem. I understand it."

He met her eyes guilelessly, and Katherine believed him.

"We can discuss it during the break if you like. And then, if you're interested, you can look up Tennyson, Shakespeare and Bacon, to see what they have to say about being the master of your own fate."

He grabbed a pencil. "What were those names again?"

Her heart twisted at his response. Who would nurture this boy? Who would see that he went to college instead of to an unskilled dead-end job? Who would tell him to make real flesh-and-blood friends instead of relying on book friends as she had?

"Lend me that pencil, Jeremy." She tore a piece of paper from her notebook. "Here's my phone number. You keep it safe. And when this class is over, after you've earned your high-school equivalency, you call me anytime. And maybe we can figure out a way, with Ms. Estelle, to get you into some college classes."

Jeremy took the paper from her as though handling a butterfly. He studied what she'd written, carefully folded the note and put it in his deep front pocket. Then he looked at her, eyes filled with love and admiration. "Thank you, Ms. Katherine. I'll never lose it."

Uh-oh! Katherine's stomach dropped to her toes as the impact of his adoration hit her. How should she handle it? Thankfully, puppy love was not fatal, but Jeremy was so vulnerable now, any rejection on her part could only inflict more hurt in his life. "Look at your desk, Jeremy. Your classmates have been thinking about you."

She caught the exact moment he understood, the moment his eyes widened when he focused on the cards. He turned back to her then as if to say, "For me?" She nodded. He picked up an envelope, but Dorothy, the mother of two, came to him. Soon Elvia, Rosa and Maria joined her. Then Luis, who sat in the last row, and John, who worked as a bellhop, joined them. And Jeremy was surrounded by sympathetic hearts.

"All your doing?" Nick's low timbre caught her by surprise.

She twirled and studied him bit by bit. He looked as tired as she felt. Tired and tempting with his scruffy beard and that stubborn dark curl falling on his forehead. She guessed he hadn't slept much better than she did. Good! Then she looked closely at his eyes. Those dark orbs burned brightly when they studied her, and didn't seem sleepy at all.

"He's made a lot of friends in class," she finally replied. "And I hope that offsets his infatuation with me."

"I do, too, but can't say that I blame him." Nick's gaze never left her face.

"What? Why are you staring at me? Do I have a smudge on my nose?"

He shook his head and reached for her hand. "It's a perfect nose. But your eyes are at half-mast, just like mine. Come with me." He pulled her into the hall and shut the classroom door behind them. "If I had done this last night, both of us would have slept."

Suddenly she was in his arms, being held and kissed with a solid strength she'd only read about in books. His familiar scent, full of spice and man, the broad chest, the hungry mouth that eventually nibbled on that special spot behind her ear, all of these sensations cocooned her, blocking out the world.

She stood on her toes, her face tilted, wanting more of him. Her usual reaction. Until a shred of sanity invaded. First, they were in a school corridor, fortunately empty at the moment. Second, and more important, she remembered his cool departure last night, and she pulled away from him. Her breath came in gasps. So did his. They stood staring at each other, wondering, wanting...

"What was that all about?" Katherine asked.

"It was the good-night kiss you were supposed to get last night."

"Then why didn't I?" she asked.

"Because I'm a jerk, that's why!"

She couldn't quite hide a tiny smile. "No. You were confused is why, between the past and the present."

A deafening silence was the only reply. Her ears rang with it, her spirits dropped.

"Pretty smart and sassy for a teacher," he finally said. His teasing words belied the unsmiling mouth, and the twin creases on his forehead. "I was scared,

Katrin. For a long moment last night, I was scared."
He stroked her cheek gently with shaky fingers.
"Give me a chance...please. We shared a lot of history last night, pretty heavy for both of us." He
looked at her with a question in his eyes.

She nodded slowly. It was the truth.

"Then it seems to me," he said deliberately, "we
could both use a new beginning."

More new beginnings. Her life had been filled with
them recently. A new city, a new job, a new man.

"A new beginning?" she said, tasting the words.
"With each other? Or with others?"

"Yes. No. Definitely not. Definitely with each
other." His words raced to her ears. His lips sought
her mouth just as quickly. "Absolutely," he murmured.

A giggle emerged from her throat at his mixed-up
response and she slid out of his hold. His kisses had
a way of becoming addictive, and the college corridor
was the wrong place.

"Let's take one day at a time, Nick, and see where
it leads."

"One day at a time, huh?" Nick repeated. "Then
I'd like to claim the next thousand days or so, to try
out the plan."

Before she could answer, the classroom door
opened and Dorothy looked at them, hand on her hip.
"Nick, are you making Ms. Kirby late for our class?
Can't you do your courtin' afterward—on your own
time?"

Nick roared with laughter, but Katherine felt her

cheeks flame. "I'll be right there, Dorothy. Five seconds."

Dorothy reentered the room, and as the door closed again, Katherine heard her repeat, "She said five seconds."

"I've got to get in there, Nick, and so do you."

"Not tonight, I'm afraid. I came here only to see you. You didn't return my voice messages, so I had to come in person. I'm loaded with work, Kat. It just can't be helped."

"But you need the preparation for the test, the practice exams I'll be giving."

"How about a private lesson, say, about eight o'clock tonight?" His eyes gleamed as he he kissed her hard and fast. Then he was gone.

She stared at his retreating back as he dashed toward the stairs, for a moment angry at Martinelli Construction and the effort Nick had to make. With such a large family, why weren't the others doing more? Weren't Nick's dreams important, too?

She'd give him a private lesson and as many as he needed until test time. A tiny smile fluttered on her lips as she realized that one day at a time also included the nights.

"SAVE SATURDAY EVENING, Kat. I'm representing the company at a big to-do for the university." Nick glanced up from the practice exam he was taking at Katherine's kitchen table. His concentration faltered every time she came near him with her never-ending legs and her round little bottom tucked into snug denim shorts.

"I'm timing you, Nick. Don't talk now."

If he didn't talk, he'd jump her bones. "The music's bound to be good. When it's slow, you'll be in my arms, and when it's fast, you'll be gyrating next to me. It's a win-win. And if we ignore all the speeches, we'll have a great time."

"I give up." She clicked the stopwatch and glared at him. "You're wasting your time and mine. Don't you want to pass?"

"Of course I do. And I will. You worry too much, Katrin. You worry about all of us, every single student, always trying to help us, always finding new ways to explain things. You never give up. And I think that makes you one fine teacher."

He'd always remember her expression after that compliment. Surprise, appreciation and wonderment. "Hell," he continued, "when I saw you standing in front of the class on the first night, I never thought you'd last two days. But you sure showed me."

"I showed myself, too. I knew I wouldn't quit, but I didn't know how effective I'd be."

"You don't have to wonder anymore." He held out his hand. "Come here, baby. You're too far away." He hauled her onto his lap and snuck in a few kisses behind that sensitive ear. She squirmed right on cue. Oh, he was getting to know her well!

"Can you be ready at seven Saturday night?" he whispered as he nibbled at the lobe.

"Oh, Nick. I'm so sorry. I can't. Suzanne and David already invited me to a predinner cocktail party before the gala. They want to introduce me to some of their university friends, including the chair of the

English Department." Her smile glowed and she looked so eager, he wouldn't diminish it with his own disappointment.

"Good for you," he said. "I understand." And he did. When it came to education, he and Kat were from two different worlds. He didn't belong in hers.

"But then we'll go directly to the hotel," Katherine continued. "How about if we meet there?"

He paused before answering. "The last thing I want to do is get in the way of your networking. If you need the evening to work the ivory-tower crowd, go for it. I'll just stand on the sidelines and drool."

Her blue eyes sparkled and she laughed as he'd hoped she would, while he suffered a mild case of frustration. He knew she couldn't ask him to her pre-gala gathering. Not only was she a guest herself, but she was hobnobbing with faculty. It seemed a fine line existed between those who had degrees and those who didn't. He'd never thought it mattered to him. And until recently it hadn't. After all, by anyone's standards, he'd proven himself again and again. But even he needed that piece of paper to write the ticket he wanted.

Although it certainly hadn't required a degree for him to provide the university with support. His hard work had done that. He wondered if the professors ever thought of all the businesses and organizations that backed the nonprofit university.

It didn't matter. Katrin's happiness with her career hinged upon employment at the university level, and he knew firsthand that the students would be lucky to have her. He also knew that Jonathan Carter had been in touch with her since his weekend in Houston. Funny, Nick wasn't worried about a romantic rival, regardless of Jonathan's intent—Katrin's responses to Nick were so open and honest—but how could he compete with her lifelong ambition? He'd be damn lucky if she found her professional satisfaction in his hometown. So he'd do whatever he could to help, even if it meant controlling his feelings tonight.

HIS GOOD INTENTIONS almost turned to dust the minute he spotted Katherine in the hotel ballroom. In a classic long sheath dress, all in white, with one shoulder bare, she reminded him of a Greek goddess. When she walked, a wonderful length of leg was revealed by the high slit at the side of the dress. A hide-and-seek gown that hung elegantly on a woman who moved like a queen.

She was his siren call. Like a bright flower attracting a bumblebee, she attracted him. And he had to sip the nectar.

But not yet. He'd promised her the freedom to do her thing.

He watched her with Suzanne, David and their group of associates. Her animated face and quick smile stirred his heart and had more than one male in their crowd hanging on to her words.

Good intentions be damned! She'd had a cocktail party and ten whole minutes at the hotel to impress them with her background. Enough. She could follow up with a résumé.

He started walking toward her, heard his name called, and spent a minute with Josie's friend. The chairpersons of the event tracked him down, and every committee member seemed to want to say hello. Lord, he knew half the guests in the room. He'd built houses for most of them, and they all seemed to have a story to tell.

From the corner of his eye, he watched Katherine dance a second time with the same guy. He excused himself and made a beeline for his woman.

"What took you so long?" Katherine asked as she wound her arms around Nick's neck. "You should have cut in earlier. If that pompous boor with the clammy hands touched me once more, I would have jabbed my high heel right into his toe."

He couldn't imagine a sweeter welcome. "So, you don't think my hands are clammy then?"

She started to laugh as he stroked her bare back for emphasis. A perfect armful of woman.

"The whole world intercepted me," he admitted.

"You know everyone here?" The incredulity in her voice made him smile.

"Not everyone, but look, see that tall guy over there, distinguished-looking, with gray at the temple. Come on, I'll introduce you."

"But who…"

"His name's Edward Stone. He's the president of the university."

"President?"

"Sure. Don't look so startled. I built his house. His wife loves it. He loves me. End of story. Relax."

He'd called it right on the nose, he thought as he introduced Katherine. Dr. Stone greeted them both

like long lost friends and thanked Nick for supporting
the expansion efforts of the school.

"Katherine is an extraordinary teacher," said Nick,
rolling back on his heels, warming up to speak about
his favorite subject. "In fact, I'm taking an evening
course with her right now at the community college.
Sort of an interdisciplinary curriculum. She makes it
so interesting, students rarely miss a class."

The other students, that is. No matter. He'd gotten
Dr. Stone's attention. The president's focus was all
on Katherine now, but heck, so would any man's.

"I'm impressed, Ms. Kirby. That's high praise
from a perfectionist like Nick."

"Thank you. I *am* a good instructor. But Nick
might be a little biased."

"I won't hold that against you or him. Send me
your résumé, Ms. Kirby. You never know when a
position might open up. See you both later."

Nick drew Katherine close to him again and led
her into the dance.

"Thanks, Nick."

"My pleasure, sweetheart. You've just learned the
first rule of business—if you want to get something
done, go to the decision maker. Seems to me, a president can make some decisions."

"But there's no guarantee."

"Only with death and taxes."

He twirled her around for eight more bars before
the next introduction was upon them.

"Are you ready for more?" he whispered. "This
one's important to me."

He saw her straighten to her full height before turning toward him. "I'm ready for anything," she whispered.

Instantly, his blood warmed and his pants felt too tight in front. "Anything?" he repeated. "Is that a promise?"

Her eyes twinkled as her lips curved into a small smile. "I'm not a liar."

The whole monkey suit felt too snug now. "Something's wrong with this air-conditioning system," he muttered as he extended his hand to the mayor of Houston.

He introduced Katherine, and watched her win an approval rating any politician would covet.

"Welcome to our city, Ms. Kirby. The public schools need good teachers. How about it?"

"Whew! You don't waste any time, do you, sir?"

"Don't believe in it. Wasting time doesn't grow our city. We're building three new schools starting late fall, which is what I need to talk to Nick about," he said.

"I'm listening," said Nick, meeting the mayor's gaze.

"I checked the list of builders who picked up the specs," said the mayor. "Don't recognize all of them. I'd prefer a local contractor to get the business. Someone I know who's reputable. Don't want any outsider looking to make a killing on the back of our city."

Nick could feel the indignation coming from a man who had pledged to lead the city forward. He watched the mayor rock back and forth—the man had tremendous energy—and wouldn't have been surprised to see him wear a hole through the carpet.

"You know that every company puts up a bond," soothed Nick. "Every bidder has to prove a history of commercial projects. The city won't get stuck as long as your engineering department reviews carefully."

"I want the best we can afford. Make sure you do your homework and submit a fair and attractive bid," continued the politician.

"Martinelli Construction is always careful to prepare the most accurate bid we can," replied Nick. "Sometimes we win and sometimes we lose, but we always do our best."

"That's the way it should be. And you'll have good honest competition, too. Just make sure you follow through with a submission."

"You'll get one from us."

"Good. But, of course, there are no guarantees."

"Death and taxes," replied Nick for the second time that evening.

The politician laughed as he slapped Nick on the back and disappeared into the crowd. Nick happily took Katherine in his arms again, and when she leaned her head on his shoulder, they tightened instinctively. Her hair smelled like roses, her skin felt silky smooth to the touch. His fingers ached to run through her blond mane, and continue across every inch of skin hidden under that dress.

He glanced at his watch. "Let's get out of here."

"But you're one of the honorees. Don't you want your company to be acknowledged?"

"All I want right now," he replied, crushing her toward him, "is you."

"Smart man," said a too-familiar voice. "And if I were thirty years younger, I'd want her myself. What do you think, Anna?"

"I think you shouldn't flirt with a beautiful girl while your wife is standing by," said Nick's mother.

Nick closed his eyes and inhaled deeply, then turned to his folks, keeping Katherine close to his side. A cold shower couldn't have been more effective in eliminating his romantic urges. At least for the moment.

"YOU'RE THE IMAGE of your dad," Katherine whispered, "except for the eyes. They're totally your mom's." She quickly turned toward the older couple and extended her hand. "Hi, I'm Katherine Kirby, and the quiet guy beside me is Nick Martinelli." She smiled at his mom and dad and jabbed him with her elbow.

A fast thirty seconds, but it gave him enough time to register that his parents weren't dressed for a party.

"What's wrong?" he asked without preliminaries. "How's Josie?" He quickly explained his sister's high-risk pregnancy to Katherine as he led them all from the dance floor.

"Sleeping," replied his mother. "And Michael looked ready to crash. So we left." She wrung her hands, suddenly looking every bit of her sixty years. *"Mama mia,"* she said, "it's going to be a long two months."

"So we left and stopped at the office," continued his dad.

"Why?" asked Nick. "It's Saturday night."

"I couldn't find my keys this afternoon, so I thought, between your mama and me, we'd look carefully."

"Did you find them?"

"Right on my desk," replied Joe. "It doesn't make sense. They were not there when I left today. This I know."

"So I said," continued Anna Martinelli, "maybe he had a little senior moment. He wasn't too happy with that."

Where did his mother come up with these things? "Dad is not having any senior moments! His memory is better than mine."

"Thank you, Nicholas," said Joe. "But there's more."

"I'm listening."

"The building alarm wasn't set. Mama and I walked right in just opening the front door with her key."

"Is it set now?" asked Nick.

"You bet, but I'm not comfortable. Two things in one day. Not good." Joe shook his head. "I called your cell number, but no answer. So we just came over."

Nick reached for his cell phone and came up empty-handed. Phones had no place in a tuxedo on a Saturday night. That was the theory, the way it should have been.

"First, we need a patrol car," he said. "Second, we change the code, and third, we change the locks. Keys go to family only. Period." He turned toward Katherine. "Did I forget anything?"

"You're assuming the alarm was set by the last

person to leave the building. Maybe that person forgot or didn't realize he or she was last to leave.''

She had a point. "Pop, who locked up?"

"Tina and I walked out together. We locked it."

Nick turned back to Katherine. "We'll call Tina to make sure she didn't return to the building for some reason. And we'll check with Danny, too."

"You need to stay here, Nicky," said his mother. "Look, they're starting to serve dinner, and then there'll be some nice speeches, including yours."

Nick glanced around and saw people gathering at their tables. He eyed the dais with resignation. Martinelli Construction was one of several contributors to the college's expansion. They'd all wind up sharing seats of honor.

"But phone calls need to be made," he protested.

"You and Katherine enjoy yourselves tonight. Dad and I will handle the calls, and maybe you can bring Katherine to the house tomorrow. We can have a nice visit. Barbecue, swimming, just relax."

He'd kill his interfering mother. Katrin wanted to take their relationship one day at a time, and his mom was pushing by leaps and bounds.

"We'll let you know in the morning." He glanced at Kat as his parents left the ballroom, and knew he'd said the right thing. She stood very straight and had that reserved look on her face, the look that protected her real feelings. A visit with the boisterous Martinelli clan evidently was not on her agenda.

KATHERINE SAT next to Nick on the dais, barely able to take her eyes from him. His broad shoulders filled out the tuxedo jacket perfectly, the cummerbund accented his flat stomach. Sexy came in all flavors with this guy, tuxedos or jeans or…nothing at all. Her imagination took flight, and she squeezed his hand.

He brushed his lips across her temple. ''Later, baby, later. Just hold that thought.''

She felt familiar heat invade her cheeks and reached for her glass of water. When she let her guard down, she was an open book. Maybe sitting with Nick wasn't such a great idea. Suzanne's table would have been safer. But she'd wanted to be with Nick.

She looked at him now as he rose to acknowledge the thanks of the university. A smile, a wave and not a single nervous gesture before he took the microphone.

''There's no doubt that I'm a better builder than a speech maker. So tonight I've decided to give you the news you wanted to hear when your homes were under construction…I'm finishing ahead of schedule.''

Katherine laughed with the rest of the crowd. Nick was a natural up there, no matter how he deprecated his public-speaking skills. She listened as he quipped his way through the shortest ''thanks for the recognition'' speech in history, and knew that no one would soon forget that Nick Martinelli of Martinelli Construction had set them laughing, or that he viewed his business as part of the community.

After publicity shots were taken of the speakers, Katherine floated in Nick's arms once again.

''This is the best part,'' she said as she stroked his back.

"This is only the appetizer, darlin'," whispered Nick. "It could be that the best is yet to come."

She glanced up quickly to see the question in his eyes. Eyes filled with desire, shining with heat...and focused totally on her. With heart racing, she nodded.

CHAPTER EIGHT

KATHERINE LAGGED three steps behind Nick as they left the hotel. She smiled at his haste, but then he turned and held out his hand, palm up, in invitation.

What could be more natural than holding hands? Katherine looked at his outstretched hand, a strong, masculine hand patiently waiting for her, and suddenly placing her palm into his seemed as intimate as sharing a bed. Her breath froze in anticipation.

She gingerly placed her fingertips on his, glanced up into knowing eyes and clasped his full palm.

Connection!

She exhaled. A shiver ran through her as Nick pressed her hand in return.

"Courage, Katrin," he whispered. "You're a woman made for loving—the giving and receiving kind—you just don't know it yet. But you will, honey. You will."

His eyes implored her. Believe me! Believe me! they seemed to say.

And she wanted to. But she also knew that to find the truth about who she was, and what she was made of, she'd have to give up something she'd nurtured for ten years. Something that had ensured her survival. Something that had become a part of her.

She'd have to shed her defenses and take a chance on life. Just like everyone else.

It didn't turn out to be as hard as she'd thought. Two hours later, Katherine rolled over in bed inhaling the novel fragrance of spice and musk, noting the strewn tuxedo on her low-back chair and wondering how she could have ever had trepidations about making love with this man. When it was good, it was very, very good. She stretched and giggled.

"Liked that, did you?" growled Nick as he caught her around the waist and hauled her against him spoon style.

She fit against him perfectly, as though she belonged, as though sharing such intimacy was as natural as breathing. Her heart filled, but she teased him. "It was…okay."

He nipped her ear.

"All right," she squealed. "It was…good."

"Just good?"

She turned over to see his woebegone face mismatched with his twinkling eyes. "How about," she began slowly, "if I say that making love with you was like tasting chocolate for the first time."

He whistled long and low. "Chocolate? Hmm. Come closer." Rising on his elbow, he leaned over and nuzzled her neck. "So how about a second helping?"

"Whenever you're ready," she whispered, turning her head a few degrees to see him better.

Ready? He was as ready and ripe as a stallion catching scent of his mares. One look at that beautiful face, one brush against her silky skin and he was lost.

Her delightful body enticed with breasts that begged to be suckled, a waist narrow enough for a man's hands to span, and those long legs of hers had his imagination doing somersaults.

She'd allowed him all that. And much more. He remembered the uninhibited joy on her face just minutes ago. Nothing beat the pleasure of watching her rapt expression as they made love.

"Nick? You're staring at me. What's wrong?"

"Not a damn thing, darlin'. I'm just enjoying the view."

He knew she'd blush, and she did.

"You know what, cowboy? So am I!"

Blushing never stopped her feisty lip. Nick grinned and knuckled her gently on the chin before claiming her irresistible mouth again. And again. And again.

Amazing. Wonderful. Extraordinary. Her dizzy mind whirled as she flew through space with him. She led, he followed. He led, she followed on a ride she would long remember. Blue flame evolved to orange fire, volcano hot and earth-shattering. Power. Exhilaration. Connection.

"Oh, my. Oh, my," she gasped in the afterglow as she lay against Nick's shoulder. "Like seeing a blazing sunset over the Grand Canyon, or shooting stars, or fireworks on the...the Fourth..." Tears flowed suddenly. Copious tears from nowhere.

Nick's arms tightened around her immediately. She heard his, "Shh, darlin', shh. It's all right," and shook her head. She'd had a close call. If it wasn't for Nick, she'd have never experienced these tears of joy. Loving him was so good, she ached with it. How would she walk away later when she had to move on?

"Talk to me," Nick begged.

She nodded. "Your wife," she gulped. "Your Donna was a lucky woman."

She felt him freeze, but his arms didn't relax their hold around her.

"Look at me, Kat," he said, providing support as she shifted position.

When she gazed into his eyes, he continued, "I never once, during this entire evening with you, thought about Donna. And that's the truth. Not at the hotel, and more important, not in this bed."

She nodded. "I know."

"You know? Then why'd you bring her up?"

"Because she was the most intimate part of you. And, I think, a good part. And now I understand how it's supposed to be."

She felt his stillness once more, felt his eyes bore through her.

"Supposed to be?" He held her closer. "Yeah," he said, "I guess so. The lucky ones know how it's supposed to be. They're the ones who know the secret—and work to keep it alive."

Secret? She needed to know. "Share it with me, Nick. Who are the lucky ones? What's their secret?"

Without blinking he replied. "They're the couples who are friends as well as lovers, and know it."

"Friends as well as lovers," she repeated slowly. "You mean, like us?"

"I mean exactly like us," he whispered.

KATHERINE LOUNGED in bed after Nick left the next morning. Sweet, sweet Sunday with lots to do, but not yet. Nick had gone to meet the alarm company and the locksmith at the office. But she—ahh—she could stay in bed and dream before she continued working on her student profiles.

Friends as well as lovers. Nick's words resounded in her mind. He'd referred to his wife when he'd first uttered them, but then had included Katherine. This relationship was a first for him also. The first since the crash. They'd take it nice and slow.

Katherine grinned. If last night had been slow, she'd like to see what a fast pace was. And afterward, sleeping next to Nick had provided its own brand of satisfaction. He'd thrown his leg over hers possessively before falling asleep. And during the night, he'd reached for her regularly, just a touch and a sigh, before dozing off again. The memory warmed her. His nearness had registered just below her conscious mind all night long.

She liked him there.

The phone interrupted her musings. Why did people call so early on Sunday? She reached for the receiver.

"Hi." His deep voice sounded as sexy as sin. She tightened her grip on the phone and eased down onto the pillows.

"Hi, yourself."

"Where are you, my little Kat?"

"Right where you left me," she replied slowly. Two beats passed before she heard his low whistle.

"In bed?"

"In bed," she repeated in a suggestive tone. "In this queen-size bed, with silky sheets tucked here and there, and that's about all." Daring, wasn't she? Katherine Kirby, participating in sexual bantering, was beginning a new chapter in her book of life.

This time he moaned. "Only a sheet? I can picture you exactly, with the little birthmark on your right—"

"Never mind," she jumped in, feeling the heat rise to her face. "Where are you?"

"In the truck on my way to the office. I've already seen my folks."

It sounded as if he'd be preoccupied for a while. "Are you going to have any time to study today, Nick? Maybe write an essay? I...I hate to sound like a nag, and I'll shut up if you want, but the test is this Friday."

"Jeez, the summer's whizzing by. I'll be back around noon and put some time in. Don't want to disappoint the teacher."

"Forget the teacher. You don't want to disappoint yourself." She hadn't forgotten about his dreams, but lately he seemed very casual about the test that would be his gateway to the future.

"I can't quite forget the teacher," he replied with a lilt, "but you're so right about finding more time." His voice became serious. "How about dinner tonight? Have you been to the Grotto yet?"

"Aren't you eating with your family?" she asked.

"Not without you. And I know you don't want to go there. So we'll go out."

Stunned, she could barely reply. "I don't understand, Nick. I never said I wouldn't go. You said it."

"Me? I was covering for you. You should have seen your expression when Mom invited us. I'm sorry, Kat. I guess I misread you."

"I thought you didn't want me to go," she replied, "so I must have…you know…put on a poker face."

"Believe me, sweetheart, if I didn't want you near my family, you wouldn't be renting from us now."

What did he mean? He'd hardly known her two months ago. "Would you mind explaining that?"

"When I saw you on the first night of class, I decided at the very worst, I was going to have a new friend."

And at the very best? She didn't ask. They weren't ready to discuss that question. At least she wasn't.

"Well, then, I guess the worst is over," she joked with a question in her voice.

"And baby, the best is yet to come."

He was on her wavelength, but didn't seem to expect a reply. For this, she was grateful.

"Should Mom set two extra plates?" he continued.

"Why not?"

JEREMY SAT QUIETLY at the breakfast table Sunday morning listening to the schedule of activities for the day and hoping a shopping mall would be included. Malls, with their video arcades and movie theaters, were air-conditioned venues, high on the approved list in the midsummer's heat. Any mall in the city had jewelry for sale and he itched to get Katherine a gift.

Today, however, he was out of luck. An Astros

game at the new Enron Field had been planned. A two-o'clock start time. He shrugged his shoulders. Baseball was all right, but he'd rather play than watch. He like doing things, being busy. Being alert.

That's why he didn't really mind his community service activity. Doing janitorial work at the boys' club allowed him to toss a few basketballs during his breaks. But now he had something better. A job with Nick. If it worked out, he'd stick around longer than he'd planned and earn some real money.

If he saved five hundred dollars, passed his GED exam, finished his community service and got an apartment, he could become emancipated from the state and be a man, living on his own, the moment he turned seventeen. All clean and legal.

But what if Nick forgot that tomorrow was his first day at Martinelli Construction? What if he forgot to pick him up in the morning? What if he forgot to tell his brother?

Nah, he'd remember. Nick liked him and he liked Nick a lot. Most of the time. But not when he was putting the make on Ms. Katherine. If it weren't for that, he'd classify Nick as being one of the coolest dudes he'd ever met. So it would be all right messing around with Nick a little every day. Even when the test was over next Friday, they'd still be able to mess around since Jeremy would be getting a ride from him every morning.

Nick knew stuff. He knew about sex and girls. He'd answer any question. Anything. Jeremy hid a grin as Nick's voice played over in his mind. *Girls are wonderful creatures, sport. I'll never understand them, but I love being around them.* Weird that he hadn't graduated high school yet, but even Ms. Katherine said not everything is learned in school.

By noontime, he felt wild. He had to call Nick. Just to be sure everything was on schedule.

"HERE YOU GO, Teach," said Nick as he handed his practice essay to Katherine later that afternoon. He stepped through the doorway, took her in his arms and kissed her thoroughly on the mouth. "Now I'll say, hi."

He loved the sound of her laughter. The sight of her blushes. The light fragrance that surrounded her. He loved the sparkle in her eye when she looked at him. All the elements added up to happiness.

"Ready to go?" he asked. She looked great. Short sundress, strappy sandals. And that megawatt smile. "Got a bathing suit in there?" He pointed to one of her ever-present tote bags near the door.

She nodded, but frowned. "I don't know. Maybe we'll just stay a little while."

"Getting cold feet?" Nick asked.

"No...it's just...I've never done this before."

"It's a new situation for me, too."

She nodded.

"And besides," he added with a slow grin, "Jeremy would be disappointed not to have time to swim."

"Jeremy? Our Jeremy?" She sounded delighted, and a smile stretched across her face. "How thoughtful of you, and generous to your *rival.*"

Content just to watch her, Nick replied, "Don't

give me too much credit. He called me. The poor kid's on pins and needles about starting his new job tomorrow, so I invited him to my parents', too. Estelle gave the okay.''

He thought she was going to cry. Women always got sappy over nothing.

''You're a good man, Mr. Martinelli. And he needs a good man in his life whether he wants one or not.''

''I'm probably not the best choice, but I'm all he's got at the moment. Anyway, it's just swimming, Katrin. I didn't give him a million dollars.''

She laid her palm on his cheek and gazed into his eyes. ''He'll remember this day, and it'll be worth more than money.''

He studied her face as she spoke, and then he saw it. Right there in her beautiful blue eyes. Love. Her eyes shone with love. For him.

But she didn't say a word.

''*I'll* remember this day,'' he whispered.

NICK WATCHED Jeremy's face light up when he spotted Katherine in the truck. He then set a speed record clambering into the back seat of the long-body pickup. It didn't take two minutes before Nick felt as if he had a couple of chattering magpies riding with him. They filled the cab with happy noise, and it sounded good to his ear. He was content to listen, to let their music wash over him as he drove.

''Almost there,'' he said as he turned into a gracious, older neighborhood with beautiful tree-lined streets. ''This was one of our first residential projects. I grew up here.''

Silence reigned in the truck now as Katherine and Jeremy craned their necks to look out the windows.

"Just like on TV," said Jeremy. "People living in real houses. Normal-like."

Nick glanced at him through the mirror and caught the awe and wonder on his face. "You've been watching too many reruns of *The Brady Bunch,* my friend. Inside these *normal* houses lurks a lot of reality." He lifted his hand and pointed. "See that house on the corner over there?"

"So?"

"Their kid is in a drug rehab program."

"Sucker."

"And in that house," Nick said, "with the big live oak in front? The mom's on chemotherapy fighting cancer." He wondered if he'd made his point. Could Jeremy understand that his definition of a normal house was just bricks and mortar, and that the people made it a home?

"So everyone has problems," replied Jeremy. "But they're not going to food pantries and sleeping in condemned buildings or under bridges. We couldn't go to the shelters because they'd call Child Protective Services as quick as a wink if we did. And at least I had my dad. We were together."

Nick heard Katherine's gasp, saw her blink very fast to stay her tears. He was shaken himself. Seemed Jeremy had a point to make, too.

It was also the first time the youngster, himself, had revealed any details about his life. Nick pulled the truck over to the side of the street and let the engine idle. He turned toward the back seat, hoping he could put the right words together.

Jeremy was studying the scenery outside his window as though he had to memorize it. Not wanting to face anyone.

"Look at me, son," Nick invited in a quiet tone.

But Jeremy continued to look out the window, and Nick could feel the tension emanating from the boy's body, permeating the atmosphere of the truck. He sensed Katherine's still form next to him, as though she was afraid to move, afraid to breathe. And then slowly, very slowly, Jeremy turned to face Nick.

It was like looking at a robot.

Nick studied the carefully controlled expression until everything clicked into place. He'd worked with enough lost boys over the years to recognize bravado. And loneliness. And desperate fear.

Suddenly, the robot blinked. That's all it took for Nick to see something else.

Want.

This boy *wanted* to belong somewhere, to someone. He'd had a pitiful father, but he'd known love.

Need.

This boy *needed* to belong somewhere, to someone. Jeremy may have lived and survived on the streets, but he was not a hardened criminal with layers of defenses protecting him. He would have been so busy protecting his dad, Nick thought, that he'd had no time to protect himself.

Nick clasped Jeremy's hand that was resting on the back of Nick's seat. "You've had a rough beginning, my friend. No doubt about it. A below-average beginning for an above-average human being.''

The boy remained silent.

''Look right into my eyes, Jeremy, so you know I'm speaking true. You are a terrific young man, and for whatever it's worth, I'm very proud of you. I'm proud you'll be working with me. In fact, I'm counting on you.''

This time, Jeremy nodded. And Nick felt himself relax a tiny bit.

''But the most important thing I want you to believe, Jeremy, is that you are *not* alone.''

''Yes, I am!'' The robot was gone and in its place was a small volcano on the verge of eruption. ''Just like she was,'' Jeremy added, pointing at Katherine. ''But I can handle it, too.''

Nick glanced at Katherine and from Katherine's caring expression to Jeremy and back again. They each had a piece of his heart. And maybe a piece of each other's as well. An idea began to form...

''How about if we handle it together?'' he asked. ''You, Katherine, and I, with some help from Ms. Estelle and the gang at Richmond House.''

Katherine spoke. ''Like a team, honey. Team Jeremy.''

Nick arched an eyebrow at her, the familiar words echoing in his mind, and his heart warmed when she smiled at him and winked.

''Tomorrow will be better,'' Katherine continued, her attention now focused totally on the youngster. ''All your tomorrows.''

Suddenly, the boy's mouth quirked up in a half

grin. "I know," he said. "I'm the master of my fate, aren't I? And I've got plans."

Then Nick heard all about the conditions for Jeremy's emancipation. All his salary would go into a special account, direct deposit, since no money was allowed at Richmond House.

"Sounds exciting," said Katherine. "Just make sure you pass your exam on Friday. Both of you!"

"No sweat," they replied together.

Nick pulled away from the curb and drove the three remaining blocks to his parents' house. He parked in front, cut the engine and looked at his two guests. "Everybody ready? Let's go. And Jeremy, there's a pair of trunks for you in that bag, brand new with the tags still on. They're yours."

The boy reached slowly for the bag. "For me? Are you sure?"

"I'm sure, Jeremy. They're yours."

"Well, thanks. Thanks a lot, Nick."

"And one more thing, sport. I need a little favor from you."

"Yeah?" Suspicion mixed with curiosity in his voice.

"Um...the GED is sort of a surprise for my folks, so let's not mention it. Okay?"

The youngster grinned. "No problem."

Katherine smiled at their interchange as she waited by the side of the truck, clutching her tote bag and not moving. Jeremy climbed down and immediately went to her side. As Nick watched, they simultaneously stepped closer toward each other.

Pure instinct. Protection mode. Nick recognized it

and understood their unique bond. But still, he sighed. They had nothing to fear. In five minutes, they'd either understand that or run like hell from the Martinelli's *normal* house.

KATHERINE STOOD with Jeremy and Nick in the front hall of Nick's parents' house. There seemed to be millions of Martinellis everywhere she looked. Running directly toward them were three noisy adorable children. Still babies, really, the oldest perhaps five.

"Uncle Nick's here! Grandma, Uncle Nick's here."

"Unca Nick. Unca Nick."

And tagging along, a toddler trying to keep up. He perambulated as best he could toward them, finally plopped in front of Jeremy and lifted his arms. "Up, up, man. Up."

"Holy Toledo. He's so small," said the man.

"Well, pick him up," suggested Nick as he hoisted an older child in each arm. "He wants you."

Katherine saw the determined look on Jeremy's face and could easily read his mind. He wouldn't let Nick down. If Nick could handle two tykes, he could handle one.

"Good going," she said as Jeremy lifted the babe. "You're a natural." In fact, he handled the child better than she would have. Nick caught her attention then.

"Meet my two favorite nieces, in fact, my only nieces. Ms. Toni Macaroni and Ms. Andi Cotton Candy."

"Oh, Uncle Nick!" responded the older between

exasperated giggles. But the younger studied Katherine with big round eyes, as dark as her uncle's, and slowly reached her arms out. "Take me."

Katherine melted. These children were irresistible. "I'll take you, gorgeous girl," she said as she enveloped the child, thankful Andi wasn't an infant. "Hmm," she said, and inhaled deeply. "You smell good."

"That's eau de baby powder," said an unfamiliar female voice laced with laughter.

Katherine turned a fraction and saw the feminine version of Nick walking toward her, minus about six inches in height.

"This is my big sister, Joanna," said Nick. "The mother of all these troublemakers."

"With gray hair to prove it," the lighthearted voice continued, but a piercing gaze examined Katherine from head to toe. "And you must be Katherine. I've been looking forward to finally meeting you."

Finally? How long had Joanna known about her? She'd just met Nick's mother last night.

And then came Anna and Joe, beaming from ear to ear. "Welcome, welcome. Come on in." The warmth in Joe's voice was as welcoming as his words.

Anna's snapping eyes seemed to take in everyone at once, and Katherine wasn't surprised to see her focus on Jeremy, who was still holding the baby.

"Well, hello. I see my grandson's made a new friend." She looked back at Katherine, then at Jeremy, before saying, "Nick didn't tell me you had a son, Katherine. A handsome son, too. You hardly look old enough." She paused, then urged them forward. "Come on in. Meet everyone else. Pool's out back."

Katherine stepped forward. The woman was a whirlwind who had to be stopped. "Mrs. Martinelli," she began, "Jeremy's—"

"She's my teacher," burst out Jeremy. "The best teacher." His face turned a bright shade of red, his eyes darted around the room looking for escape.

"Jeremy's not only my student," said Katherine quickly, "he's also a special friend." The kid looked so miserable, she was sorry they'd come. It hadn't taken two minutes.

"And he's also our newest employee," inserted Nick. "Jeremy Tucker, meet the folks who started the company."

Recovering nicely, Nick's parents greeted Jeremy again, welcoming him warmly.

"How about a swim?" asked Nick. "We all brought suits, and I can smell barbecue from here."

"And if you don't like barbecue, I have meatballs with my special sauce..."

"Put me down, Uncle Nick. I want to swim," said Toni.

"Down, man, down," echoed the baby in Jeremy's arms.

"Me, too," said Andi.

And suddenly it was quiet again, the children and their mother disappearing through the kitchen door to the backyard, the grandparents following.

Katherine caught Jeremy's eye, and they both started laughing. "It's sure different than my house was," she said.

"Wow," said Jeremy.

"You're not kidding." Katherine held her waist to ease the pain of the laughter.

"What?" asked Nick, looking from one to the other. "What?"

Katherine shook her head and said nothing, happy to gasp air and breathe again.

Finally Nick nodded and grinned, one of his slow sexy grins. "Welcome, folks, to the Martinelli style of normal."

"I guess this is one of the good houses in the neighborhood," drawled Jeremy, hands on hips and a slight question in his voice.

"You're right, son. I guess it is. Full of noise, and love, and fighting, and caring."

This is what Katherine had missed for ten years. And in the back of her mind she'd known it. Of course she'd known it. But she hadn't seen it, or felt it, or smelled it, or touched it, or heard it. Or *wanted* to do any of those things. Not until now. Not until Nick brought her home.

She looked at the family pictures on the foyer wall, a rogues gallery of children at every age, then walked to the kitchen and looked out at the yard where a dozen people milled around the pool.

Her heart filled. She missed her family. She missed her loving parents. She missed her old house. Not as noisy a house, without brothers and sisters, but the warmth, the kitchen aromas, the feeling of belonging. The feeling of home.

She took a deep breath. She'd always miss her mom and dad, yearn for them, but she couldn't run from them anymore. Even her work—the work she'd devoted herself to—couldn't eliminate the memories.

She blinked hard and looked out the window, once more focusing on the crowd outside. The Martinellis made a happy sound. The sound of family.

And damn if she didn't want it again!

EDDIE JENSEN WANTED something, too. He wanted in. Into the offices of Martinelli Construction Company.

And Sally didn't like it. She bit her fingernail as she watched her brother wear down her rug with his pacing.

"The friggin' cops were around all last night. I never had a chance to get in. How the hell did they know? That's what I can't understand." Eddie looked at her, and for a moment anger and desperation warred for dominance in his expression.

She was afraid. For him. For herself.

"Forget it, Eddie. Whatever you're involved in, you don't have to do it. We'll go to the police."

His small explosion nixed that idea. "I need those quotes, and I need them soon. Because I get a big piece of the action on this, and…" He let his voice trail off.

Sally rubbed her stomach to ease the burning. "And what?"

"I get to stay in one piece."

She downed two antacids. "My God, Eddie. What have you done?"

Suddenly, the fight went out of him. His complexion turned pale; he ambled to the couch and slumped down.

"I lost fifty thousand to Stan Willard, Jay Willard's brother."

"Fifty thousand!" She stared, bug-eyed, at her brother. He must have hit it big a few times then lost it all. An old story. "Fifty thousand," she repeated. "To Willard." She knew the name. "Jay Willard's in construction. Commercial. Does his brother work the business, too?"

"Sometimes. Like now when he wants dough. And I tell you, Sally, he wants those numbers from your place. And I have to get them. Then the debt's paid, plus we get a bonus if Willard gets the contract."

He turned to her then, animation back in his face. "So it's not all bad, sis. We'll both be riding high soon enough."

She'd need more than antacids to get her through this nightmare. Woozy for a moment, she felt like passing out. Her brother didn't seem to notice, however, he was so caught up in his own musings.

"Everything went like clockwork yesterday when I showed up for lunch. Before we left, I picked up the old man's key ring. Afterward, I made copies and returned the ring. He never knew it was gone and neither did you."

"What are you talking about?" she asked, but really didn't want to hear him confirm her sudden understanding.

"I did owe you a lunch, sis. And you got overtime for Saturday. So we both got what we wanted."

She put her head in her hands. "You used me to get into Mr. Martinelli's office. You took his keys."

Eddie would never change. Why couldn't she just accept it?

"Sleep tight, Sal. You didn't know. Just like you didn't know when I borrowed his keys a few years ago. You're still so naive."

"What?" She sat straight up, spine rigid.

"Yeah. When you first started working there. Remember, I used to drive you sometimes, before you had the car."

She nodded.

"Nobody fussed at me being there. They got used to me after a few times. I was Sally's brother, giving her a ride."

"And that's about when you found a new gambling buddy whose brother's in the same business as my boss." She had no trouble reconstructing the events now.

Sally stood up and slowly walked toward Eddie. She bent over him on the couch. "Listen to me, Edward Jensen. Listen hard. I can't help you. Even if I wanted to, I can't. Because I'm not involved in the project." Thank goodness.

She gulped for air. "Understand? I'm not near those figures. I don't know where they are. In fact, I don't even think they're in the office. So stay away."

His eyes narrowed. She held his gaze and hoped she'd said the right things.

"I believe you," he said softly.

Before she could sigh in relief, he added, "So if the figures aren't in the office, we'll just have to look somewhere else. Won't we?"

CHAPTER NINE

KATHERINE ZIPPED UP her short terry robe and stretched out on a chaise lounge near the shallow and shaded end of the pool in the Martinellis' backyard, glad to be out of range of the horseplay in the water. Every activity Nick's family engaged in was done at full throttle, and the chicken game was no different. She scanned the pool, her radar attuned to Jeremy and Nick, the boy sitting squarely on Nick's powerful shoulders, facing the opposing team of brother Danny, and Richie, Tina's fiancé.

These last two hours were the first time she"d seen Jeremy truly having fun. He could have been any kid, in Anytown, U.S.A. She sighed with contentment and closed her eyes, now totally relaxed in this family environment, until a shadow blocked the late-setting sun and Joanna started speaking.

"Are you really sleeping down there or just escaping?"

Katherine felt her lips quirk. "Maybe a little of both," she replied without moving a muscle.

"Well, I'm wide awake and curious," continued Nick's sister as she stretched out on the chaise next to Katherine. "Tell me about yourself. Jeremy said you were his teacher. But school's out now."

Katherine chuckled. "There are always summer sessions for GED classes."

"Oh! You're a high-school teacher."

"Well, not exactly," Katherine replied. "I teach at the community college, and Jeremy's in my class there."

Joanna sat up in her chair, eyes focused on Katherine. "So you're a college professor?"

"Afraid not, not yet, anyway," Katherine replied. "But I'm working on it. A Ph.D.'s not required for the GED program."

"Oh…" Joanna drew out the word. "A doctorate. Wow. So your current position is only temporary—salvaging kids who failed in regular school." She turned her head to look at the sixteen-year-old as he splashed in the pool. "So, what's Jeremy's story? Why's he here with you? And how did Nick get mixed up with you both?"

A flush of anger charged Katherine's pulse, as well as concern about not revealing Nick's attendance in her class. She took a deep breath, determined to hold on to her temper, protect Jeremy's privacy and Nick's secret. "You sound more like a detective than a nurse," she said with a laugh.

"Nurses ask a lot of questions, too," Joanna replied, her already tanned face turning a shade darker. "We try to protect our patients, especially from themselves."

Katherine kept eye contact with Joanna and said quietly, "You're not at the hospital now, and there's no one in danger here."

Joanna rested her gaze on Nick for a moment before replying to Katherine, "That remains to be seen."

Katherine waited, sensing the woman wasn't done delivering her message. She was right.

"I'll be straight with you, Katherine. Nick's been through a lot and you're the first woman he's brought home since Donna died. I'm just...worried that he'll get hurt. You're going for a Ph.D. and my brother doesn't even have a high-school diploma. And you'll be searching for other positions—who knows where."

Katherine waited a heartbeat before replying. She tried to modulate her voice to take the sting out of her words. "Nick's a big boy, Joanna—thirty-four years old—and certainly entitled to make his own decisions."

Joanna's eyes flashed. "Nick's wife," she said, "also happened to be my best friend. A very hard act to follow. I want my brother to be as happy as he was before. I see the way he looks at you—his eyes are glued to you—and if this blows up, he'll be heading for more pain."

"Is this a private party, or can anyone join?" Nick's voice saved her from having to reply to his sister. Katherine watched as he strode to her side from the pool, water streaming down his body.

"This party's breaking up," replied Joanna with a trace of a smile. "Your date has a quick tongue."

Nick's eyes twinkled. He leaned over Katherine and snatched a kiss. "Delicious, too."

Katherine felt the heat rise to her face, not totally due to embarrassment, despite Joanna's presence. For some reason, Nick's touch ignited her anytime, any-

place. But now, after Joanna's conversation and
Nick's kisses, she needed to cool off in the pool.

She started to rise, but Nick barred her way.

"One more kiss, Kat. Just one," he begged with a
hangdog expression.

Before she could answer, Jeremy's voice interrupted. "Hey, Nick, aren't you coming back in?"

When he turned to respond, Katherine ducked under his arm and rose from the chair. She waved to
Jeremy. "We're both coming in," she called. "And
you and I, buddy, are going to drown him."

"Great!"

Katherine slipped her robe off, her heart light again
as she absorbed the picture of a grinning Jeremy. She
looked at Nick, broad chest, muscled arms, a body to
die for. "So, big man. Think you can handle the two
of us?"

A delighted grin slowly spread across his face.
"It'll be my pleasure."

Katherine pushed Nick toward the water and ignored Joanna's still form as the woman paused to
watch their horseplay. However, Katherine couldn't
ignore her parting words, aimed for her ears alone.

"Whatever happens, Katherine, please don't hurt
my brother."

Not exactly a threat, but a plea that echoed in Katherine's mind.

THREE HOURS LATER, Katherine leaned back in the
front seat of the pickup next to Nick. She glanced at
him, admiring the strong profile, the capable hands,
the depth of personality. The longer she knew him,

the more she liked him. And maybe that was more telling than love.

She looked over her shoulder at Jeremy, quiet now, and stretched out as best he could on the narrow rear seat. He stared at the interior roof, and Katherine imagined the impressions of the day were being sorted through his memory.

Nick started the engine, and impulsively she stretched toward him and kissed his cheek.

His breath quickened.

"Hold that thought, baby," he whispered. "The evening's not over."

Her pulse raced. Anticipation. A familiar reaction to the thought of making love with Nick. As though she were a teen discovering herself to be in love. Or a twenty-year-old who's sure she recognizes what she wants. How had she gotten to be almost thirty without feeling the passion that sang in her veins now?

She shrugged. Other goals. Narrow paths. A road not taken, until this splendid summer.

Images of the day kaleidoscoped in her mind. The general camaraderie of the family. Conversation about Tina and Richie's upcoming wedding. Concern about the absent Josie and her husband, Mike. She'd felt Joanna's eyes follow her on and off for the rest of the day, although the woman hadn't spoken to her again about what was on her mind.

And then her thoughts had veered to Jeremy. She'd watched him surreptitiously exchange Nick's can of beer for a can of soda. Three times. Nick kept scratching his head and opening a new can. In the end, Katherine doubted he'd had more than a half can of the malt. She'd speak with Nick about it later.

Jeremy. He'd called her Kathy today, following Danny's example. It had popped out naturally in the informal surroundings and Katherine was pleased. "Just not in school," she'd whispered with a wink. "One more week, then do what you want." His happy expression was worth everything. And he'd deferred to her, too, putting on sunblock when she reminded him.

The boy needed people to care about him. People of his own. In particular, someone who'd walked in his shoes—the last survivor of a family. She'd had Suzanne as an anchor in a choppy sea. But Suzanne had been a kid too, like Katherine, just nineteen and part of her own family. Not alone. But Jeremy could have her, Katherine, not a kid anymore, for as long as he wanted her. Or needed her. Just as they'd discussed on the way to Nick's parents' house.

"ALONE AT LAST," said Nick as he reentered the truck after dropping Jeremy off at Richmond House. "I had to promise him—a swear-to-God-and-hope-to-die promise that I wouldn't forget to pick him up in the morning."

"Very nice of you," Katherine joked, "since he swiped three beers from you today."

"He what?" Nick jerked the wheel.

"Relax. You know he wouldn't drink it himself. I saw him go into the kitchen with each can and return a minute later. He probably spilled the beer down the sink and got you soda instead."

"Well, well. We're going to have to talk to him about that. In fact, Kat, we need to talk about a lot of things."

He heard the silence. And her voice, now soft with a bit of a tremble in it. "Whenever you want."

He wanted everything right now. He wanted to take her and keep her forever. But he couldn't say it yet. Not when Helen Kowalski wanted her to marry an educated man. A deathbed promise. His stomach had knotted as soon as he'd heard Katherine mention it earlier.

His mom had asked about Katherine's parents, in a general way, and he'd wished he'd warned his folks about her having no family. But Kat had responded quietly, with dignity, about the accident, and her rush to the hospital. Naturally, his mom's eyes had filled up, and he knew Katherine had been taken into the fold. And then he'd heard her say something about how her parents thought education was everything, and that on her deathbed, Helen had spoken about her marrying an educated man. He could understand a dying mother's thoughts for her young daughter. Sure he could.

But he'd walked away from the group after that, wondering why she kept going out with him. Well, not exactly. He thought he knew why. He swore he'd seen love shining in her eyes. So, maybe she didn't know what she wanted. For the first time since he'd met her, he felt there was a piece he hadn't figured out. He'd have to keep peeling the layers away.

"We'll talk soon, Kat. I hope real soon." He'd burn the midnight oil this week, practicing for the damn exam. He knew a high-school diploma wasn't exactly what her folks had had in mind in their definition of educated, but he'd offer it as a down payment.

KATHERINE DROPPED her bag by the door, kicked off her shoes and flipped through her mail as she walked to the kitchen. A couple of bills, a couple of ads and no responses yet to all the résumés she'd sent out. It was too late for the fall semester, but she was hoping for a midyear opportunity. Although Jonathan Carter at UT-Austin, and Dr. Stone at the University of Houston, had been encouraging, no promises had been made by either one. Her job search was still at the top of her agenda.

She threw the envelopes on her desk in the study and massaged her temple. Tension had crept into the class tonight as the reality of test day approached. And suddenly, her own responsibility for coaching the students seemed very heavy.

"They won't all pass," Dr. Goldman had told her weeks ago. "Don't expect it or you'll be disappointed. An average pass rate for a class is approximately fifty-five percent. It's virtually impossible for some folks, mature adults or not, to make up for years of no schooling in ten weeks. But we try. And many do succeed."

It had seemed reasonable at the time. But now after working on their biographies, she knew every student, every face, every hope and every dream. And she couldn't bear the thought of their disappointment. She also felt her own fate riding with them. Her own talents and ability. And maybe pride as well. Despite the rough beginning, she'd given it her best shot. But Rosa still mixed up her verb tenses when she wrote, and John still had trouble manipulating negative numbers. And there were only three days left.

Katherine's head hurt, her feet hurt, and she needed dinner.

She opened the door to the fridge, and happiness filled her heart. Staring at her was the care package Nick's mother had pressed on her two days ago, meatballs with special sauce. She reached for them just as a familiar knock echoed at her door. She glanced into the container, relieved to note sufficient dinner for two. Right now, happiness was a full stomach.

She opened the door, saw the concern on Nick's face and walked right into his arms. She needed to be held, wanted to be held. Just for a moment. And he obliged. With tenderness and warmth, he encircled her, comforted her. She closed her eyes and could have stayed forever in his embrace.

Feathery kisses rained down along her forehead. Strong fingers massaged her scalp, the pins securing her hair scattering on the floor. She purred, and heard him laugh. Happiness, she decided anew, was having Nick with her, a purely selfish desire when he should be at his own place, hitting the books. Then she noticed the container in his hand.

"Meatballs?"

"Mama's best. Come on. You looked whipped in that class tonight. I even brought you a bottle of aspirin."

"You *are* good. How'd you know I had a head-ache?" she asked.

"Your eyes. I notice these things." He tapped her nose. "I get paid for noticing details. Let's warm this up. Bring out the veggies and I'll toss us a salad."

True to his word, he did. Quick, efficient, and no mess.

"Now," he said after they'd eaten, "feeling better?"

"You wouldn't believe how much." And it was true. The pounding at her temples had stopped.

"So, tell me what's wrong. You're not usually a headache person." Nick leaned back in his chair, patiently waiting for her answer.

"Just worrying about the exam."

His laughter filled the room. "But you're not the one taking it. We're the ones who should be worried." He got up from his seat and walked toward her. "Come here, my little Kat." He reached for her hand.

She rose easily, snuggled against his wide chest and wrapped her arms around him. "I've never been privy to so much of my students' lives before," she said. "When I taught in the past, I focused on how well they understood the material, but now their understanding affects their lives. Directly. Immediately." She lifted her head to look at him. "Did you know that the air force is waiting for Hector to pass his GED and he's in? All the arrangements are made. The kid's already packed. Everyone's just waiting for the results of the test."

''Hmm. I know,'' whispered Nick as he tightened his hold a bit.

''And about half a dozen students have already visited college admissions offices both at the community college and the university. They're all so primed and anxious.''

''Don't fret, sweetheart,'' said Nick. ''We won't let you down.''

She shook her head. ''This class,'' she said, ''is turning out to be a lot more challenging than I thought, for a lot of different reasons. I'd always taken high-school graduation for granted. But I was wrong. This diploma has broad ramifications. It's affecting lives right now!''

''You have no idea how much,'' Nick replied with a rueful laugh.

WITH A FISTFUL OF PENCILS and a box of tissues under her arm, Katherine stood inside the official testing center that Friday morning, greeting her students as they arrived. Extra pencils always came in handy, and tissues…well, she'd been advised to bring some for any student suffering extreme stress. Frayed nerves sometimes led to tears.

She'd arrived early, but five students had preceded her by half an hour. She sympathized with them. Who could sleep the night before a big exam? Even Nick had returned to his own place last night.

Most of the others had already arrived, Jeremy included. Not Jeremy anymore, she mentally corrected herself. His new handle was J.T. for Jeremy Tucker. That's what Danny and the guys building the new subdivision called him. And he loved it. Couldn't wait to tell her about it Monday night in class, after his first day on the job.

"Sounds great," she'd said. "Has a certain panache." His smile faltered. "Here." She scribbled on a pad and gave the paper to him. "Go look it up."

Two minutes later, he'd reappeared. "The dictionary said 'dash' and 'style.' But I just think the name is cool."

"Me, too," she'd replied. "Very cool, J.T."

Well, J.T. was already inside the test room, while N.M. hadn't shown up yet. She should have called him this morning before she left. Maybe he overslept. Maybe he got stuck in traffic. She continued to pace, eyes scanning the hallway in both directions.

He came toward her suddenly, at a fast clip, looking exhausted. She knew something was wrong.

"Josie's back in the hospital," he said without preamble. "Dad called me an hour after I left you last night. He and Mom went to see her. Now she's stable again, and they're home sleeping. I can't leave Tina alone at the office with so many things going on." He paused for breath. "You look beautiful, Kat. I always forget how much until I see you again."

Warmth filled her, but her mind raced to his explanations. He wouldn't test today. That was the bottom line. She knew it, and began to realize that unless something changed, the family business would always come first. The sense of responsibility he felt to his family and to their customers weighed in stronger than his secret dreams. And perhaps he, himself, didn't realize it.

"I'll help Tina," she heard herself say. "Take the test, Nick. I'll stay at the office all day until you get there. I'm a quick study. I'll free up your secretary so she can handle more critical things."

He shook his head, and impatience slowly filled her. Didn't he think she could handle a phone?

"No, Katrin. I want *you* to sit in my office. Sally knows she's been reassigned for a while." He shook his head and looked away for a moment. "You know the story. Family only." His eyes met hers once more when he continued. "My subcontractors will call on my direct line. Talk with them. Guarantee them a return call from me by this evening."

She answered with a smile. "No problem."

"I'll trade you my keys for a pencil."

"Absolutely," she said, offering him several.

"And I need one more thing," he said slowly.

She stared into his warm brown eyes and smiling mouth, and felt her legs weaken. That look of his. That I-can't-take-my-eyes-off-you look that always preceded something delicious. "And what would that be?" she whispered.

"This." He leaned down and claimed her lips with a sense of possession she hadn't felt from him before. With pulses throbbing, she met his urgency with urgency of her own.

"Just a little kiss for luck," he finally whispered.

She stroked his cheek. "I willingly give you all I have...but while you're in there, don't forget about brainpower."

He saluted. "See you later, boss. Don't tell Tina

where I am. You read a lot of fiction. Now's your chance to make up a story.''

KATHERINE NEEDN'T have worried. After explaining that Nick would be along later, Tina seemed so relieved to have help that she never asked for the details. It was pretty neat, Katherine thought, to be accepted so easily by some members of the family.

Sally didn't seem to have a problem with her either. In fact, the woman was rather quiet, talking softly with Tina, and accommodating with any task that needed to be done. Sweet and quietly efficient.

Katherine sat at Nick's desk, taking so many detailed messages, her fingers began to ache. She started to appreciate the amount of information Nick kept in his head or at his fingertips. The school project was not the only one in the works. She received calls from the sales offices in several new subdivisions where Martinelli homes were being sold.

Danny called. Did Nick know about the big open house at Echo Lakes this Sunday? Every real estate broker in the city was going. Did he want someone to be there representing Martinelli Construction? And where was he, anyway? Katherine promised to deliver his questions as soon as possible. ''And by the way,'' he added, ''J.T.'s a real good kid once you get past the defenses. He usually tries to please but sometimes he resents criticism. He's a fast learner though. Hard worker. Got lots of potential.''

''That's what I think,'' replied Katherine with deep satisfaction. ''I'm hoping the rough edges will smooth out in time. Thanks for telling me.''

"Anytime."

She hung up and let her mind wander to Nick and Jeremy, as it had on and off all morning. How were they making out? She glanced at her watch, amazed to find it was past lunchtime. They probably still faced a couple more hours of testing before it was over. Just as she stretched and rose from the chair, wanting to check with Tina about ordering a sandwich, Tina, herself, burst through the door.

"We have a baby!" she announced, almost tripping over herself in her excitement. "A tiny, beautiful girl. Perfect, they say. Four and a half pounds...not too bad."

"How's Josie?" asked Katherine, surprised at her concern for a woman she'd never met.

"Exhausted. Ecstatic. Come with me for a minute."

Katherine followed her into the general reception area where they saw Sally ready to leave for lunch. Tina waved at her.

"I've got to go to the hospital, Sal. Can you and Katherine cover by yourselves for an hour or so?"

"I think Sally's got plans," Katherine said, nodding to the big man waiting for Nick's secretary.

Tina looked up, studied the visitor, then smiled. "Hi, Eddie. It's been a while." She introduced Katherine to Sally's brother, and then asked, "Taking your sister to lunch?"

"Sure am."

"Well, how'd you like to order in today? Lunch is on me."

"We'll be happy to and you don't have to treat

us,'' he replied immediately. ''You just take your time at that hospital. It's not every day you get a new baby in the family.''

Tina beamed. ''You're so right. It's a special day. Thanks for sticking around. I won't be long.''

Quick and graceful, Tina grabbed her purse, threw some money at Katherine and flew down the corridor to the main entrance of the building.

Nick's going to rake her over the coals. Katherine watched the younger woman disappear, then pasted a smile on her face as she looked at her lunch companions.

''Tina wasn't thinking clearly, folks. There's no reason you can't go out to lunch as planned. I'm perfectly capable of covering the front desk, and Sally's been working nonstop all morning.'' She looked at Sally and felt her smile relax. The young woman really had worked tirelessly.

''No, ma'am,'' replied Eddie. ''The boss's sister needs Sally to stay, so we'll all stay, unless...unless *you* want to leave!'' He grinned broadly. ''Hey, it's no problem. Sally and I can take care of things. There are two of us.''

Katherine felt goose bumps on her arms as she studied Sally's brother. Unkempt, his shirt loosened from his waistband, his hair only finger-combed. The man looked almost hopeful as he made his suggestion to cover the office. Katherine quelled a shiver and glanced at Sally, but Sally stared at the floor.

''I have no plans to leave here,'' she said, turning back to the brother. She met his gaze and was glad to note the steadiness in her voice. "Why don't you call out for something, Sally?" Katherine continued as she walked toward Nick's office, "I'll be back in a few minutes."

She crossed the threshold, closed the door behind her and tried to gather her wits. Something was not right between Sally and her brother. That much was true. But why did Katherine feel uneasy with him? She'd never met him before, didn't know him. Why did she have the distinct feeling that Eddie wanted her gone?

Everyone else in the building was on the second floor, at lunch or scattered. So that left her to deal with the siblings. She walked to the desk and grabbed Nick's keys, visualizing the employee lunchroom she'd steer them to while she covered the phones.

"So what kind of topping do you want on the pizza?" Eddie's voice boomed into the office.

Katherine whirled around, her heart racing fast enough to choke her. Sally's brother filled Nick's doorway, his head moving from side to side as he studied the room.

"Don't you believe in knocking?" Her voice was sharp. She didn't care. "This is a private office. Visitors are asked to remain in the reception area unless accompanied by an employee."

He raised his hands, palm forward, in mock alarm. "Sor-ry. Just wanted to know the kind of pizza you like."

So maybe she'd overreacted. But it promised to be a long lunch.

IT WAS a never ending lunch. When Eddie finally left, Katherine breathed a sigh of relief. The man asked too many questions about Martinelli Construction. And Katherine didn't like it one bit. It took him a while to realize that she wasn't sharing information.

She didn't like him walking down the halls, even to visit the men's room. He strolled, he examined, he acted nosy. And she didn't like his suggestion of them eating lunch in Nick's office. He'd seen the conference table there, however, so it could have been an innocent idea. But she didn't think so.

"A great place to put the pizza," he'd argued.

She'd smiled sweetly, but had eyeballed him without a blink. "Not on my watch," she'd said as she turned the key in the lock. If looks could kill, she'd be a dead woman.

But an hour later, Eddie was gone, and when Nick and Jeremy bounded through the door, all noise and grins with a bouquet of flowers and a large box of chocolates, her concerns about Sally and her brother blew away like fallen leaves in an autumn wind.

"But you don't know that you passed yet," Katherine protested as she exclaimed over the flowers.

"True," said Nick, "but I had time at the end to review each part. And our boy wonder," he continued, slapping J.T. on the back, "took a nap while waiting for me." He paused for a moment. "I'm feeling lucky. Very lucky."

His eyes shone as he looked at her, and she couldn't look away. "That's wonderful," she whispered, almost as a prayer.

"Me, too," said J.T., as he handed her the chocolates. "I think I passed, too. Thanks, Kathy, for everything."

One look at his piquant face, and Katherine felt tears well in her eyes. She wrapped one arm around the boy, then turned toward the man...reached out with her other arm and clutched them both.

CHAPTER TEN

KATHERINE LEFT the endless line of traffic and glanced at her watch, relieved to note she'd be on time for her meeting with Dr. Goldman. She chuckled nervously. In her mind, meeting was too weak a word. Maybe summit, reckoning, or moment of truth would be better. This *meeting* had only one item on the agenda: the GED results.

Her stomach flip-flopped whenever she considered her students' possible test scores, and now, when the revelation was near, she didn't appreciate the delays of morning rush-hour traffic.

She finally pulled into a spot and cut the engine, wishing her nerves would be as quiet as the now-silent car. An impossible feat at the moment. With thoughts of Nick and Jeremy in the forefront of her mind, she navigated to her supervisor's office as quickly as she could.

When she saw the smile on Rose Goldman's face, a tiny bubble of joy surfaced, and when the older woman stood up and embraced her, the bubble inflated with the speed of a helium balloon. Something special had happened.

"Congratulations, Katherine, on an outstanding job," the diminutive woman said. "Your class attained a seventy-five percent pass rate. Very high, un-usually high. Remember what I told you when you began teaching the class? The average pass rate is fifty-five percent.''

Wow! Katherine wanted to dance around the of-fice...for a moment. "But it still means, Dr. Gold-man, that twenty-five percent failed. What about Nick and Jeremy?'' Her pulse raced so hard, her fingertips throbbed.

"Look for yourself," replied Rose, reaching for a sheet of paper on her desk. ''They're both high-school graduates now. Letters were mailed out this morning, and the certificates will be sent in about ten days.''

Katherine scanned the list and collapsed into a chair at the same time. It seemed forever until she focused on their names, but yes, yes, they'd passed. With respectable scores. And Hector would be going into the air force. Dorothy's daughters could continue to be proud of their mom, and the three cousins could justify higher salaries. Or continue their education.

She released a pent-up breath and started to shake. The corners of her mouth trembled, her palms tingled, then felt damp. She needed to inhale deeply.

"My dear, you're crying!"

Katherine raised trembling fingers to her cheek and felt the wetness there. With a tissue from her con-cerned boss, she wiped the unexpected tears from her face.

"They worked so hard," she whispered in a broken voice. "They wanted it so badly. Every one of them. Not just seventy-five percent." She rose from her chair, now too restless to sit. "I'll call the ones who didn't pass and personally invite them back. I don't want to lose them, because I know they can do it too.''

She paced the floor as she spoke. ''We'll have a celebration. A little fiesta. We'll honor both the GED grads and the pre-GED students who worked so hard. I'll invite them all. How about this Saturday night? At my place. Can you come, Rose? And your husband?''

''Wouldn't miss it for the world,'' replied Dr. Goldman. ''A beautiful ending to a successful summer. Or a lovely prelude to the fall semester, which begins in two weeks.''

''I'll be ready,'' promised Katherine.

Rose didn't reply immediately, and Katherine saw a flash of indecision cross the older woman's face. For a moment, she feared for her job, but that didn't make sense. Not with Rose talking about the prelude to a new semester. She reseated herself and leaned forward in her chair.

''What's the matter, Dr. Goldman?'' She heard Rose take a deep breath before answering her question.

''I have another challenge for you, Katherine. In addition to the GED class. If you want it.''

She *wanted* to teach advanced composition and comparative literature, but dismissed the thought. Not possible on this campus, and certainly not in the Developmental Education Department. Rose's tone of voice, however, captured her attention and she focused on her colleague.

''We have an opening for a part-time ESL instructor,'' explained Rose. "English as a Second Language classes, as you know, are part of our department, just as GED classes are. Between the two areas, you'd have a full-time position, with full-time salary, health benefits, retirement plan, faculty perks—the whole enchilada.'' She leaned toward Katherine and took her hand. "I think you'd be a natural for it. In fact, I'll mentor you myself.''

Katherine's mind raced. It wasn't what she wanted. Not at all. In fact, the longer she stayed at the community college, the further away her own goals seemed. But she'd be financially set for the fall semester as long as she did a good job. She nodded. No problem there. She'd give it her best shot, just as she had with the GED class. And if a better offer came through from a university, she'd be able to accept it for the spring semester. Perfect timing.

She looked at her mentor and extended her hand. "It's a deal, Rose. And thank you. Thanks very much.''

KATHERINE CHECKED the buffet table one more time before going into the bedroom to get dressed. She couldn't remember when she'd last felt this excited. And then she chuckled. She felt plenty excited while being held in Nick's embrace. But that was different. Very different. Very personal.

She selected a white, peasant-style blouse with lots of eyelets, a gathered, off-the-shoulder neckline and embroidered flower petals in poppy red scattered throughout, and matched it with a long red skirt and a pair of sandals. Her silver earrings swung jauntily when she moved her head and played peekaboo in her loosely flowing hair.

She smiled in the mirror at her altered persona, an adopted ethnicity to go along with the piñata hanging from the ceiling, and the nachos, salsa, fajitas, rice and beans on the borrowed-from-Suzanne tables in the dining room.

She'd made personal phone calls to every student in her class and had hopes they'd all come to her little fiesta, *una fiesta pequeña,* to celebrate their efforts. She wanted not just seventy-five percent to attend, but as close to a hundred percent as possible. A celebration for everyone.

She'd already made up her mind to try different techniques next semester; maybe start a tutorial program on the side. Students helping students. Anything was possible with time and imagination.

The doorbell rang and her evening began with Gloria Ramos, the bank teller, who had to return to class.

"I will come back, Ms. Katherine. Don't you worry. Now I have what you call baseline scores, so we can plan a strategy. No?" The young woman beamed, hope shining in her eyes.

"Yes," replied Katherine as she looked at the enthusiastic face and dabbed the tears from her eyes. "We certainly can and will."

In the next hour she greeted more people than she'd ever entertained in Chicago. As promised, Dr. Goldman came with her husband; Estelle King brought Jeremy; Suzanne and David showed up, as did Anna and Joe Martinelli, who, Katherine soon realized, didn't have a clue as to what the celebration was about.

"Why didn't you tell them?" Katherine whispered to Nick.

Nick shrugged, his complexion turning ruddy. "Let it be a surprise." He reached toward his neck to loosen a tie that wasn't there. "It's not such a big deal," he muttered. "Thousands of people get a GED every year. I don't even know why I brought them."

"Oh, yes, you do," she replied gently.

He laughed and bestowed a quick kiss on her mouth. "Maybe I do at that. They've waited a long time for their firstborn to bring home a piece of paper."

"How did you ever convince them to come here? What did you tell them?"

Nick looked around and waved at his folks standing at the buffet. "They think they're supporting you and Jeremy. Your first class and all. And they appreciate how you've helped out in the office this week. But I guess they came...because I asked them to."

Good parents, thought Katherine. Lucky Nick. And tonight, Anna and Joe would be well rewarded.

Just then, Jeremy approached and pulled her to one side. "I got you something," he said as he took a small package from his pocket and thrust it into her hands. "A present. I really liked your class. You are so great.... I hope you like the gift. The diamond ones were prettier but—"

"Diamonds?" Katherine gasped. "Jeremy, what have you done? You shouldn't spend your hard-earned money on me!"

"No, no, Ms. Katherine. They're *not* diamonds, but I wish they were." And he slipped away to join his classmates.

Katherine stared after him and shook her head. Estelle wouldn't have allowed him to use more than a few dollars for a gift, so it was probably all right. She quickly put the package in the bedroom and returned to the party. It was time to present her own Certificates of Completion to each student, both graduates as well as returning students.

Looking forward to their reaction, she kept one eye on Nick's parents as she handed out the awards, and watched them clap politely as each person was recognized. They applauded loudly for Jeremy, their youngest employee. But when Katherine, full of anticipation, finally announced Nick's name, she thought they hadn't heard her. They stared and were dead silent...for a moment. Then came the grins, the laughter, the slaps on the back. And then Katherine watched Joe Martinelli turn the celebration into a major event.

"So any of you—Katherine's graduates—who want to go to a Houston city college and need help...you come to me. In fact, I want to see every one of you doing that. Go to college. Get a future."

Next to her, Katherine felt Nick stiffen. Lord knew how much money Joe was committing himself to, she thought. But Nick's mind didn't seem to be on the money.

"Does that include your own son, Dad? You want to see me go to college?"

"You bet," Joe replied without a pause. "If that's what you want, do it."

Wow! Joe sounded confident. Katherine bit her lip in concentration. Too confident for a man who depended on Nick's partnership in running an expanding business.

Katherine glanced up at Nick, expecting to see a quizzical expression. Instead she saw twinkling brown eyes and a grin inching across his face. She felt his body relax against hers and heard him exhale a huge breath.

"Yup," he replied. "That's just what I want. Earn my degree as quickly as possible, and get my architectural license. My own stamp of approval can go on Martinelli designs."

Joe's eyes lit with pride. "Not to worry. You'll have it all. Go to school full-time. Get your license. Should have done it years ago." He turned toward his wife. "See, Anna," he said with a lilt in his voice. "I can't retire now. Nick's going to college. The business needs me. And besides, the doctors don't know what they're talking about. I'm as healthy as a horse."

Anna said nothing. Just closed her eyes and pressed her lips together.

NICK'S DREAM DIED at that moment, and he barely noticed the pang. Not then. Not when he looked at his mother's drawn expression. How could he possibly relinquish responsibilities at Martinelli Construction if his dad was ill? Nothing on earth had the power to make him leave. Nothing.

An image of Katherine flashed through his mind's eye, and he shuddered at the possibility of loss. She'd be disappointed. Education meant everything to her, more than money, more than fame. *Marry an educated man.* He couldn't forget that deathbed promise she made to her mother. And all he had to offer was his GED.

"I'll walk them to the car and find out what's going on." Nick nodded toward his parents as he spoke directly to Katherine, but wasn't prepared when she gripped his arm, her normally fair complexion abnormally pale.

"What's wrong, Kat?"

She turned to the side a bit, away from Anna and Joe, and looked at him with fear-laden eyes. "Your dad would do anything for you, but you can't let him do this! It would kill them both. I really hate to say this, Nick, when you're finally on your way, but you might have to postpone your—"

He kissed her hard on the mouth. He was the world's biggest idiot, a lucky idiot to have a wonderful woman in his life. A woman who responded to his hasty kiss the way a man in love dreams of his woman responding. Even with a crowd of people in the room. Even with a couple of wolf whistles and cheers from the younger set.

He pulled away and was relieved to see the usual pink blush on her cheeks. "Hold that thought, sweetheart, until I get back." He took a step then turned back to her. "I'll get that degree, Kat. At some point, I will. I promise."

Katherine's smile wobbled, but she gave him a

thumbs-up before she turned toward his parents and hugged them first together and then separately. He watched his mother cling to Kat for a moment, and despite the cause, took pleasure in knowing the two women had connected.

"I've got plenty to do here," said Katherine as she escorted them to the door. "Take your time, Nick. Talk to them."

"You bet I will," he replied, hurrying down the outside stairs after his high-energy parents. His father strode like a man twenty years younger. How could anything be seriously wrong with this vibrant senior?

"A LOT OF MEDICAL mumbo jumbo," grumbled Joe Martinelli in answer to Nick's questions. "Those doctors use lots of words."

"Let's hear them."

His dad glared at him. "Whose side are you on anyway?"

"Yours."

"Hmm. Just a little plaque, a little clog in my arteries, some angina…maybe angioplasty."

Nick's stomach dropped. Surgery.

"It's just a *procedure*," insisted Joe.

"That's right," confirmed Anna. "A procedure in an *operating room!*" She drew out the last words into twenty syllables. "You are not going to work full-time anymore!"

"We'll see, Anna, we'll see. We need more tests. Don't worry. Finally, Nicky wants to go to college. You think I'm going to stand in his way? Never!"

The pride on his dad's face almost made Nick cry.

Why couldn't he have recognized the love years ago when he was sixteen? He would have been through school by now and all the heartache he'd caused his folks would have been avoided.

"I'll go to school part-time," said the man in question. "It's not a problem."

"Part-time is good," said Anna.

"Full-time is better," replied Joe.

And so it went, Nick thought with a laugh. The senior Martinellis in high gear. Arguing, compromising. Still wanting a say in their children's lives. And always finding their way. His parents would always find their way...together. They'd done it for thirty-eight years, and he wanted them to go on forever. An impossible dream. He knew that. He could personally attest to the uncertainties of life. But the boy in him could still wish for the impossible.

He promised a quick visit the next day, and waved as their car rolled away. He started to say good-night to other departing guests and thought of Katherine waiting for him upstairs. Thirty-eight years with her... His heart pounded as the man in him focused on the possible.

"Hey, Nick."

He turned at the sound of Jeremy's voice, and felt the corners of his mouth curve into a grin. The kid had a way of doing that recently. Making him laugh, making him proud.

"Calling it a night?" Nick asked.

J.T. looked at Estelle King and shrugged. "I guess." And then he turned to Nick. "So, what's

wrong with Mr. Joe?'' The boy's nonchalant stance
was at odds with the anxiety in his voice.

Nick stared at his young friend and relaxed his own
posture to match the kid's. He'd have to be careful.
Jeremy's life was still fragile, too fragile to handle
the specter of another loss, as improbable as it might
be.

''Nothing that can't be fixed, sport. Don't worry
about it.''

''Yeah, right, Nick. Like they can really fix a heart.
I heard what he said. It's not like kidneys, where
there's one to spare, so don't lie to me.'' Jeremy
turned quickly and started toward the parking area.

''Don't walk away from me, J.T.,'' Nick's voice
commanded, but doubts filled him as he stood poised,
looking at the sensitive boy hidden beneath the brittle
shell. The kid wanted to run, cut his losses before he
was in too deep. He was crazy about Joe, just like
everyone else in the family. And he was afraid.

The boy paused, but didn't turn around.

''Heart problems *can* be treated, Jeremy, and here,
in Houston, we have the best facility in the world.
But just as important, we're all in this together,'' said
Nick. ''You and me, and Kat, and Danny, and my
sisters, and the kids. Remember, we talked about it
recently. This time, if there's trouble, you're not
alone.''

Now he got a reaction. Jeremy twirled and captured
his gaze. ''I *am* alone. I always end up alone. I'm not
really part of your family, Nick, no matter how many
times we swim or buddy up. And that's okay. I'm
almost seventeen and almost on my own anyway, out

of Richmond House. I don't need to be part of anybody. I can survive by myself.''

Oh, kid. Survival's not enough. You need to learn to live.

"Come here, Jeremy," Nick said quietly. And waited until the boy stood in front of him before he casually placed a hand on his shoulder. "That's where you're wrong. No one survives well alone. No one. And if you think you're not already part of me and part of my family, you're wrong about that, too. Just because we don't have legal documents doesn't mean the feelings aren't there. Why am I going out of my way every darn morning to pick you up and take you to work? Why do I call Estelle all the time to ask about you? Why are you the subject of so many conversations Kat and I have?''

The boy's eyes almost popped out of his head. His mouth dropped open, too. Jeremy stood close enough for Nick to see the sheen cover his blue irises. Nick reached for him, gave him a bear hug. "Why am I so damn proud of you?''

Jeremy looked at him. Didn't say a word, just shook his head. "I don't know," he finally whispered.

"Because I love you! Because you are one terrific young man who has a lot to offer everyone around you. A lot to offer the world. So don't go running away from us. You need us and we need you. Get it?''

"I'm not sure.''

"Then think about it.''

Estelle King stepped forward then. "Can I take this

prize boy home now, Nicholas? Some graduates need their sleep.''

Nick grinned and nodded.

"And, by the way,'' she added without missing a beat, ''call me in a week or so. We need to talk.''

''Yes, ma'am.'' By next week he'd devise a plan for Jeremy's future with him. With Kat. With his family. Maybe as a foster parent, maybe just as a committed friend.

Part of the answer would lie with Jeremy. Part with Kat. It would be easier now that he was beginning to understand what made the kid tick. All that toughness, all that anger. Just a cover for fear. Lashing out at one moment; trying to please the next. The poor kid was trying to survive. He just didn't know how.

NICK TURNED and walked toward his own condo. He'd grab some clean clothes, his shaving gear. He'd already taken his laptop from the truck into Katherine's house. Tomorrow promised to be a sweet Sunday for the two of them, with just a short side trip to his folks'.

He strode up the outside stairs to his apartment, inserted his key and turned the doorknob. And that's when he realized his door wasn't locked anymore. In fact, it swung open with just the weight of his hand.

Nick froze where he stood and peered into the darkened room, straining to hear anything at all, any sound that would indicate someone's presence. He heard nothing but the slight rustle of a live oak behind him as its branches swayed in the warm evening breeze. He ran his arm along the inside wall and switched on the light.

His apartment had been ransacked. Bulldozed. Decimated.

He needed a moment to appreciate the destruction. It was no random act of violence, but rather a deliberate search-and-destroy mission. He buried his immediate outrage and reached for his cell phone.

"Lock yourself in, Katherine. Don't open the door to anyone, even me, unless I'm singing 'Happy Birthday.' Then you'll know the coast is clear." He hung up before she could argue, and took a step inside.

In the living room, every seat cushion on his leather couch had been slashed and ripped wide. Doors on his entertainment center swung crookedly, and his CDs were spilled all over the floor. His eyes scanned the mess until he found the CD he wanted and slipped it inside his pocket. Then he selected a few others at random.

In his office, the devastation was total. He could barely find a spot to place his feet. Desk drawers stood on end, with their pencils, rulers, paper clips, postage stamps and maps spilled to the floor. His checkbook rested on the phone. Bookcases sported gaping shelves.

He searched for the photo of Donna and Jenny that he'd kept at eye level, and finally spotted it under *The Fountainhead*. The glass had shattered. He knelt and picked it up as carefully as he would a newborn infant, despite his shaking hands. He swallowed hard and reburied the outrage bubbling to the surface, while he placed the picture gently on the desk.

He forced his way forward to the computer, which, surprisingly, seemed untouched, the screen saver's graphics rotating steadily, as always. He shrugged. He might have left the machine on. He touched the mouse. The graphics were replaced by a message:

NEXT TIME WE'LL FIND IT.

Nick reached for the phone just as he heard Katherine's horror-laden "My God! Nicky. What's going on?" Startled, he whirled fast enough to create a breeze.

"I asked you to lock yourself—"

"Are you all right?"

He couldn't allow her to ignore him. She could have run right into...he didn't want to imagine what... "Didn't I ask you to stay in the apartment? Didn't I ask you to wait for me there?" His rage found an outlet. He heard the anger in his voice, but tasted fear—metallic and cold—instead. He pulled her toward him with one strong hand and punched in 911 with the other.

She squirmed as he barked into the receiver. His embrace tightened until he finally felt her puny punches, and he dropped his arm as though it was on fire.

"I'm sorry, so sorry. Did I hurt you? Stay behind me." The door was half-open still, not even latched into place. He had to keep her safe in whatever way he could. He stepped in front of her and turned his attention back to the phone. "No sirens. Whoever came in is gone now, my house was the deliberate target, the only target. No one else is in danger.''

He glanced back at Katherine and hoped like hell his words were true. ''And be prepared to dust for prints,'' he added into the phone before he hung up and turned his attention to Katherine once more.

''Now,'' he said in the quietest tone he could manage, ''what are you doing here?''

Katherine squared her shoulders and met his gaze. ''Helping my best friend when he's in trouble,'' she said calmly. She drummed her fingers on his desk and examined her surroundings. ''Big trouble.''

He didn't know whether to laugh or cry. She was so sincere, so sweet with her concern, but she'd only put herself in danger. Just where he didn't want her.

''You never even considered doing as I asked?''

''I've taken care of myself for ten years,'' she replied. ''In a city larger than Houston. I'm not used to taking orders from anyone and I'm not going to start now.'' Katherine took his hand. ''I thought I could help,'' she explained softly.

He shook his head as one idea after another raced through his mind. ''It's not over yet, Katrin. They didn't find what they were looking for tonight, and they'll try again.'' He paused as his thoughts coalesced. ''Whoever's behind this knows me, knows where I work, knows where I live. And most likely knows about you. So I need to keep you safe.''

His brain stopped right there. Safe. A precious word. A precious woman. If anything happened to her… God, not again. Never again. What was the best thing to do? Should he keep his distance? Not see her. Not call her? Should they go their separate ways to throw the perpetrator off the track?

But if the perp already knew about Katherine, knew she lived two buildings over, knew she and he were a pair, then Nick would be leaving her totally defenseless…when he wasn't around. He shivered at the thought. She'd be a sitting duck.

He had to decide and he didn't have all the facts. The image of Katherine as a victim made it easy in the end. "The best way to keep you safe," he explained slowly, "is for me to move in with you."

HER THOUGHTS WERE as scrambled as a dozen eggs in an omelette. She knew she'd scared him by coming up to his condo as she had. He hadn't wanted her there and he certainly wasn't expecting her. That was obvious when she saw his reaction to her presence— fear and anger. Typical male. Women cried, but men got angry when afraid. And she couldn't really blame him. His mind was on the police, on his apartment. Or what remained of it.

But he was delusional if he thought she'd bite her nails behind closed doors when she could be helping him. She was not one of his employees who had to follow the Martinelli rules.

And now he wanted to move in with her. Not because he loved her, but because he felt obligated to protect her. She blinked hard. Right move. Wrong reason. She'd dreamed of them taking a next step together, but not like this.

"Sorry, Nick," she said. "We're not ready."

"Ready has nothing to do with it," he replied without hesitation. "It's logical. Makes sense." He looked at her then, his eyes twinkling, back to the usual warmth he reserved for her. "Will I be such an onerous burden to have around?"

Under ordinary conditions, she'd welcome him gladly. Under these circumstances, however, her heart was heavy. She didn't want a chauvinistic protector; she wanted a partner.

"Yes," she answered without meeting his gaze. "You will."

Nick schooled his features to hide his shock and disappointment. Before he could protest her response, however, he heard footsteps, a loud knock, and two of Houston's finest were inside.

The questioning went on for half an hour; the computer keys were dusted for prints as was the mouse, and every hard surface in the apartment. Nick called his locksmith in the middle of the night for the second time in a month.

"Be right there, Nick. Looks like you're not too lucky these days. First the office, now your apartment."

"Nah, just temporary setbacks."

But he had second thoughts when he saw his bedroom. The perp had gone all out. Left nothing untouched.

Seeming to feel the same way, the younger police officer whistled long and low. "Whoever it is really wants something bad."

Nick stood still, again stunned at what met his eyes. Not one item, not one piece of furniture had been overlooked. The end tables lay on their sides, the dresser drawers pulled out, and even the mattress was halfway off the bed. But worse, his big down pillows had been slit wide open, their feathers covering the ground like a six-inch snowfall. Thick and white.

He glanced at Katherine standing on the threshold to the bedroom. Her complexion had turned an unbecoming shade of green. He strode to her, blocked her view of the room and took her in his arms. "Come on, baby." He kissed her head, her ears and neck as he walked her out of the room. He turned to the cops.

"Can one of you escort Ms. Kirby back to her apartment?"

He felt Katherine shiver as he held her. She clasped him tightly. "No, Nick. I'm staying here. With you."

"You look ready to keel over."

"Doesn't matter," she replied. "This whole thing is so ugly. Does it have to do with the school project? Is that what it's all about?"

"Probably."

"Why are they cutting mattresses? How could big blueprints be hidden there? I don't get it."

He glanced at the officers who had joined them in the corridor and spoke to all three of them. "They didn't find paper copies of anything—cost estimates, blueprints, material lists—so now they're looking for computer disks. We use a CAD program to design everything on computer first. Computer Aided Design. Then we print out and work from there to develop blueprints and compute how much of everything we need. They're probably looking for the spreadsheets delineating costs rather than the design itself.''

''Are there any hard copies of the spreadsheets lying around?'' asked one of the cops. ''Or haven't you printed them out yet?''

''Under lock and key,'' Nick replied. ''Nothing's lying around. And the numbers aren't final yet anyway.''

''But probably close enough,'' inserted Katherine. ''You've been working on them all summer, and they're due soon.''

Nick nodded. ''In three weeks. September 15.''

''Seems like forever.'' Katherine's voice quivered, and Nick wrapped his arm around her again.

''Do you have any idea, Mr. Martinelli, about who could be behind this?''

Nick shook his head at the younger officer. ''Martinelli Construction has some tough competitors in the city, but there's never been anything personal or violent. Certainly nothing on this scale.''

''What about your employees? Have you fired anybody lately? Ticked somebody off? Demoted anyone?''

''No. No. And no.''

Suddenly Katherine stepped out of his embrace and turned to him. ''What about Sally? She was sort of demoted.''

''Sally?'' Nick was incredulous. ''She works as hard as any of us. No way.''

''I like her too, but...there's something not right. I've been helping out for a week now and I know she does anything she's asked, but she won't look at me…it happens all the time…especially when her brother's there.'' She snapped her fingers and paced two steps back and forth. ''In fact, do you know why her brother is hanging around her so much? What do you know about Eddie Jensen, Nick?''

Nick's forehead wrinkled. ''I don't know anything about him. But, Kat, he's not in the construction business. That I do know. I think he changes jobs pretty regularly, although Sally doesn't mention him much.'' He let that information sink in a moment before following up. ''Why do you ask?''

She smiled a little self-consciously before meeting his eyes. ''He gives me the creeps.''

Nick wanted to laugh, but controlled himself. ''Afraid we can't arrest him for that, sweetheart.''

''He was too darn curious when he came to the office. Asked a lot of questions. I just didn't like him.''

The older police officer took out a pad of paper and a pencil. ''Can't hurt to look him up,'' he said. ''And if he's got a good alibi for tonight, no harm done. We're doing our job by conducting a thorough investigation.''

Nick nodded. ''Maybe you'll get some fingerprints also.''

''We'll know tomorrow.''

''Sunday?''

''Perpetrators don't take a day of rest, Mr. Martinelli, and neither do the police.''

THIRTY MINUTES LATER, after the new lock was installed on his door, Nick walked hand in hand with

Katherine back to her apartment. With a clean set of clothes tucked under his arm, he was spending the night with her.

"I wasn't trying to be macho man tonight," he said quietly. "I just want to keep you safe."

She lifted her face to his, her eyes wide and luminous, then she kissed him. "I know. I know. Because I wanted to do the same for you. That's why I came."

He shook his head, loving her but exasperated. "And if the crook had still been there with a gun or a knife, what could you have possibly done except get into big trouble?"

"If the crook had still been there, you couldn't have called me on the phone!"

Women! This woman in particular had an answer for everything, but he had to laugh despite his frustration. She was saucy and adorable.

"Come here, Kat," he commanded as they approached her doorway. He turned her in his arms and covered her mouth with his own. And felt the instant sizzle. Her arms tightened around his neck, her lips opened in invitation. He accepted eagerly, and still managed to maneuver them inside the apartment and slam the door with his foot.

"I love you, Nick."

"I know, sweetheart, I know," he said as he locked the door and led her into the bedroom, thankful she'd agreed to him staying with her temporarily.

Threatening her with a full-time bodyguard or a trained police dog seemed to do the trick. After due consideration, she'd settled for him.

CHAPTER ELEVEN

WHY DIDN'T he say the words...the three words she wanted to hear? Katherine leaned into Nick's chest, loving the way his arms surrounded her, loving the fragrance of musk and man. She nuzzled closer.

He loved her. She knew it as surely as she knew the sun rose in the east, as surely as she knew her own birthday. He showed his feelings every time he made love to her, every time he conjured up a tasty dinner when she would have settled for a tuna sandwich. He showed it every time he asked about her day, and then listened as she replied.

But she'd never heard those three special words because he'd never said them, at least not to her. How ironic, when for the first time in her life, her heart was open to love and trust.

Nick blew gently into her ear. A delicious chill swept through her, head to toe, and she hugged him tighter. No, she wasn't going anywhere. She'd have to trust a little longer.

"Love those low necklines," said Nick as he bestowed a series of kisses along the top of her breasts and shoulders. "Love them more when they disappear." He scooped the blouse from her body, baring her breasts, while she quickly unbuttoned his shirt.

"Fair is fair," she murmured as she leaned in to tongue his nipples. She had the satisfaction of hearing him inhale then groan. And suddenly, she was wrapped in his arms again, his lips on hers, experiencing a kiss born of desperation.

She returned it full measure, sensing his need for her, but concerned about it, too.

"What is it?" she asked when she could breathe again. "What's wrong?"

She felt him startle, saw a mask slip over his normally expressive features. "Everything's fine, Kat. When you're in my arms, safe in my bed, nothing's wrong."

"I agree," she laughed, "but we can't stay in bed forever!"

The mask disappeared; his eyes sparkled and a teasing grin crossed his face. "I'd sure like to try."

She returned his grin. "Well, if anyone can do it…"

"There's no time like the present," he replied as he reached for her again.

She offered no resistance, happy to see his smile back in place, happy that she'd been the one to put it there. But afterward, she had a hard time falling asleep. The events of the evening had cast a shadow over their lives.

THE NEXT MORNING, Nick watched patiently while a new alarm system was installed in Katherine's apartment.

"It'll take me a year to learn how to operate this contraption—" protested Kat. She glared at Nick, then turned to the installer and pasted a smile on her face. "No offense," she said, "but I think Nick's overreacting."

"It's an excellent system," replied Nick soothingly as he leaned against the kitchen table. "I guarantee you'll learn to use it in five minutes. I'll teach you myself." And if it took five *hours,* so be it.

"If the system's so great, why didn't it work in your apartment?" She stood with her hands on her hips, a challenge in her eyes.

"It didn't work," he admitted, "because I didn't have it on. I didn't set it."

"You didn't…"

She started to laugh, and he let her go on for as long as she wanted. He deserved it, and he could afford to be generous now.

"I lived in a fool's paradise," he admitted when she finally controlled her giggles. "But it's not going to happen again. Understand?"

To his horror, she began to cry. "Of course, I understand, Nick, but I don't have to like it."

First laughter, then tears. Not a good sign.

He crossed to where she stood and drew her close. "I know, Kat, I know. And I don't like it one bit either. But it's the smart thing to do. The reality is that we live in a big city and safety bolts and alarm systems are a way of life."

She didn't seem to be listening. "When I think of what your apartment looked like last night," she began, "my heart just stops. What if you had been home?"

He wished he had. He wished he could've confronted the perpetrator, put a face to him, and put an end to the whole business. But he'd had enough experience with females to know that Katrin didn't want to hear that.

"But I wasn't, sweetheart," he soothed. "I was with you, celebrating my graduation."

Finally, he saw a smile. A little wobbly, but a real smile.

"It'll be a night to remember," she said. "Everyone happy, celebrating, and Jeremy was so sweet. I forgot to mention it, Nick, but he gave me a gift."

"He did?" A small frown marred Nick's face. "What kind of a gift? Something homemade, I hope?"

"I'm afraid not," she replied. "A pair of earrings. Lovely rhinestones. Probably ran him about forty dollars or so. But it could have been worse, Nick. He said he'd wanted to buy diamonds."

Nick slammed his eyes shut for a moment. Damn! The kid had screwed up. Big-time.

"Of course, I told him not to spend his money on me," continued Katherine. "He's working so hard for it."

"Will you show me the earrings, Kat?"

"Sure...but you're scaring me. What's the matter?"

What wasn't the matter? Why did everything happen at once? Wasn't it enough they had to handle the break-in? Now they also had to deal with Jeremy. And he knew that would hurt Katherine's heart more.

"Jeremy has no access to money, sweetheart. All

his earnings are deposited directly into a trust account.''

He watched as she digested this information and put the facts together. Her mouth formed a perfect O. Her expressive eyes reflected the concern, worry and disappointment he felt himself.

''He stole them,'' she whispered.

''Afraid so,'' he confirmed.

''Oh, God, Nick. What are we going to do? He's such a great kid. I don't want to get him into trouble.''

Nick took her by the arm and walked her into the bedroom. He held the earrings in his hands. Pretty. The kid had good taste. He slipped the box into his pocket.

''*Jeremy* got *himself* into trouble. You had nothing to do with it.'' He turned Katherine to face him. ''You're going to have to trust me with this, Kat. It's not going to be pretty, and Jeremy's not going to like it. And he won't like me or even you for a while.''

''I thought we were making so much progress,'' she said. ''I thought he was doing so well, considering everything.''

''He was. And he will again. We've just got to stop him in his tracks right now before he does other foolish things and gets into real trouble later. He's not thinking straight, but theft is theft. And there's a penalty for dishonesty.''

Her shoulders slumped. ''Ah, well. You're right. So what happens next?''

Nick led her back into the kitchen. ''The first thing on the agenda is learning to operate the alarm system.

And then I'll call Estelle and we'll work out a plan ASAP."

AN HOUR LATER, Katherine stepped out of the shower, her thoughts tumbling one over the other, but then focusing on the break-in to Nick's apartment. From whom were they defending themselves? She wished she knew.

She'd promised Nick to set the alarm not only when she left the condo, but even when she was in the apartment alone. He had already arranged for a guard service to patrol their street at night. Now he was at his place with the investigators from the police lab. Hopefully, they'd find clues as to who the perpetrator was.

She shook her head in concern. Nick was orchestrating a big defense, including his parents' house, the main office of Martinelli Construction and the sales offices on the various sites. His strategy made sense, but it brought home to her that all of them were vulnerable. There were too many locations, too many innocent people.

As she dressed to visit Anna and Joe, Katherine stared wide-eyed into the mirror as the truth dawned. *Nick was the target. The only target.* The employees out in the field weren't working on the school project. The engineers working in the office all reported to Nick or Joe. And with Joe now ill and out of the picture for a while, the walking target had to be Nick.

She took a deep breath. She'd stick to him like glue for the next two weeks, until she started teaching again.

With that plan firmly in mind, she set the alarm and walked to Nick's building, hoping the police had picked up enough clues in their search so they'd be able to close the case quickly.

"ALL THEY GOT was half a print!" said Nick in disgust as he started the truck. He glanced at Kat, relieved to see her looking as good as ever. "Even the cops were surprised, because the ransacking was the work of an amateur. They expected the place to be loaded with fingerprints, considering that he'd been in every room."

"He must have worn gloves."

"That's just what they said."

"So maybe he's brighter than we think. Maybe he's done this before." Her voice quavered, and he reached for her hand.

"Nothing's going to happen to you, Kat. I really will hire a personal bodyguard if it'll make you feel better."

"Me?" she exclaimed. "I'm not the one they're after. It's you I'm worried about."

He started to laugh and raised her hand to his lips. "It's not me they want, it's the work."

"Same difference," she grumbled.

He shrugged. "Relax, honey. The burglar won't return to City in the Woods. His thorough search produced nothing. And you saw how every inch of the apartment was messed up. Nah, he won't come back. They never return to the scene of the crime," he added dramatically.

"So he'll look somewhere else."

"So?"

"So where is all the data he wants? Where do you keep it?"

He glanced at her and winked. "That is one piece of information, baby, that you do not need to know." And maybe that was the best piece of protection he could provide.

TEN MINUTES LATER, Nick pulled up in front of his parents' house. Anna and Joe greeted them like long lost relatives, and were still exclaiming over the graduation party.

"What a lovely group of people," Anna said. "I managed to speak with most of them. They sing your praises, Katherine. You've opened doors for them. Raises, promotions, college. You must be very proud of what you do."

"You know, I actually had a great summer," she replied as she felt a smile slowly cross her face. "I did work hard, but I'm sure the students worked harder. I'm proud of them."

"Well, they were lucky to have you," replied Anna. "My son, too." She elbowed Nick.

"Absolutely, Mom. She's the best. The very best. See." And with that he bent his head and kissed Katherine full on the lips.

She felt the heat rise as quickly as a sandstorm in the desert. Her face had to be bright red. She'd kill him for embarrassing her, she vowed as she tried to push his immovable body away. And she'd do it right in front of his mother.

But then he softened the kiss and nibbled the corner

of her mouth. "Isn't this more fun than worrying about last night?" he whispered, and she knew he'd never reveal to his parents what had transpired after they'd left Katherine's house the evening before.

"Mmm," she replied.

"See, Mom." He tucked Kat next to him and looked at Anna with innocent eyes. "I told you she was the best."

Anna's dark eyes twinkled. "She has to be to put up with your shenanigans. Now, both of you come with me and meet the newest member of the family."

Nick turned to explain. "Josie and Mike must be here. With the baby."

They followed Anna to the family room, but Katherine paused on the threshold, transfixed by the stunning picture of mother and child rocking gently on a tightly upholstered white antique chair. Katherine turned to comment to Nick, but found him staring at his sister, too.

"And this is what happens when little sisters grow up," he said just loud enough to be heard.

"Nicky! You're here. Now everything's perfect," said the little sister. Her delighted expression gave credence to her statement, and she turned toward Katherine then, her smile welcoming. "Let's introduce our ladies," she said to Nick. But she didn't wait. "Hi, Katherine. I'm so happy to meet you finally. Everyone's been speaking about you and Nicky."

"You mean the old phone lines have been humming as usual?" joked Nick. He looked at Kat.

"There are absolutely no secrets in a family of sisters. Ask Danny. He'll vouch for me."

He complained but he loved it. And maybe needed the teasing, the support, more than ever in recent times.

"Your sisters are crazy about you," Kat replied, "so don't go complaining to me." She spoke the truth. They were crazy about Nick...to the point they could make a visitor uncomfortable. She thought of Joanna.

But they were an attractive bunch. Elfin Tina with the gamine face, classically pretty Joanna, and this madonna-like Josie. And similar in their loyalty and love. No wonder Nick was so comfortable around women.

She watched him kiss Josie, watched his expression as he looked at the baby, and looked some more. She saw a flash of pain, of wistfulness, before it changed to admiration for a gorgeous niece.

"Good job, Josie," Nick said as he finally straightened up. "She's absolutely perfect. Does she have a name?"

"Of course she has a name!"

"Well, no one's told it to me. Whenever I asked, they said you weren't sure yet."

"Her name," said Josie, "is Nicole. We're going to call her Nikki." She reached a hand toward her brother. "Mike and I would like *you* to be Nikki's godfather."

Katherine heard his breath as he inhaled, saw his free hand search for hers, then felt him squeeze it. Tears gathered in her own eyes. This man was born to be a dad. In his heart, he wanted a family of his own, but maybe wasn't ready to admit it. Maybe he just needed more time before he took that last step.

"I'd be honored, Josephina," he finally said in a hoarse voice. "Count on it."

"Thank you, Nicky."

"So where's the proud father?" asked Katherine.

"Celebrating with Dad," replied Josie, but I get the feeling Mom's not too happy. What's going on around here?"

NICK'S THOUGHTS CHURNED. The better question would be, what's *not* going on around here? But of course, he wouldn't say that.

"Dad just has to take a few tests to check his heart. Nothing to panic about," said Nick, hoping he spoke the truth. "So he won't be in the office much for the next couple of weeks."

Josie's forehead wrinkled. "Maybe I'd better get back to work then. I could take Nicole in with me."

She was nuts! Nick stepped toward the rocking chair and squatted on his heels next to his sister and niece. "No way. My goddaughter has been in an incubator for two weeks. She's just out of the hospital. There's no way you're surrounding her with everybody's germs. And you need to recover, too."

Josie's eyes glinted. "I'm as healthy as a horse, bro, but thanks for your concern." She looked at the infant in her arms, her face softening, and nodded. "I'm not going to argue. I think you're right. She needs more time before she faces the big wide world."

Nick sighed with relief. One less person to worry about, or rather, two.

"How about me?" asked Katherine. "I can help out at the office for the next two weeks. At least part-time, while I prepare for my new classes. And I can also write the introduction to *Changing Lives*—the collection of autobiographies we've assembled."

Nick stood up again and turned to Katherine. "I thought you were planning to spend the two weeks at the library." And he wished she would. A nice quiet, safe college library. "Doing the research for your dissertation. We wouldn't think of getting in the way of that."

Katherine started pacing. "You won't. I'm extremely disciplined when I get involved with my work. I'm going to research the social history, family structure, and most importantly, the home life, of nineteenth-century England, then see how and if the country's major female writers have incorporated these ideas into their literature. Maybe I'll use a couple of time lines. I'm not sure yet. I still need to work out the details. Speak to my adviser in Chicago."

And this is where he couldn't help her. Not when she almost spoke another language. The language of academics. He smiled wryly, thinking about his high-school equivalency.

"How can I help? Do you need airfare to Chicago? Do you want to buy your own reference books or a more powerful computer?" At least he could offer financial assistance.

"Why, thanks, Nick! But money can't buy what I

need. I just need time to think. And to get an outline down on paper.''

He walked to Kat, kissed the crease on her forehead, and put his arms around her. ''You'll do it like you do everything else—well.''

Her smile almost blinded him. ''Thanks, Nick. It's nice to hear.'' She leaned closer, raised her head and kissed him right on the mouth.

Hmm. Maybe he *did* do something for her, which had nothing to do with schoolwork.

''So, count on me for the office. Sally, Tina and I can make it work...if Tina's not still at the sales office at City in the Woods.''

''She'll go where she's needed.'' He squeezed her hand gently and turned her toward the baby. ''Come on over. Meet my godchild.'' With that, he scooped the infant from Josie, burrowed his nose in her neck and inhaled the delicious smell of baby. He walked toward Kat. And watched his intrepid Katherine take a step backward.

''She's...she's awfully small, Nick. I don't think...''

He gently placed the baby in Katherine's arms. ''Don't think at all, sweetheart. Just cradle her like this... See how snugly she fits. Come on, sit down on the couch next to me.''

He glanced at his sister's sparkling eyes and winked, before turning his attention back to Katherine. ''You're a natural, honey.''

''Oh, I don't think so,'' she replied breathlessly. ''Don't leave me. I won't know what to do.''

''You're doing just fine, Kat. You can't drop her,

because you're sitting down. So just relax and enjoy.''

"Hmm."

He watched Katherine concentrate on her tiny charge. Watched her poke through the receiving blanket to view the delicate fingers. Heard the ''oh, my!'' she whispered when she beheld them. Felt her body finally relax next to his on the sofa as she continued to hold Nicole.

''This is really something,'' she murmured.

He choked up when he looked at her again. Images of another woman, another child, another time, superimposed themselves for a moment, faded in and out until finally there was only Katherine. Katherine and a baby. His Katherine, with his baby.

But not until everyone was safe.

EDDIE JENSEN WAS NOT a happy man. His florid complexion worsened as he shouted at Sally that same afternoon at her apartment.

''I tore his place apart for nothin'—ya hear me—nothin', and the cops made a house call just to talk to me.''

''Whose place, Eddie? Whose place did you tear up?'' Dread filled her as she waited for his reply. Everything was getting way out of hand. Her brother was in over his head and nothing good would come out of this escapade.

''Whose place, Eddie?'' he mimicked in a falsetto. ''Whose do you think?'' he bellowed. ''Who has the stuff I need for the Willard brothers? Your big boss, baby. The guy you worship so much. I left his place a mess, but the damn work wasn't there. No disk and no printouts.''

His eyes looked wild, his breath labored. ''So where are they, Sal? I need that information now.''

''Well, I don't have it. And I don't know where it is. And I told you that from the beginning.''

''But you're gonna find out, Sal. You're the only one who can because you're his secretary. You're closer to Nick Martinelli than anyone—except maybe the blond bitch he's sleeping with. And you're gonna find out because you're my sister and blood is thicker than water, and you don't want me dead.''

Sally closed her eyes. Don't panic. Don't panic. You'll figure out something as soon as he leaves. Her brother continued to ramble. She let his words wash over her until she heard him talking about the ''bitch'' again.

''Now, I ask you, why did the cops come to my place? Out of the whole damn population in this city, why would they single me out when I didn't leave even one fingerprint in the joint?'' He leaned forward and poked his finger at his sister.

''I don't know, Eddie. Why did they visit you?''

''Because of her. She doesn't like me. I could tell when we had lunch there that day. Snooty voice, snooty walk. She looked at me like I was dirt.''

''She did not! She was polite to you, that's all. And visitors are not allowed to walk through the building unless accompanied by an employee. And you thought you could wander anywhere you wanted. Well, you can't. Real-life business doesn't work that way.''

"Just listen to you. Think you know everything, don't you, Sally?"

"I don't know everything, Eddie, but I know a few things. And I know a drunk when I see one." She turned her face away from his sour, beer-laden breath. "Why don't you just go home? Sleep it off."

"I ain't drunk, Sal. Not so's you'd notice."

"Well, I noticed, Edward. You're stinking drunk. Now get out of here." She kept her voice low, her words clear. "This is my house, and I don't need this. I told you to leave me out of your wild schemes from the beginning."

She hated him the most when he was drunk. That's when her anger overruled her fear. Most people she knew got scared when their guys drank too much, and she didn't blame them. But she was different. She got angry. Her brother brought all the bad stuff with him when he visited her like this. All the old stuff that she'd left behind a few years ago. Obviously, she hadn't left it far enough behind. Not when her brother could still ruin everything for her.

"Well, I ain't too drunk to forget about the blond bitch. Because if Nicky boy don't have what I need, then she's gotta have it. And right after she hands it over, she's gonna get hers. The snooty bi..."

With a sweeping gesture and a grand belch, Eddie fell on his sister's couch and passed out.

Sally packed a suitcase and left the apartment.

CHAPTER TWELVE

"I DON'T BELIEVE THIS," said Nick the next morning as he read the letter he held in his hand. It had arrived by courier not five minutes earlier and now he stood in the reception area of Martinelli Construction, where Katherine sat, trying to make sense of it.

"What is it?" she asked.

"Sally's resigned."

"Sally? Your Sally? Your Sally who's supposed to be at this desk right now? Just like that? With no notice?"

Katherine reached for the envelope Nick held out to her. "Any explanation?"

"If you can believe it."

She perused the message. "Her aunt's ill and she's gone to care for her. In the Hill Country, miles west of here." She looked at Nick. "And she's very sorry not to be able to give two weeks' notice, but she had to leave in a hurry."

Katherine reread the entire letter again. "No forwarding address or phone number. Not even for any salary due her." She handed the missive back to Nick. "Has she ever done something like this in the past?"

"Never," replied Nick. "In fact, she's always on time and dependable. Makes a point of it." He reached for the phone, but then returned it to the cradle. "Something's not right here. I'll use the phone in my own office."

"Who are you calling?" asked Katherine.

"The officers we met Saturday night. I want to know about Sally's brother. Maybe, my girl, you were on the mark about him."

But ten minutes later, he wasn't sure. Both detectives had spoken with Eddie, and the guy had a strong alibi. He'd been at a club on the Richmond strip—one of his regular haunts—and the bartender remembered him being there Saturday night. They were still checking him out, and they'd keep Nick posted about any new developments.

"Good. Maybe you'd better keep a tail on him or visit him again," said Nick after he told them about Sally's resignation letter. "Sally worked for us for three years. I would swear she enjoyed her job and liked it here. Her absence is too coincidental. Something stinks."

"You're right, Mr. Martinelli," said Officer Roberts. "In our business, there's no such thing as coincidence. We'll follow up. What's she driving?"

After giving the police whatever information he could, Nick replaced the phone and returned to Katherine's desk. A typical Monday morning at Martinelli Construction and calls were coming in at a steady rate. Katherine seemed to be fielding them as best she could.

"Two calls are holding for you, Nick. Get back in there."

"Yes, boss," he said with a grin. "Just wanted to

tell you that the detectives haven't dismissed Eddie Jensen yet as a possibility. They're still on it.'' He leaned down and kissed her nape. ''Delicious. Couldn't resist.''

She squirmed and turned around. ''I can't work when you do that,'' she laughed.

''I love to hear you laugh,'' he said. ''I love to see you happy.'' He kissed her quickly on the mouth and returned to his office. And he'd make sure she stayed happy…and healthy.

His thoughts circled one another, and returned to Eddie Jensen. With Sally's disappearance, he was willing to admit Kat's instincts might have been right, but the guy wasn't even in the construction business. He had an erratic work history. So what was his motivation? What could he possibly want badly enough to risk a break-in?

Nick sighed with disgust. Absolutely nothing. But someone did. The question was, who? And finding the answer was like looking for the proverbial needle in a haystack. Construction companies abounded in the Houston metropolitan area. And then there were any number from Dallas, Austin or parts unknown who were interested in bidding. It was impossible to guess which competitor would use illegal methods to obtain information. If it was a competitor at all. There was no guarantee about that either.

So if he couldn't concentrate on the impossible, he'd focus on the possible. Keeping his family safe. And that included Kat and Jeremy. And speaking of Jeremy, he reached for the phone to call Estelle. Hopefully, they'd set up a meeting with all of them—

Jeremy, Katherine, Estelle and himself. But he'd leave it to Estelle to set the stage. She was an old hand at dealing with wayward boys. Hadn't she and Joe conspired years ago to straighten Nick out?

AT THE END OF THE DAY, Katherine and Nick left for home in separate vehicles. After parking in their respective spots, Katherine, as usual, collected her mail from the designated cluster of boxes before heading upstairs. Nick walked right beside her, key in hand, to open the door before she entered.

"The alarm's on," she protested with a laugh. "You watched me set it this morning."

"Indulge me, baby," he replied as he pushed a series of buttons to disengage the system.

As if she could do anything else.

"I'm going to my place to check on the cleaning crew's progress," he said. "Be right back, but lock up after me."

"Aye, aye, Captain." Katherine saluted and followed his directions, but then sighed heavily. She'd never been a paranoid person, and she didn't want to become one. She wished the police would catch the perpetrator and put an end to this way of life.

She glanced at the small pile of envelopes she'd brought in and quickly flipped through it. "Phone bill, community coupons, bank statement, and at the bottom...a return address from the University of Texas in Austin. She ripped the flap open and forced herself to calm down enough to read. And absorb.

A smile crept across her face as the words started making sense. She carried the letter into her office and flopped at her desk. She'd been invited for an interview. The letter was signed by the chair of the English Department regarding a pending position available in January. Seemed that Jonathan Carter had suggested she be considered.

Katherine folded the letter and sat quietly. The initial rush had ended before it began. Why wasn't she more excited? Why wasn't her heart racing? Why weren't her nerves jingling? A position at a prestigious university was what she'd always wanted! Four months ago she would have been walking on air. Even one month ago, she would have been very pleased. But now? All she felt was…confused.

How could she want something and not want something at the same time?

Because her life had changed since she'd moved to Houston. Nick had entered it. Oh, she still wanted that doctorate. Nothing would change that. Her Ph.D. was the key to her future in higher education. But now she wanted more.

Because Nick lived in Houston, not Austin. A slight hundred-fifty-mile difference!

But he's never admitted his love for you. He's never said the words.

Katherine rubbed her temples and placed the letter in her desk drawer. He loved her—she felt it—but he was afraid. Afraid to reach for happiness again. Afraid to lose it again.

She jumped from her chair, too impatient to sit. She understood those fears all too well. Hadn't meeting Nick enticed her out of her own cocoon? Now it was his turn to let go.

She closed her eyes, crossed her fingers and said a silent prayer. She might wind up hurting badly, but with hope in her heart she left the letter inside and closed the drawer.

ESTELLE KING SAT behind her desk Tuesday evening, facing her most recent graduate. A smart boy. Basically a good boy. With a lot of tough breaks. Sometimes a lot of attitude. But a survivor. It was her duty to guide Jeremy on this critical rite of passage to adulthood. Not that she thought a boy of almost seventeen was an adult, but those were the state's rules and Richmond House followed them.

Based on his progress, they would have released Jeremy as soon as he turned seventeen. But this shoplifting incident could change everything. It all depended on what happened in the next couple of hours.

She settled back in her seat and looked at the youngster across her desk. "Jeremy, I'd *like* to tell you how pleased I am with your progress. You've come a long way and you're very close to realizing all of your goals."

He grinned and sat back in his seat.

"You've got your high-school diploma, a good job, money in the bank, community service almost done and educational plans for the future—as well as two good adult friends who care about you. In a few months, you'll be seventeen and emancipated."

"Yup, I'm almost there. I knew I could do it."

"I knew you could do it, too, but unfortunately, Jeremy, we have a real problem. Big enough to jeopardize everything."

There was no hiding the disappointment in her voice or in her heart.

"What problem, Ms. Estelle?"

"I think you know exactly what I'm talking about."

"No, I don't," he said quickly. Too quickly.

"Then let me help you remember." She paused. "Nick Martinelli called me yesterday."

"Yeah? So what? I see him every day."

"He called me about a pair of rhinestone earrings.... Ring a bell?"

She saw his eyes narrow, his mouth compress. "They were a gift for Ms. Katherine. It's none of his business that I gave her a present."

"Where did you get the earrings, Jeremy?"

"I bought them."

"With what? You don't have the money to buy that kind of gift."

"I borrowed it." He led with his chin as he continued, "I like Kathy and she likes me. And she helped me with a lot of work."

"I understand that," Estelle replied. "But I don't understand the money part. You have none and neither do your friends."

Jeremy's silence answered her.

"As it turns out," Estelle continued, "the earrings pinch her and Katherine has to choose something else." The counselor paused and extended her hand, palm up. "She's going to need the sales slip to return them to the store." Jeremy would never know that legitimate gifts could be returned without a slip.

"I lost it."

"You're going to lose more than a sales slip if you continue to lie." She leaned across the desk now, needing to shake him up. "The name of the store was with the earrings, on the card. We've already called them."

"So what? That doesn't prove anything." His eyes roamed the room, focusing on everything but her.

"Look at me, Jeremy, and listen hard. They've got you on their security tape. You slipped up, my friend, and I'm glad."

Estelle glared at him, waiting for a reaction. Some kind of reaction. Anything.

He said nothing.

She held his gaze. "This is not going to go away. The longer it takes, and the harder I work, the worse it will be for you. All the good things you've accomplished will go out the window. Instead of being emancipated, you'll go before a judge. Once it's out of my hands, *I can't help you.* You choose."

Now she got the reaction she wanted. The kid slumped back in his chair, eyes closed. His complexion paled, and for a fast talker he didn't have much to say for a moment.

"What's going to happen?" His lips trembled, but his words were strong enough.

"For starters, *if* you go before a judge, you won't be treated as a juvenile anymore. You'll have a record. And you might go to regular jail. With adults, Jeremy. Men doing time for things you haven't thought about yet."

If his skin tone turned any whiter, she'd call for a

doctor. But the kid managed to rally. "I don't think a judge would do that to a kid."

"You want to find out?"

"And Nick shouldn't have called you," he retorted. "Wasn't any of his business. He's just jealous that I gave her a gift. He thought he had her all to himself."

Whoa! thought Estelle. The puppy love hadn't dissipated yet. Well, they'd deal with that also.

"You may be angry with Nick," said Estelle, "but he's very concerned about you. In fact, he's here and wants to talk to you."

Jeremy's head snapped up straight then. His body, too. "Well, I don't want to talk to him."

"It's your decision, Jeremy. Either you'll speak with Nick, or with the judge. That's your choice. But I urge you to choose Nick. Listen to him. Share things with him. Remember, he was once one of my boys, too."

That got his attention. "And afterward, you'll speak with me again and we'll resolve everything tonight. But if you'd rather go to court, you don't have to speak with anyone. The store will press charges and you'll take your chances."

She could almost hear his mental gears shifting in ten different directions searching for the smartest maneuver.

"So, Ms. Estelle, you're offering me a hard road or a harder road?"

She never thought the kid was dumb, just dealing with hormones and life circumstances.

"No, son. I'm offering you a road so easy you can almost slip right down into a real life."

"Yeah. Sure. All right. You might as well send him in and we'll get this over with."

Nick walked through the door and shook hands with Estelle. "Thanks for giving me the opportunity to speak with J.T. alone."

"No problem." She waved to the boy as she left.

"I didn't have much choice," said Jeremy. "And you know it. And I don't feel like talking to you at all. You had no right to call Ms. Estelle. You had no right to get involved with Kathy and me."

Nick grabbed a visitor's chair near Jeremy and sat down. "We'll discuss rights later. In the meantime, you'll listen. You'll listen and you'll think! And when I'm done, you'll make choices one way or the other."

His firm tone caught the kid's attention; J.T. leaned forward and sat at his chair's edge. *So far, so good.* Nick relaxed against the back of his seat.

"When I lived in Richmond House," he began, "there were no doors on the bedrooms, and one of the counselors was always around." He quirked an eyebrow at Jeremy.

A quick grin illuminated the kid's face for a moment. "Same garbage today," he said. "No privacy."

"I remember that, probably more than anything else. Except for how many times I ran away from home. My parents' house."

"How many?" Jeremy asked.

"Six."

"How far'd you get?"

"Twice I returned on my own. Four times the cops

brought me in.'' Nick's memories were as sharp as ever. ''And then there was the problem of who I hung around with and some of the stupid things I did. Worse than what you did.''

''You were bad, man.''

''My dad was the one who sent the cops after me.'' Nick would never forget the look on his dad's face every time he was brought home.

''Mr. Joe?''

''Yup.''

''Then what happened?'' asked Jeremy.

''Then my dad got the judge to throw me in Richmond House. Said he wiped his hands of me, and if I was so miserable at home, I didn't have to live there.''

''But Mr. Joe's a great guy! He wouldn't have done that. He loves you and the whole family. You're lying!''

Jeremy's eyes almost glowed with heat in his defense of Nick's father. Nick silently cheered.

''He *is* a great guy and I promise you I'm not lying. All I knew when I was in high school was that I was miserable, angry and hated school. I barely passed anything. Back then I was hyperactive, a poor reader, always the last one finished. And I hated everyone. Including my parents. One day I just quit, and watched all my friends graduate and go on to college. Making lives for themselves.''

''But you're so smart now. You run a whole business.''

''Well, back then I wasn't so smart about anything,

and they didn't know what to do with me. They were frightened every time I ran away.''

''So they put you in Richmond House for that?'' Jeremy asked.

''That and well...there was a neighbor's car, a high-speed chase and a few six-packs. I guess that's what pushed Dad over the edge.'' Nick leaned closer to Jeremy. ''By then he was scared—*real* scared. He called his friend, the judge, and the next think I knew, I was in Richmond House.''

''Gee, I wouldn't have thought Mr. Joe would do that,'' said Jeremy.

''Well, he did. It's called tough love. When you break the rules, you pay the price. But it's for your own good.''

''Right,'' said Jeremy, sarcasm extending the one syllable.

''Want some proof?'' asked Nick, one leg crossing the opposite knee.

Jeremy nodded briefly.

''I stayed in Richmond House for three months. I wanted to go home sooner, but they wanted me to learn a lesson.'' He paused, amazed at how clear the memories were after so many years. ''The boys that were here with me...they weren't so tough underneath. Mostly scared. Their families were...not good. I bet not much different than your friend Trevor's family or some of the others that are here now.''

Jeremy nodded.

''I was the luckiest son of a gun in the place, J.T. Bar none.''

''What happened then?''

"I started working at the business with my dad. He worked me longer hours than anyone else." Nick laughed at the memory. "That was also tough love."

"Yeah. He wanted you too tired to do anything bad."

"Right. He told me that if I wasn't going to school, I had to work full-time. I was too stupid to understand what he was saying. He really wanted me to go to school, but I hated school so much I thought he was giving me a chance to work. Either way, he was going to make me do something with my life."

"Because you were his son, and he loved you," replied Jeremy.

"I know that now," said Nick softly, "but I didn't then. And that's the reason I'm going with you when you return the earrings to the store. I love you, J.T. Like my dad loved me."

Nick thought Jeremy had turned to stone, but he couldn't stop trying to convince the kid. "And if you choose instead to go before a judge—which I don't advise—I'll be standing right next to you."

He still wasn't sure if Jeremy heard anything he said. The youngster looked stunned.

"But...but...how can you stick by me? I love Kathy, too. That's why I got her the earrings."

Nick didn't know whether to laugh or cry. "The thing is, J.T., that Kat loves you, too, but do you really think she'd want to keep the gift knowing that you stole it?" He leaned in closer and squeezed the boy's shoulder. "Come on, sport. Figure it out."

Jeremy sighed deeply, and Nick hoped all the boy's remaining defenses were gone.

"I guess not," Jeremy finally replied. "Not Kathy. She's straight."

Nick nodded. "She sure is. And she's worried about you. And she wants to see you."

Jeremy jumped from his seat as though it were on fire. "No way."

"Yes way. But you have a short reprieve before she comes in here, J.T. I need to hear you say to my face that you took those earrings without paying."

"You already know it."

"But I want to hear it from your mouth. Taking responsibility is part of growing up and becoming a man."

Nick held his breath, watching the boy pace the room. *Own up. Own up.* It seemed like hours before he heard the boy's voice.

"I took them. I took them because she's been so good to me and I wanted to thank her and show her how much I care for her. I would have stolen diamonds if they weren't locked up." He looked at Nick defiantly. "And if I had your money, I would have bought them for her, and someday I will."

Nick swallowed his grin. The kid was so earnest. "I know you will," he replied. "Someday. But right now, J.T., I'm proud you fessed up." He held the boy's gaze and hoped Jeremy could read the truth there. The youngster blinked; swallowed several times. Nick saw his Adam's apple working hard.

"Come here, champ," said Nick.

Jeremy walked toward him, his step tentative.

Nick met him halfway and pulled him into a bear

hug. "You're doing great. And after you apologize to Katherine we'll put this matter behind us."

"Does that mean it will all be over?"

"Among the three of us, yes. After that, it has to do with the store and Ms. Estelle. You've made a good beginning. Let's see if you can finish it."

Jeremy nodded, and Nick walked to the door. He turned around and said, "Do you want me to stay while you speak with Kat?"

Jeremy's head moved from side to side. "No, I want to be alone with her."

"No problem."

Jeremy turned and collapsed into his chair. He heard the door close, then the light tap of Katherine's shoes as she crossed the floor. He didn't know what to say when she sat down opposite him. She'd been the focus of his thoughts all summer. And now everything had blown up in his face.

After what seemed like an eternity, Katherine's voice broke the strained silence.

"Hi, Jeremy," she said quietly.

He could barely look at her. "Hi," he replied. "I have to tell you something."

"I came to listen."

"I gave you the earrings because I wanted to say thank-you for the help this summer."

"The thought was nice but...J.T., I don't need expensive gifts!"

He felt himself squirm in the seat. He hated this. Hated talking about the feelings for her he had inside. And she sounded so upset, when all he wanted to do was make her happy.

"It was for more than just the course work and the help at school. It was because you came to my dad's funeral, the way you put your arm around me and held my hand when we walked away. The poem you gave me, the hugs and good times. Being with you made me feel good. Even when you told me to put on sunblock. No one ever cared about me like this before. No one ever took care of me that I can remember. I took care of my father. Besides, I wanted to show you I loved you as much as Nick does, so I...I...stole the earrings for you."

He managed to raise his head and look her in the face. Tears glistened in her eyes, and Jeremy thought his heart would stop. He'd made her cry!

"Oh, Jeremy, honey. You don't have to give me presents. I love you without gifts. I love you differently from the way I love Nick. I love Nick in ways that I can never love you. But you, you're special. You're the kid brother I never had, the kid brother I always wanted. You and Nick are the two men in my life."

Jeremy stared at her. She *did* love him...he'd felt it...so that part was good. He'd just gotten the kind of love mixed up. Kid brother, huh? Well, he was only sixteen.

She rose from her seat. "Come over here, J.T."

He slowly got up from his chair and walked right into her arms. "What do you want me to do about the earrings and the whole mess?" he mumbled.

"What did Nick and Ms. Estelle tell you about that?"

"But I got them for *you. You* tell me what to do."

He wanted to make her happy. He didn't want to make any more mistakes.

"You need to do whatever you think is right."

He had to take a minute and figure it all out. "There's no easy way out, is there?"

"No. But we'll be with you."

He nodded, and his voice trembled. "Then I guess the first thing is to say I'm sorry for all this trouble. I didn't mean to make such a mess. I didn't mean to let you down."

"Apology accepted. You're moving in the right direction." She tousled his hair. "Come on. What else?"

"Next I have to return the earrings to the store, and I have to work something out with Ms. Estelle. I bet I'll be doing community service forever. I'll never get out of Richmond House now."

He looked at her, hoping he was doing everything right.

Her smile was answer enough. "This is the best present you could have given me."

To his horror, Jeremy felt wetness on his face and there was nothing he could do about it. He just let the tears roll down his cheeks and hoped the mess he created would come to an end.

He was running on empty. His stomach felt more knotted than a child's shoelace, and he was sweaty, lonely and tired. He wanted it over. Maybe he really *was* still a kid. He wanted someone to take care of him.

"Kathy," he said in a low voice, "will you still

help me prepare for the TASP test so I can get into college?''

"Of course," she said as she got up. "In fact, we can start tomorrow afternoon if possible. Let's go see Estelle and Nick and try to put everything to rest.''

Fifteen minutes later, Jeremy sat with Estelle in her office. "You had us all worried, son, but now I'm proud of you. We'll go to the department store in the morning—Nick also—and you'll apologize to the people there. They probably won't press charges if you're sincere, so your record will stay the same. This time. There'd better be no next time.''

"Yes, ma'am.''

"Now, what else is on your calendar for this week?'' she asked. "Still working and watching your account grow?'' Of course, she knew his schedule to a T.

His familiar grin peeped out. "I'm way over the five hundred dollars I need in the bank," he reported, "and I'll still be working full-time for the next two weeks until school starts again.''

"What about the TASP test requirement?'' she asked.

"I've been studying, sort of," he admitted. "But Kathy's going to work with me tomorrow afternoon. She's leaving the office early and picking me up so Danny doesn't have to go off-site. She said she'll work with me on Sunday, too, so I can still do my community service on Saturday.''

"You've got some good people in your corner," she said.

"They're the best.''

AT ONE O'CLOCK the next afternoon, Katherine pulled into the work site where Jeremy had been assigned. Lakes on West Memorial. A residential development of single-family homes, with construction crews active in several areas. She drove slowly, absorbing the scope and energy needed for projects such as this. The manpower, the materials, the landscaping, the design. A variety of homes. One-story and two-story residences of all sizes.

She wondered how many of them Nick had designed. He had to have a wealth of information at his command, from knowledge of all the building trades to awareness of the latest in kitchen appliances, standard and luxury. A million decisions. Tremendous responsibility.

She spotted Jeremy at the curb of a cul-de-sac, waiting for her, very macho in his leather work boots and tool belt. She couldn't suppress a grin. He was still so skinny, they must've drilled a hole near the middle of the belt to make sure it stayed around his hips. A good excuse to take him to lunch.

"Hey, cowboy," she said as she rolled down the window. "Come on in and cool off."

His million-dollar smile tugged at her heart, especially after yesterday's events.

"Hey, Kathy. I'll get your car all dirty."

She handed him a towel. "Sit on this, J.T. I came prepared."

He gave her a thumbs-up, climbed in, adjusted the seat and stretched his legs out in front of him. Then he snapped his seat belt closed.

His deliberate movements reminded her of Nick

and she couldn't help smiling. "I hope you're hungry today."

"Are you kidding?" the boy said. "I eat more than anybody on this work site. Danny says if his mom didn't provide our lunches, I'd starve to death. The stuff I bring from Richmond House isn't enough."

"Well, I'm providing lunch today, J.T. How does Fuddrucker's sound? All the hamburgers you can eat, nice and healthily broiled. Add your own toppings. Have a salad."

"And fries?" He glanced at her sideways.

She laughed. "Sure. Have fries."

And he did. Two orders of them with two hamburgers, two sodas and a salad. And Katherine thought she'd talk with Anna about teenage boys and their eating habits. Just what was normal?

"So," began Katherine as the first wave of hunger was satisfied, "how did it go this morning at the department store?"

Jeremy met her gaze, turned away for a moment and then slowly lifted his head again. "Not so bad. But it seemed like a million people were in the room. I apologized to everybody. But I don't think I'll go there again too soon. They all know who I am now."

"But you did the right thing, J.T., and I'm proud of you. Estelle and Nick must have been, too."

Jeremy looked at the floor. "Yeah," he said softly. "I think they were okay with it."

Katherine smiled to herself. Estelle must have been popping her buttons. "And now it's over. Learn from it and go forward."

"That's what I think, too."

"Good. Are you ready to hit the books again?" Katherine asked as they left the restaurant and got into the car.

"Sure. I still read a lot at night at the House."

"Great. Like what?"

He glanced at her and said matter-of-factly, "Oh, like Shakespeare—lots of him, and Homer, and Robert Browning, and—"

"Give me a break, J.T. I wasn't born yesterday."

He burst out laughing. "You are *great,* Kathy. Just *great.* The truthful answer is anything by John Grisham and Stephen King. But I really did read *The Odyssey.* Do you know that one?"

"Only the best adventure story ever written," she said. "We'll talk about it sometime."

"Okay."

She peeked at him as he relaxed back in his seat, and a warm glow filled her. She really loved the kid, and no matter what stupid things he did, she'd be there for him. She'd almost cried when he called her great. It was more than the words. It was the look on his face. She wished she'd had a camera to capture it forever.

She needed to call Estelle. See what the options were for a single woman to make a home for a teenage boy. And then she'd tell Nick.

FIFTEEN MINUTES LATER, Katherine turned her car down Lake Avenue toward home. Her home. How quickly a once-empty apartment had changed into a home since Nick had come into her life.

She looked around the familiar landscape. She still

took pleasure in the tall palms lining her route, the lush green lawns and numerous trees—crepe myrtle, Bradford pear and shady live oak—interspersed throughout the property. Nick had done an outstanding job.

"Nick said he'd be here early," said Jeremy as they walked to her apartment.

Katherine glanced at her watch. "Then it's a good thing I told him not to. Our lunch out cost us time. You and I have a lot of work to do."

"You think that's going to stop him? No way! He likes being with us. And he really likes you. He'll be here just when he said. Early."

Katherine shrugged. If truth be told, she liked when the three of them were together, too.

She took her keys out, turned the tumblers of both locks and opened the door. The alarm system activated and she quickly stepped inside, waving Jeremy ahead of her. She reached for the control panel on the wall. Punch, punch, punch, punch. Beep, beep. Punch, punch. Quiet and done. She'd finally gotten the hang of it.

"That should make him hap...*ohh!*..." Katherine yelped as something shoved hard against her shoulder, sending her spinning to the floor. As she lifted her head she saw Jeremy pivot and look beyond her toward the door. His look of horror sent shivers up her spine. She got to her feet clumsily, turned and stared in the same direction he did...and almost choked.

A hulk with no face. All in black. From the top of

his head to his feet. Including the gloved hand holding a gun.

"Stay behind me, J.T.," she cried, trying to battle her rising nausea. She thrust her arms behind her, needing to assure herself the boy was there.

"That's as far as you go," growled the voice behind the stocking. He filled the doorway, blocking most of the sunlight. Then he stepped into the room and kicked the door back with his foot. "One more step and someone's gonna get hurt."

Katherine's heart pounded like a jackhammer. She'd never seen the business end of a gun in real life. But even more terrifying was the covered head. As dark as night where a face should be. She took two steps back and forced herself to keep looking at the intruder.

"What do you want?" Her voice quavered. "Money? Take my purse. It's there on the floor. Here's my watch. Then leave."

"Don't you wish, blondie. Not so quick."

Fear dried her mouth, but she kept her gaze steady on him. Keep calm, Kat. Keep calm. "What do you want?" she asked again.

"First, you're gonna tie the kid up." He reached behind him and pulled out a wide roll of duct tape. "Once he's out of the way, you're gonna give me exactly what I want."

JEREMY'S EYES DARTED around the room looking for anything that might help. Damn! They were in the entrance hall. No knives from the kitchen, no paperweights from the desk, no fireplace tools. No nothin'!

If only he hadn't left his tool belt in the car! He could have thrown his hammer at the creep's face, mashed his head with the wrench. He had to do something right this time! How could he just stand there and let Katherine be raped? His mind revolted at the thought. He'd watch for an opportunity and he'd act. He'd think of something. He'd show them all what he was really made of.

"IF YOU WANT ME, then let the boy go." Katherine forced her trembling leg muscles to be still and faced the intruder defiantly, staring directly at his covered face. She tried to judge where his eyes should be and focused her glance there. The whole body image seemed familiar, the height, the weight, the stance, the carriage of his head.

And suddenly, like the pieces of a puzzle slowly falling into place, she instantly knew with whom she was dealing. And everything made sense.

Except the gun.

Searching her apartment shouldn't have required a gun.

Which meant she couldn't reveal to Eddie Jensen that she recognized him. In the movies, weren't guns used to eliminate witnesses? She wasn't ready to be eliminated. And she damn well wasn't going to risk Jeremy's life.

The biggest irony of all, she thought, was that she had no idea where Nick's estimates were. All the information relating to the bid was under lock and key somewhere. Nick had never revealed the place. But Eddie didn't know that. He didn't have to know that.

Maybe she could buy time… She had to get them out of this mess. Somehow.

"The kid stays. Now, catch," ordered the gruff voice.

Using peripheral vision, Katherine automatically reached for the roll of duct tape the man threw, and caught it.

"Get busy, blondie," said Eddie as he took a step toward her. "I'll be watching. Wrap him good and tight."

"No way." Jeremy cried out as he lunged.

CHAPTER THIRTEEN

NICK WHISTLED HAPPILY to himself as he left the office, even though he carried a ton of work with him. He glanced at his ever-present laptop. Great inventions. Being able to live a portable life was great. And it had other advantages. It had provided him with a perfect hiding place.

Eager as always to see Katherine and Jeremy, he hopped into his truck with a light step and a light heart. Kat and J.T., his two favorite people. He knew they'd had a lunch date followed by a study date. And if they were still poring over the books, he'd gladly join them. His own dream might be temporarily on hold because of Joe's health, but it wasn't abandoned.

He pulled into his regular guest spot in front of Katherine's building, right next to her Honda, and glanced inside her car as he locked his own. His lips tightened with displeasure. Jeremy's tool belt lay on the front seat. He'd have to talk with that boy again. Tools with which a person earned a living were not to be left around carelessly. He jiggled his key ring, selected Katherine's spare car key and took the tool belt with him.

He flexed the belt. The leather was still stiff, barely broken in. But the hammer had gotten used. Plenty of scratches. Nick smiled at his memories. The hammer claw got used as much as the head in the beginning. Pulling out all the mistakes was important, too. Looked like Jeremy was no different than anyone else. And the boy had taken the time to oil the belt and wipe down the tools.

Nick automatically buckled the belt around himself. A comfortable, familiar feeling. Suddenly his hands itched for a project. Maybe Kat could use another bookcase. Heck, there was no maybe about it. She was always adding to her library.

He locked Katherine's car, grabbed his computer and started walking toward the building, tipping his head to look toward her second-floor apartment. Damn! Was her door open? He squinted against the sunlight to see more clearly, then started to jog.

Didn't anyone ever listen to him? First Jeremy left his tools lying around, and then Katherine left her door open. When he gave advice, did they think he was talking to himself?

Nick climbed the stairs toward the landing and was just about to call out when he heard muffled voices. A low bass tone. Certainly not Kat's or Jeremy's. Instantly, all Nick's senses came alive. He placed the laptop on an upper step, cursing himself for not hiring a daytime guard.

He flattened himself against the wall next to the door and listened intently. He heard Katherine's voice.

"If you want me, then let the boy go."

Nick pulled the hammer out of the tool belt.

"The kid stays. Now, catch," said the deep voice.

Nick hefted the hammer and peered through the door. He saw the back of a huge figure, all in black, with an arm raised straight out in front of him. At the end of the arm was a gun. Pointing at Katherine. His Katherine.

"Wrap him good and tight."

A red-hot anger filled Nick. An anger so intense, he could barely contain it. His hands shook with the need to smash. Kat's face was a white as parchment.

Suddenly her eyes met his and widened. But she didn't react, didn't gesture. *Good for you, Kat.*

Clutching the hammer near the bottom of its shaft, Nick raised his right hand and, at the same time, opened the door with his left. He added muscle as he swung the hammer in a downward arc, catching the intruder on the side of the head.

It should have been a knockout blow. But the guy's damn mask cushioned the impact, and the intruder fell to his knees before hitting the floor full length. Almost immediately, he tried to stand.

At least he'd dropped the gun.

Nick was ready to strike again, when suddenly Jeremy leaped on top of the goon, fists flying and feet kicking. From the corner of his eye, Nick saw Kat kick the gun across the floor. With the biggest problem out of the way, he turned and dived into the fray. Landing a dozen good punches would feel awfully good now.

KATHERINE TOOK one horrified look at the fighting men and raced across the room after the gun. She grabbed the weapon, placed her fingers on the trigger, pointed at the ceiling and fired...with two hands.

She got their attention. Lowering her arms, she stepped toward the intruder. "Don't move," she ordered. "Not a single muscle. In fact, don't even breathe. I fired this thing once, and I'll do it again."

Nobody needed to know her hands were so damp with perspiration the gun felt slippery. Or that her legs felt so weak she had to consciously stiffen her muscles just to continue standing.

In as strong a tone as she could muster, she said, "Jeremy, go call 911. Right now." From the corner of her eye, she watched the kid limp to the phone.

"Katherine, sweetheart."

Nick's calm voice seemed to come from a million miles away. She felt her lips shape themselves into a smile—sort of.

"You can put the gun down now, darling," he cajoled. "I've got this poor-excuse-for-a-man under control. See, I've got him in a headlock. So, you can put the gun away, Kat. Everything's fine now."

"He's awake...." she whispered.

"Not for long."

She watched, fascinated, while Nick shifted his hold on the hulk. He grabbed him by the shirtfront, pulled him almost to a standing position and punched him in the jaw.

"That's what you get for messing with my family."

Nick's breathing was deeper than usual as he tossed the hulk to the ground, watched him collapse and not move. He then leaned over, grabbed the mask and ripped it off.

"It's Eddie Jensen," Katherine said.

"You're right. It *is* Jensen, out cold."

Nick turned quickly and looked at Kat. She still held the gun pointed at Eddie. He walked to the side of her and gently pried the weapon from her stiff fingers. "It's over, baby, it's over."

"Tie him up, Nick."

"Sure."

He grabbed the duct tape and quickly had Jensen looking like a birthday gift for the police. He then reinforced his handiwork with a length of cord—a remnant of Katherine's move to Houston.

"Feeling better now?" he asked gently when he returned to her side.

"Yes," she replied, just before passing out in his arms.

NICK THOUGHT his heart would stop when Katherine fainted. He placed her carefully on the sofa and barked at Jeremy, "Get me ice. In a bowl. And a cold, wet washcloth, paper towels, anything for a compress."

He rubbed Katherine's hands. "Come on, Kat," he cajoled. "Wake up. Open your eyes."

And she did. For a moment. "That's it, sweetheart. Come back to me."

"Hmm," she sighed before settling down again, eyes closed as if preparing for a long sleep. Nick looked around. Where was Jeremy with the ice? The sound of sirens interrupted his thoughts and he glanced across the room to the hallway at the still form of Eddie Jensen. A dozen questions filled his mind, and his hands itched to pull answers directly from the man's throat. But not yet. Right now, nothing was more important than Kat.

He looked down again, this time into beautiful blue eyes, now wide open.

"Hi," she whispered.

"Hi, yourself, sweetheart. Feeling better?"

Her forehead wrinkled.

He bent down and kissed her cheek, firmly tucking her hands in his own. "It's okay, baby," he whispered. "It's over now."

But Katherine turned toward the hallway, agitation in every movement. "Is he still in there?"

"Not for much longer," replied Nick as he took a cold compress from the bowl Jeremy had returned with and placed it on her forehead.

"Hear the sirens?" he asked. "The cavalry's on its way."

"The cavalry's a little late," Katherine replied. "Seems to me, we did all the work ourselves."

Which is exactly what she told the police five minutes later when she also berated them for not arresting Jensen days earlier.

"We did check him out," the detective answered her. "Jensen had an alibi. The bartender remembered him being at the club."

"Sounds like you need to revisit the bartender," said Nick. "Maybe he was having a busy night and wanted your men out of there fast. Maybe he needs a reason to cooperate."

"We'll get the job done, Mr. Martinelli, and get back to you. But...uh...do you want us to call an ambulance?" The detective nodded at Katherine.

"Does who want an ambulance?" asked a familiar voice from the doorway. "What's going on, Nicky?"

Tina! He'd never been so glad to see his kid sister.

"I assume this is yours?" she asked, lifting his laptop for him to see.

"Thanks. Will you slide it under the couch, out of the way?" In all the excitement, he'd forgotten about leaving it on the landing. The contents seemed unimportant anymore; he'd have donated all his work to the city if it would have guaranteed Kat's and Jeremy's safety.

"What took you so long?" he grumbled. "I figured you'd hear the sirens coming right past the office."

"Sorry, bro. I was closing on a unit, and hoping the buyers wouldn't notice the excitement we generate around here."

She turned from him then, and Nick noted how she focused on Katherine. Entirely solicitous and concerned. Not her usual wisecracking Tina style. His heart warmed and he smiled in appreciation before returning his attention to the police. "No ambulance. We'll handle it by ourselves. But, thanks. Just haul Jensen away."

"He's already gone, and he'll be interrogated as soon as legally possible. As you all will be. Whoever was involved."

"Not now," insisted Nick as he reached for the blanket Jeremy held. "First things first. And Katrin is number-one priority."

"I'm okay. You can stop fussing." She looked at Jeremy. "Guess we didn't get much studying done, huh, J.T.?"

"No, ma'am. I think we got a little distracted."

His understatement had them all smiling, and Nick felt himself relax for the first time since he'd walked up the steps to the condo an eternity ago.

"So, what exactly was this all about?" asked Tina. "Do you know?"

"Yeah," said Jeremy.

"Yes," said Nick at the same time. "It was about our bid on the three schools."

"Schools?" asked Jeremy, looking totally confused. "What schools? I thought the hulk wanted to…you know," he said, turning away, "uh…rape Kathy."

Nick could hear Kat's gasp, and saw her turn pale again. Shoot! No more.

"Well, you thought wrong, champ. And it's over," Nick said, thinking to put an end to the conversation.

But Kat wasn't finished. "Jeremy…you thought…and you came to my rescue…"

"Oh, no! She's going to start crying again," wailed J.T. "And it's my fault."

Nick closed his eyes. If the situation hadn't been so serious, it could have been funny at this point. He opened one eye. Tina, alone, had a grin on her face. Figured.

"You know, Katherine," he heard his little sister say, "life in the quiet Martinelli family sure has become more exciting since you've been around!"

And then came the sound he'd missed hearing all day. The sound of Kathy's laughter.

KATHERINE LAY on the sofa an hour later, feeling more than fine, but not allowed to move by order of J.T. and Nick. They were treating her like a queen and it had been nice for a little while. She was about ready, however, to rejoin the world.

She raised her eyes to the windows where early-evening sunlight still streamed in. The afternoon had seemed so long, but in reality only a couple of hours had passed. And no wonder! Each moment of danger had seemed like an aeon.

Both Nick and Jeremy were showing aftereffects of the fight. Nick had taken a couple of punches in the ribs and was walking gingerly. Both of his hands were bruised as well, with knuckles swollen. And Jeremy's eye was almost completely shut at this point. The black-and-blue hues were impressive.

She, herself, had gotten away without injury thanks to her brave champions. However, she'd never forget shooting that gun. Never! Even now she shivered with the memory. But when she pictured skinny Jeremy trying to pummel that monster, and Nick wacking Eddie Jensen with the hammer, putting himself in grave danger for her, she knew she'd grab the weapon again in a heartbeat. So the best therapy she could give herself now was to put it out of her mind and think about Nick instead. An easy transition.

He'd used an interesting word while he wreaked havoc on Eddie Jensen. Mighty interesting indeed if her memory served her well. She wondered if he realized what he'd said in the heat of the moment.

Family. Not once during their months together had he said I love you to her, not even during their most intimate, glorious lovemaking. But the sentiment came through loud and clear dozens of times when he wasn't aware of it.

The doorbell rang and she braced herself for visitors. The police would be back, the rest of Nick's family would show up. Her friends, Suzanne and David, would come over. And God knew who else. But it was better this way. If they visited with everybody that night, they'd be left alone tomorrow. The story would hit the local papers the next day, and they could not let Anna and Joe find out that way. Nick had put Joanna in charge of informing their folks. As a nurse, she'd keep a sharp eye on his dad.

But of all the visitors Katherine expected, she couldn't help hoping the pizza delivery would be first. She'd need every bit of energy she could get to handle the rest of the evening.

NICK GLANCED at his watch two hours later, more than ready for everyone to clear out. Kat looked wiped, Jeremy needed a respite from Joanna's ministrations to his eye, his folks finally seemed satisfied that all was well and the police surely had enough information for now. They must have asked more questions of Kat than they had of Eddie. Tomorrow was soon enough to learn all the details.

He wanted to call Estelle to get permission for J.T. to spend the night. But mostly, he needed to hold

Katherine. Feel her warmth, see her smile. Reassure himself that she was alive.

His mental snapshot of Eddie Jensen's gun pointing at her was a nightmare he'd live with for the rest of his life. He could feel his blood churning just thinking about it. No wonder Sally had disappeared! He could imagine her feeling trapped between a lousy brother and a good boss and not knowing what to do. She was young.

He shook his head. No, her actions had almost cost him…cost him…he couldn't think about it. Sally could have prevented tonight's drama. She was old enough to know the difference between right and wrong.

And if she had spoken up? a little voice questioned. Would her own life have been in danger? Nick had to admit he didn't know. In fairness, he'd postpone judgment.

He walked toward the woman who'd become the center of his life. She stood in the living room chatting with Suzanne, but moved into his embrace as if she'd spent a lifetime there. Still standing, she snuggled up and leaned gently on his broad chest. Nick held her in his arms and in his heart. He looked down and saw her lids close, her eyelashes fanning her cheek. His wonderful woman needed a night's sleep, while he was still revved up enough to celebrate their futures.

Of course, he hadn't really spoken to her about their future. Or Jeremy's future. Not yet. A flicker of apprehension swept through him. Yes, he had a creative mind. But how did a person finesse a proposal to a woman and a boy at the same time?

He knew Kat was fond of Jeremy. She'd stood by his side through every crisis and turning point during the summer. But being fond of a youngster and taking permanent responsibility were two different things. She was single, used to caring only for herself. It was a neat, clean lifestyle. She'd been an only child. Was used to peace and quiet, and an academic life. He and Jeremy offered none of these things.

Sure, she'd whispered words of love to him. But did she really know what she was saying? Sexual compatibility coupled with affection could make a woman think she was in love.

Excuses! If he dug deeper, he knew he'd unearth more excuses. It wasn't Katherine who was afraid. It wasn't Jeremy. *It was him!* He was the fearful one. Afraid to try again. Afraid of losing everyone again. Another wife. Another child. Maybe even another infant. He lifted Kat into his arms and walked with her to the couch, impatient for their visitors to leave.

As he inhaled her light floral scent, and memorized the face he treasured, he knew his fear didn't matter. It was too late. He'd been willing to protect her with his own life. He loved her. So his heart was already at risk.

HE GATHERED his courage later, in the middle of the night, when Katherine turned to him in her sleep. Her hand reached out, touched him, before she drifted off again. She'd found her comfort. Amazed at her trust, he nestled her closer to him, tucking the sheet securely around them.

He'd left their bed twice to check on Jeremy, sleeping on the living-room couch. He needn't have bothered. The kid was out cold. Rather miraculous, considering the shape and color of his eye. Nick leaned over and briefly touched his lips to the boy's forehead. Cool. He kissed him gently. A good kid with a lot of heart. A good kid who needed a family.

"Nick?" the boy mumbled.

"Yeah. It's me."

"How's Kathy?"

"Sleeping. Like you should be."

"She okay?" Jeremy asked.

"She's terrific."

A beatific smile crossed the sleepy boy's face. "Good. G'night, Nick." He rolled onto his stomach, instantly returning to dreamland.

The kid loved her, too, but hopefully now more like Kat's little bro. They'd both had their points to make with Jeremy the night before. Nick had high hopes that he and Kat both had handled him well.

Nick walked quietly back to the bedroom and climbed into bed, delighted when Kat unconsciously turned to him again in her sleep. He tucked her close, leaned back on the pillows and felt himself relax. Stars still twinkled in the early-morning sky, and Nick settled down to wait for dawn. For Katherine. For a new beginning.

His eyes closed. He wanted to celebrate his feelings for her. Do something special, something she'd really enjoy and cherish. Maybe write her a poem. The thought lasted a full second before he shuddered. He wouldn't get past roses are red, violets are blue. No, he'd have to borrow a real love sonnet from one of her favorite poets. It wouldn't be hard. Her shelves were filled with more choices than he'd need. It would be a perfect way to propose.

He'd buy her a beautiful ring so she'd know he loved her every time she looked at it. If he hadn't been so fearful, he would have already purchased one. His thoughts drifted further. He'd reserve a private room at Tony's for a romantic dinner, with candles on the table, and fresh flowers. He'd recite the poem, give her the ring, make it a night to remember. He felt a grin spread across his face. It would be perfect.

HER KISS WOKE HIM the next morning. Still cuddled to his side, Katherine's slender form felt like part of him. She peeped at him from under her lashes, her blue eyes soft and full of warmth.

"Good morning," she whispered with a smile that shot all his plans straight to hell.

"It'll be a better morning if you'll marry me." Whoosh! His words filled the room.

He watched her eyes widen, then to his horror fill with tears. But she didn't move away. He stroked her head, her back, and wished he'd kept his mouth shut. "Don't cry, Katrin. Please don't cry."

She lay across his chest, sobbing harder.

He felt like crying himself, but plunged ahead. "You heard me last night, Kat, and in my heart you're already my family. Your tears are killing me because I love you so much. I want to see you happy.''

She quieted, and he felt encouraged enough to continue. ''I wanted to read you a poem, and give you a ring and flowers, and take you to a romantic restaurant. I had it all planned, and then when you woke up…''

She sat up then, facing him, her hands squeezing his. ''What did you say? Would you repeat that?''

''I wanted to read you a poem…''

''No, not that. Before that.''

He paused. What had he said? Ah. ''I love you, Katrin,'' he repeated quietly. He bent his head and kissed her gently on the lips. ''I love you with all my heart, with all my soul, with all my being…''

She flung her arms around him. ''Finally,'' she whispered. ''You finally said the words I've wanted to hear. And very poetically, too!''

As he looked at her, twinkles replaced the tears in her eyes as she returned the favor, giving him the answer he wanted. ''Yes,'' she said, ''I'll marry you. What took you so long?''

''I guess I'm a slow learner,'' he replied as he kissed her again. ''But once I get the hang of something, I never forget.'' His next kiss proved the point. His next I love you reinforced it.

''Hmm,'' murmured Kat between his onslaught of kisses. ''You're not a slow learner at all, in fact, I think you were one of my best students.''

But he was not a natural scholar. Never had been, and that was at the root of all the trouble years ago. He pulled Katherine up higher so they sat side by side against the pillows. He reached for her hand and brought it to his lips before turning to face her.

"I'm not an educated man, Kat. I'm not the kind of man your mom wanted for you. The kind of man *you* had planned on." His eyes locked with hers. He was giving her an out, not because he was a gentleman but because he wanted no regrets.

Love and laughter shone in her eyes. She moved herself on top of him and wrapped her arms around his neck. "I love you, Nick. And you're wrong. My mom would have thought you're the smartest man on earth. Smart enough to want her daughter!"

"Smart enough to love her daughter!" He zoomed in for another kiss.

"Mom told me something else that night," Katherine continued a minute later. "Something I didn't think about very much because it was so obvious."

Nick studied her thoughtful expression and waited. And when she spoke, her words came slowly. "She also said that I should marry a *good* man, like my papa." Her big eyes met his and remained riveted. "I've never met a better man than you, Nicholas Martinelli. You are everything my folks could have wanted for me."

He vowed right then to never let her down. But when he leaned over to tell her, she put her hand up. "Wait, you need to hear more. You need to know that I'm not that frightened young girl anymore. A girl who tried to substitute a campus for a real home. Who tried to live by the rules there because they were easy and comfortable. And safe."

He appreciated her insight but reveled in her honesty, her expressive features communicating her thoughts as clearly as her words did. She placed her hands on his cheeks.

"All I received from school was a diploma. I learned about real life and love when I left. In Houston, Texas, I learned that a man is measured by so much more than a degree. My dad would have loved you—your warmth and humor, your protective instincts—and your business savvy." A tear fell then. Followed by another, and another. "And my...my mom would have rejoiced in my happiness."

He cradled her on his lap, stroking her shoulders and back with a slow, steady motion.

He leaned down to kiss her cheek. "Katrin, my love. Together, we're quite a team."

She peeped up at him and was about to reply when the sound of running water and clattering dishes came through to them.

Instantly Kat sprang out of bed. "Jeremy," she said. "He needs breakfast."

"He can wait a minute." Nick slowly left the bed, too, and looked at her startled face. "We need to talk."

She said nothing for a moment. Then she made the connection.

"About J.T.?"

He nodded.

SHE NEEDED TIME to sort her thoughts. A marriage proposal was a huge way to start the morning. But to be followed by an equally important topic required a clear head. She wasn't sure she had one now.

"Okay," she replied. "He's been on my mind, too. But I'd like to get washed and dressed first. And maybe you could peek in there and see what he's concocting. His meals of choice sometimes prove to be very interesting."

Nick chuckled. "So you noticed that, too?"

She nodded and smiled.

"Take your time, Kat. I'll also check on his eye before I meet you back in here."

Ten minutes later, a refreshed Katherine in capri-length pants and matching turquoise blouse, rejoined Nick in the bedroom. He devoured her with his eyes. And then she was in his arms.

"You did say yes before, didn't you?" he murmured as he rained kisses on her face. "I wasn't dreaming?"

"If you were, I was in the same dream." She hugged him tightly and returned each kiss. "I am so happy."

He finally pulled away from her, as breathless and flushed as she was.

"If we continue," Nick said in a husky voice, "we'll stay in this bedroom all day, which would be a great idea if Jeremy wasn't in the kitchen."

Jeremy. Their new topic.

"Sit yourself at the foot of the bed, Nick, and I'll stay up here." Katherine grinned as she scooted to the pillows. "Otherwise, we'll never have a conversation!"

A slow smile covered his face and he winked as he followed her suggestion. "J.T.'s gathered all the ingredients for a big breakfast," Nick said. "Especially for you. He thinks you need to get your strength back after yesterday.''

She shook her head, feeling her eyes mist. "He is quite a kid. I've been thinking a lot about him recently.''

"So have I,'' Nick replied. "He's a great youngster...a fantastic boy...but I don't think he should be on his own, even when he turns seventeen.''

"Neither do I.'' Her heart started to pound. "In fact,'' she bravely continued, "I was on the verge of calling Estelle.'' She met his interested gaze.

"So was I.''

"Really?'' Her voice squeaked. Yes! Oh, she wanted this to work out. "I wasn't sure they'd allow a single woman to foster a teenage boy, but I was going to ask...just in case.''

"In case I didn't want to?''

She nodded.

"Katrin! Katrin!'' he chuckled. "That kid is me all over again, without the reading problems. Hungry to prove himself in a man's world, prove his independence. But this kid has no parents to guide him. To love him.''

"Whereas you had Joe and Anna,'' she said.

"Did I ever!'' he said. "Sweetheart, Dad invented tough love before there was a tough-love theory. My teenage years were hell for all of us,'' he admitted. "But my folks never gave up.''

Katherine left her end of the bed, scooted toward Nick and kissed him full on the mouth. "They loved you, and you loved them. And I think, darling, we need to speak with Jeremy.''

CHAPTER FOURTEEN

JEREMY WATCHED Katherine and Nick walk hand in hand from the bedroom to the kitchen where he'd finished setting the table. He stared at their clasped hands and then at the goofy smiles on their faces. *Something was up.* They weren't even trying to be cool, and Nick was one of the coolest guys he knew. Oh, well. He'd have to reeducate him.

"Hey, dudes."

"Good morning, J.T.," said Katherine. "How're you feeling?" She left Nick and walked closer to the youngster, now focusing all her attention on his eye.

"I'm cool, Kathy. Hardly hurts at all."

"Well, it looks gross, but in my view, it's a badge of honor."

He flushed at the compliment, felt the heat climb right up to his face. He hated that. Then she gave him a quick hug, which was okay. She did that a lot. But when she leaned in to kiss him, he knew again that something was up. She was a hugger not a kisser. At least not so far.

"Nick and I are going to make breakfast today," he said, glad to focus on some action. "So you can just sit down and relax." He figured she must still be nervous from yesterday. Man, she was something shooting that gun.

"No argument from me," said Katherine as she complied with his invitation. "I like to be waited on once in a while."

Ten minutes later, Jeremy scanned the tabletop, noting the piles of scrambled eggs and bacon, the toast, the coffee, the milk. "Did we forget anything?"

"You forgot to sit down!" Katherine laughed. "It's great. Dig in."

He was starving and didn't need a second invitation. When he picked his head up after the first satisfying bites, Katherine and Nick were looking funny at each other again.

"What's with you two?" he finally asked. "You're acting weird."

He saw Nick give Katherine a look and a nod, and braced himself. *Something was up* and he suddenly had the feeling it involved him. He put his knife and fork down, stared at Nick and waited.

When Nick's eyes began to twinkle and his smile stretched across his face, Jeremy felt himself breathe again. It had to be something good.

"Kat and I want to share something special with you, Jeremy."

He sat up straighter. Jeremy was now his serious name.

"Of all the people in our lives," Nick continued, "you are the first person to know that Katrin and I are going to get married."

Married? Married. Like grown-ups did. He thought about it. Tasted it. Yeah. Nick and Kathy. He nodded, then laughed out loud. "Married? Is that why you're acting so goofy? That's great." And to his surprise, he jumped out of his chair, kissed Katherine and pumped Nick's hand. They'd probably invite him to the wedding. He'd never been to one before. It would be fun with Nick's whole family. "You guys are the best," he added. "And your kids are going to be so lucky."

"You really think so?" asked Nick softly.

"Sure."

"Well, J.T.," said Katherine, looking him square in the eye, "*we* think our kids would be even luckier to have an older brother."

He couldn't breathe. He plopped back into his own chair. Two pairs of eyes were trained on him, waiting. Silence surrounded him except for the sound of his own heartbeat reverberating in his ears.

"Wha...what do you mean...*exactly?*" he managed to ask. Nick and Kathy were still looking at him. He wasn't sure if they were breathing either.

Nick leaned across the table then, and put both his hands over Jeremy's. "What we mean *exactly* is that we're hoping you'd want to be part of our family. You, Kat and I. Together."

"You...you want to marry both of us?"

"*Exactly,*" Nick said. "But in your case, it's called adoption."

Sheesh. Adoption. He'd never before considered such a thing, not even when chatting with Estelle about foster families. "Have you told Estelle?" Jeremy asked.

"We'll tell her today. All of us. If you're willing."

What was the downside? There was always a downside to everything. "This is big," he replied. "I've got to think about it."

He saw a flash of disappointment cross Katherine's face, but she smiled at him. "While you're thinking, sweetheart, remember the most important point of all."

Jeremy waited for her to continue, and saw her eyes shining with hope and light.

"We love you, J.T. From the bottom of our hearts." Katherine took his hands and pulled him from the chair. She hugged him and kissed his right cheek, then his left.

Since when did she change from being just a hugger to being a kisser too? *Maybe when it's important enough.*

His thoughts discharged like lightning bolts crisscrossing the sky. What about his emancipation? What about living in the woods at Walden Pond? What about his own apartment near Nick?

"What apartment?" asked the man in question.

Jeremy turned toward the older man. He must have spoken his thoughts aloud. "I was thinking that maybe I could live in an apartment near you and Kathy when I turn seventeen. Emancipated. I had it all figured out. My job, my savings, finishing my community service, and now more school. I'd be on my own, like an adult."

"But Jeremy," Katherine's soft voice chimed in. "You've already been an adult...for years. All the responsibility you took on with your own father, looking after him, looking after yourself." She squeezed his hands gently. "And you're still only sixteen. Isn't it about time for you to be a regular teenager whose biggest worries are about girls and acne?"

He looked at her face filled with such concern, and suddenly his chest felt tight. He tried to breathe but started gasping instead. His head buzzed. From somewhere inside him, a big wall started to crumble. Some kind of harsh sound was escaping through his mouth. Some kind of wetness was flowing down his face.

He rarely thought about what *should* be and what was because he'd always been too busy going from day to day. There were loads of kids on the streets like him. And if occasionally he did think about his life—about kids in a normal house, in a normal family with a normal dad—he got angry, not sad. Kathy, however, had a way of getting right to him.

But it was Nick who wrapped his arms around him and held him like a little kid who'd hurt himself. Who made him feel that it was okay for a boy to cry. Hell, when he looked up, Nick had tears in his eyes, too.

And Kathy stood right there, hovering. These were the best people in the world. They loved him, and…God almighty, he loved them! Why was he even hesitating?

He pulled away from Nick and wiped the back of his hands across his eyes. "Let's go see Ms. Estelle."

AT SEVEN O'CLOCK the next evening, after a day of biting his lip and keeping Kat and J.T. away from the office, Nick welcomed his family to the private back room of his favorite Mexican restaurant near the Martinelli building. The serving tables were loaded with a fajita buffet. He could have asked Anna to gather the clan at the house, but on a Friday evening after a roller-coaster week, everyone deserved a treat.

He felt the electricity in the air as his brother, sisters and brothers-in-law began to arrive. He hadn't divulged his and Kat's plans to anyone but his parents, and that had happened only about an hour earlier.

It had been a sweet visit. Anna had cried and fussed over Jeremy and Katherine. Joe had had tears in his eyes. But now they were both with him, standing next to J.T. and Kat, greeting all the new arrivals.

He was glad to see how everyone checked out J.T.'s eye, as though he was already a member of the family. And how the little ones all ran to him, his toddler nephew still wanting to go "up, up" in Jeremy's arms.

"So what's going on, Nicky?" asked Tina, almost dancing toward him. "Richie and I have our theories!"

"Stick around and find out." He shook his soon-to-be brother-in-law's hand and winked at his high-energy, youngest sister, before adding, "You're going to like it."

She darted a look toward Katherine and raised an inquiring eyebrow, but Nick just shrugged. It wasn't often he could put one over on the minx; he'd enjoy every minute of it.

He glanced at Joanna, surprised to see the normally bustling woman standing quietly, almost at attention, her eyes darting from him to Katherine and back again. He'd speak with her later, discover if something was wrong.

Finally everyone, including baby Nicole, was in the room. Nick signaled the waiter to wheel over an iced magnum of champagne. And suddenly there was silence. He beckoned Katherine and Jeremy to either side of him and wrapped his arms around them before addressing his larger family.

"The last twenty-four hours have turned out to be the most extraordinary day of my life. A wonderfully extraordinary day—and we're celebrating." He held up the champagne and heard the murmur of excited voices. High-pitched sister voices. He frowned at Tina and Josie, and they shut up. He nearly fell over in shock, but took advantage immediately.

"In front of you stands a new Martinelli family. By Christmas, Katrin and I will be husband and wife, and Jeremy will legally be our son."

First silence, then came the whistles and cheers. Long and loud. And a thumbs-up from Joanna, whose smile removed his concern.

Nick glanced at the woman beside him and felt his heart fill with love for her. Jeremy, still holding the little boy, looked a bit overwhelmed.

"Hey, sport," Nick whispered. "How does J.T. Martinelli sound? Or Jeremy T. Martinelli? Or J. Tucker Martinelli?"

Jeremy grinned for the first time since they'd arrived at the restaurant. "I'll think about it. And you know what's weird?"

"What?"

"Danny's going to be my uncle!"

"Very weird."

Joe stepped up to the front then and shook Nick's hand, kissed Katherine and put his arm around Jeremy. Then he turned to the rest of the family. "This day is more than wonderful. It's stupendous. I get a beautiful new daughter and a handsome new grandson. Because of them, the sun is shining for my Nicholas again. And for this, Mama and I are very thankful."

Nick heard a spontaneous chorus of amens around the room. He'd gone from first love to tragedy to miracle, and his family had watched and worried. He put his arms around his almost wife and son and counted his blessings.

"And now," Joe continued, "as long as we're all here, I have another announcement."

Nick's mind suddenly went on red alert. He'd had enough of Joe's announcements lately, and he wasn't sure he wanted to hear any more.

"After my medical tests this month, no matter the outcome, I'm going to semi-retire."

"Wrong!" interrupted Anna. "You're going to retire. Period."

Nick had trouble keeping his mouth from falling open. Retire? Even semi-retire? Joe had too much energy. What would he do with himself?

He soon found out.

"First of all, we now have two weddings in the next few months." Joe nodded at Tina and Richie as well as at Nick and Katherine. "After that, Mama and I are going to travel a little, visit relatives in Italy, spend more time with the grandchildren. Enjoy our time together. We're not getting any younger, so if not now, when? It's what we want to do.''

Nick's gaze flew to Danny. Danny shook his head. He searched out Mike, Josie's husband, and got the same response. The same with his three sisters. None of them had known about Joe's grand announcement in advance. He sighed and rolled his shoulders, glad they were broad enough to carry more responsibility. He glanced at Katherine and felt his strength double. With Katherine's love, he could do anything.

A MONTH LATER, Nick sat behind his desk at Martinelli Construction and stared at the contract in his hand. The contract for three Houston public schools. No small accomplishment, and under other circumstances he would have been elated. The cost of procuring this assignment, however, had been too high. No project on earth was worth the danger they'd faced because of one desperate man. Eddie Jensen had had enough imagination and cohorts to bamboozle a bartender into believing he'd played pool all night in the club's back room. But he hadn't had enough smarts to avoid trouble in the first place. Stupidity and a gun. A dangerous combo that Nick hated to think about.

Despite his feelings about Jensen, Nick had submitted their bid because business was business, and Martinelli Construction depended on him to make logical decisions and continue to grow the company. And that's just what he would do to the best of his ability.

He leaned back in his chair, happy to discover his renewed interest in running the show, and not surprised that part of his eagerness came from knowing his dad's condition could be controlled by medication, at least for now. Josie's husband was going to assume more management responsibilities, and the company would continue to thrive.

His renewed eagerness also came from a woman named Katherine. His Katrin. She hovered at the edge of his mind all day long, and each evening he looked forward to going home.

What a difference a few months made. In the time before Kat, he'd found excuses to stay at work late into the night. No more. All because of his beautiful, sexy, warmhearted Katrin. One wiggle of her derriere caused instant perspiration on his upper lip and emptied his brain of coherent thought. Sexy, beautiful and clever enough to wangle the truth out of him. A truth that had no power to hurt them anymore. So he'd told her about transferring information from his laptop to a CD each night—a CD with John, Paul, George and Ringo's picture on front of the plastic case.

He'd read enough mysteries to know that hiding in plain sight was the best hiding place of all. He'd made a nightly printout and brought it into the office the next day. So nothing critical was ever left in the office overnight or on any of his hard drives. But that system would be changing. Nothing vital was ever going home with him again.

His thoughts drifted to all that had transpired that month. Danny was back in school, his nose buried in medical textbooks fat enough to cause a hernia.

Tina and Richie were now husband and wife. The wedding had provided J.T. with his first taste of being a normal teenager at a table full of Richie's young cousins. Except for having to wear a new suit and new shoes, he'd had a blast.

And Sally Jensen had called from Dallas, apologizing and crying at the same time. Even with her brother behind bars, she wouldn't return to Houston. Nick had wished her the best of luck and had offered to serve as a business reference.

Now Nick lifted his head and gazed out the window, refreshing his eyes on the green-and-gold foliage of a southern autumn. His life couldn't be sweeter. He and Kat would create a home, cement it with love more solid than the brick and mortar he used every day. He glanced at his watch and rolled the chair back. It was after six on a Friday night. Time to go home, take her in his arms and strengthen the foundation.

NICK TURNED his key and let himself into the apartment, eager to find Katherine. The aroma of roasting *something* made his stomach growl. He sniffed appreciatively and glanced at the oven, caring little about what was inside. He knew it would be delicious.

He took three steps before he heard voices. Kat's and a man's, somewhat familiar. Nick could almost place him, but not quite, until he approached the study. Jonathan Carter.

Nick stood where he was for a second, trying to grasp the essence of their conversation. All he heard was "a great opportunity." Words that were spoken by Carter.

It was time for Nick to be informed.

"Hi, darling." Nick crossed the room to Katherine, gratified at the sparkle in her blue eyes when she realized he was home. Her smile wasn't bad either.

He kissed her, turned and extended a hand to the other man. "Good to see you again, Jonathan."

A solid handshake as the other man replied, "I'm glad you're here. Maybe you can help me talk some sense into Katherine."

Nick glanced at Kat and lifted an eyebrow.

She shrugged but didn't meet his eye. "There's nothing to talk about, Nicky. There's a position open at UT-Austin, but I've decided not to interview for it. Our friend, Jon, doesn't seem to understand the word *no.*"

Nick looked at the other man. Decent enough, connected to Kat's best friend, Suzanne, who certainly would have informed him of Katherine and Nick's relationship. So, what was his motivation?

"It's not a run-of-the-mill opportunity, Nick," said the visitor while his eyes remained on Katherine. "It's a chance of a lifetime."

The guy had the hots for Kat. No question. So that answered the motivation issue, and made their visitor less than a gentleman. At this point, Nick could ignore that. But he couldn't ignore the truth. Was this the opportunity Katherine had been searching for?

"I'm a grown woman, and I think for myself." Katherine's eyes flashed warnings at the two of them, which Nick ignored also.

"Tell me more, Carter."

"It's not just a job. She'd be a graduate student in

residence. She'd teach, she'd be guided in her research, she'd be paid, and be exposed to everyone who's anyone at the university. The campus is crawling with nationally recognized writers, poets and visiting professors. I've read some of her stuff. Her poems. She's damn good.''

Poems? Kat wrote her own poetry? Nick hadn't known that.

His ignorance hurt, but he managed to refocus his attention on their visitor.

''Suzanne made me promise to stop by here and speak with you, Katherine,'' continued Jonathan. ''She's told me that this was exactly the kind of opportunity you'd been seeking. Professionally, it's a no-brainer.''

''I'm no longer—''

''Wait a minute,'' interrupted Nick as he faced Jonathan. ''You said Suzanne is in favor of this?''

Jonathan paused as though to weigh his words. ''Suzanne said something about what happened to Katherine in Chicago. Was it bad luck? Or a lack of qualifications? She wanted to make sure Katherine understood the magnitude of this opportunity.''

The professor turned to Kat again before walking toward the door. ''Think about it, about the opportunity to discover the talent inside you. Think about the resources available to you there. I haven't pulled your application yet, so it's not too late. I'm in town for the weekend. Leave a message with David and Suzanne before Sunday and we'll talk again.''

He turned once more to Nick. ''If you really want

her to be happy, achieve her dreams...well, you know what you need to do."

The ground slipped beneath Nick's feet, but he met the other man's gaze without flinching. "What I need to do is hear what Kat has to say. It's totally her decision."

Silence followed Jonathan Carter's departure. An uncomfortable silence. For the first time since he'd met her, Nick felt an awkwardness between him and Kat, and a piece of his heart started to die.

He walked toward the woman he adored and crouched next to her chair. He took her hands and squeezed gently. "You know I can't leave Houston, Kat, not now," he said, trying to be calm and sensible, even generous. "But if your hopes and dreams lie elsewhere...we'll figure something out. Commuting on weekends...or...something... Hell! I'm dyin' here, baby. Say something. Fast!"

"I love you, Nick." She slid off the chair and into his arms, toppling them both to the floor. He didn't need a college degree to understand her message.

"I love you," she said again as she almost tore his shirt from him. "I've got more options now—jobwise and otherwise—than I've ever had before and they're in Houston."

His pants were down to his ankles in a jiffy, and suddenly they lay skin to skin, communicating without words. Hands, mouths, tongues. Stroking, caressing. Kissing. Quivering. Celebrating. He followed her lead. She followed his.

"Nicky, Nicky...more...more..."

A sweet request.

And then they were one.

He held her close and listened to her gasp for breath. Felt her arms clinging to him, her lips nuzzling his neck, until finally she snuggled and relaxed against him.

Now he was home.

A HALF HOUR LATER, Katherine sat across the table from Nick, enjoying his appreciation of her simple roast beef and baked-potato dinner. Although not quite as indifferent to the culinary arts as Suzanne, Katherine knew Julia Child didn't have to worry about competition from her. But she'd start to gather recipes for meals that were simple and large.

She reached for his hand across the table, enjoying the close attention he always paid to her. "I wasn't kidding earlier, Nicky, about my career. I'm very proud of our work this summer, including the students' *Changing Lives* journal—which, by the way, will be included with any future grant applications the school makes. Rose is retiring next year...so her job's a possibility...and the year after that I'll have my degree. So, who knows what may happen then. But one thing I can promise you right now, darling...I've never been happier or felt luckier."

His eyes shone with love for her as he squeezed her hand. "Do you write happy poems?"

She laughed. "Oh, Lord. I write all kinds of poems, stories, too. I'm a closet writer, Nick, just like most English teachers."

"A closet writer? You mean, you're afraid to show anyone the work?"

"Sort of. It's really personal stuff. Private."

"Well," said Nick with a smile, "the professor seems to like your work."

"I sent in a few poems because they'd asked for writing samples, not because I expect to become the next poet laureate of the United States," she replied. "I write because I have to. And it doesn't matter if I ever get paid for it or not. It's something I do. Period."

He nodded and smiled. "I get it, Kat. Just like my designs. I don't get any recognition but I keep playing with ideas."

"That'll change when you become licensed—the recognition and payment part. I know you'll keep playing with ideas for the rest of your life." She smiled, her heart full of love. "It's who you are."

He avoided her gaze. "As a part-time student, Kat, it'll take me years to graduate. Too bad it took me so long to get the hang of it all."

"Maybe," she said with a laugh, "you just needed the right teacher."

JEREMY STOOD in the entry hall of Richmond House Saturday morning waiting for Nick and Kathy to pick him up. He shifted his knapsack to a more comfortable position, and toed his overnight bag to the side of the doorway. Peering out of the small window next to the door, he scanned the circular driveway. Seemed like he was always waiting to be picked up by someone. One day very soon, he'd be picked up and wouldn't be coming back. At least not to live. He knew Nick would always return to see Ms. Estelle, to help out when he could. And Jeremy would go with him.

It was too weird that just a few months ago, he didn't even know Nick Martinelli or Katherine Kirby existed in the world. And now they were becoming his whole world. And they weren't even getting any money for adopting him. Not like foster parents did. In fact, Nick had to pay court fees and lawyers' fees and stuff like that.

The other kids said he was too old to be adopted. And that he was nuts for wanting to be. He was almost free to do anything he wanted. Get his own apartment, buy a dog, stay out late and meet hot girls. Why did he want to trade in Richmond House for someone else's house with rules? None of them would have made the choice he did. And maybe they were right *for them.*

But none of the kids had ever been in his situation with two great people who hugged and teased him, and made a guy feel good about himself. When he was with them, he didn't think about being too old. Heck, he didn't think much about any of their ages. Nick and Kathy were real grown-ups and smart, and he'd rather be with them than with anyone else. Even more than being on his own. The three of them really liked each other, they even loved each other. And that was good enough for him.

Ms. Estelle said that he'd learned love from his own father. Despite all the problems. And that he'd never lost his basic trust in people. Some of his friends at Richmond House hadn't been as lucky, and had a long way to go until they learned to trust again.

A horn sounded in the driveway, and almost instantly Kathy was beside him, giving him a quick hug and signing him out for the weekend.

"Ready to go? Nick's got a surprise for us after we hit the stores."

Ugh. The stores. He'd forgotten. Now that he was attending college, Katherine insisted on sprucing up his wardrobe. "Just a few things," she'd promised. In his mind, a few meant three. A pair of jeans and two shirts would be okay. He hoped she'd read the same dictionary he had.

Two HOURS LATER, Nick pulled into Lakes on West Memorial, the newest residential project they were building, the project Jeremy had been assigned to all summer.

"Do we have work to do here today?" asked the boy. "Are we falling behind?"

Nick laughed. J.T. had a feeling for the business already. "No, sport. But I want to show you and Kat a work in progress."

His palms slipped on the wheel and he realized he was nervous. He should have discussed this with Kat first. Maybe she'd rather stay in a condo development with close neighbors. Maybe she didn't want the extra responsibility of a house. Heck, it wasn't too late to change their minds. After all, he was the builder.

"The houses are all in different stages of completion," Katherine commented as Nick drove around the large center lake.

"That way buyers can walk through lots of models," said J.T., "and choose the one they like best."

"We also have three different model homes," said Nick. "Totally furnished. But that's not where we're going right now."

He could feel Katherine's eyes on him, almost hear the wheels turning in her mind as her curiosity took hold. But she didn't say a word until he pulled in front of a newly framed house sitting on a double parcel in a small cul-de-sac. One of the development's man-made lakes lapped beyond the backyard of the property.

"It's a nice setting," she commented when he shut the engine.

"I thought so, too," he said. "Just walk through it and tell me what you think."

He didn't have to ask Jeremy twice. The kid flew out the door as soon as it opened.

Nick grinned at the boy, but had second thoughts about Katherine being able to see what he saw. The ground outside the house was bare of any landscaping so far; the house itself consisted of a bunch of two-by-fours and a concrete foundation; no walls or roof to give it shape. But the blueprints were in the truck for reference...if she was remotely interested.

He watched her scramble from the vehicle, take a few steps, then turn back to wait for him. She extended her hand. He clasped it and they walked to the house together.

"Talk me through it," Kat said. "Give me a tour. And then I'll do as you asked, and tell you what I think."

Nick drew her to the framed front door. "Right now the family interested in this house has only one child—a teenage son. But hopefully, someday there might be one or two more. Maybe even three.''

She almost tripped at the last number.

"But it doesn't have to be," he backtracked as he steadied her. "Careful where you walk."

She listened as he lovingly described the features of each room. The fireplace in the large family room, the vaulted ceilings, and like her condo apartment, the specially designed loft in the study. Each room took shape with his vivid commentary. A teen room over the three-car garage, fully air-conditioned and connected to the main house.

Within the first few seconds, Katherine knew he'd planned it for them. How many hours had he worked to present her with this gift? With the attention to detail, with the concern for the needs of his new family?

Family. That's what this was all about. The greatest gift. She turned her imagination on, allowing Nick's voice to infiltrate her heart, visualizing a life within strong walls, under a solid roof.

Hearing the noise and the laughter yet to be.

She glanced up through the framework of those walls. The late-morning sun shone down on them through the clear autumn air. Occasional white clouds floated in a cerulean sky. She closed her eyes and allowed the beauty of the day to seep into her soul.

"Katrin...my Katrin...marry a good man. A man like your papa."

Her mother's voice came to her as clearly as if she'd heard it yesterday.

She turned to Nick then, her heart bursting with love.

"I am, Mama. I am."

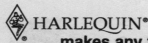

*Harlequin truly does
make any time special. . . .
This year we are celebrating
weddings in style!*

A
Walk
Down
the Aisle
WEDDING CELEBRATION

To help us celebrate, we want you to tell us how wearing the
Harlequin wedding gown will make your wedding day special. As
the grand prize, Harlequin will offer one lucky bride the chance to
"Walk Down the Aisle" in the Harlequin wedding gown!

There's more...

For her honeymoon, she and her groom will spend five nights at the
Hyatt Regency Maui. As part of this five-night honeymoon at the
hotel renowned for its romantic attractions, the couple will enjoy a candlelit
dinner for two in Swan Court, a sunset sail on the hotel's catamaran, and
duet spa treatments.

HYATT
R E G E N C Y
M A U I®
A HYATT RESORT AND SPA

MAUI
The Magic Isles™
Maui • Molokai • Lanai

To enter, please write, in, 250 words or less, how wearing the Harlequin
wedding gown will make your wedding day special. The entry will be
judged based on its emotionally compelling nature, its originality and
creativity, and its sincerity. This contest is open to Canadian and U.S.
residents only and to those who are 18 years of age and older. There is no
purchase necessary to enter. Void where prohibited. See further contest
rules attached. Please send your entry to:

Walk Down the Aisle Contest

In Canada	In U.S.A.
P.O. Box 637	P.O. Box 9076
Fort Erie, Ontario	3010 Walden Ave.
L2A 5X3	Buffalo, NY 14269-9076

You can also enter by visiting www.eHarlequin.com
Win the Harlequin wedding gown and the vacation of a lifetime!
The deadline for entries is October 1, 2001.

HARLEQUIN®
Makes any time special®

PHWDACONT1

HARLEQUIN WALK DOWN THE AISLE TO MAUI CONTEST 1197
OFFICIAL RULES
NO PURCHASE NECESSARY TO ENTER

1. To enter, follow directions published in the offer to which you are responding. Contest begins April 2, 2001, and ends on October 1, 2001. Method of entry may vary. Mailed entries must be postmarked by October 1, 2001, and received by October 8, 2001.

2. Contest entry may be, at times, presented via the Internet, but will be restricted solely to residents of certain geographic areas that are disclosed on the Web site. To enter via the Internet, if permissible, access the Harlequin Web site (www.eHarlequin.com) and follow the directions displayed online. Online entries must be received by 11:59 p.m. E.S.T. on October 1, 2001.

    In lieu of submitting an entry online, enter by mail by hand-printing (or typing) on an 8½" x 11" plain piece of paper, your name, address (including zip code), Contest number/name and in 250 words or fewer, why winning a Harlequin wedding dress would make your wedding day special. Mail via first-class mail to: Harlequin Walk Down the Aisle Contest 1197, (in the U.S.) P.O. Box 9076, 3010 Walden Avenue, Buffalo, NY 14269-9076, (in Canada) P.O. Box 637, Fort Erie, Ontario L2A 5X3, Canada.

    Limit one entry per person, household address and e-mail address. Online and/or mailed entries received from persons residing in geographic areas in which Internet entry is not permissible will be disqualified.

3. Contests will be judged by a panel of members of the Harlequin editorial, marketing and public relations staff based on the following criteria:

    - Originality and Creativity—50%
    - Emotionally Compelling—25%
    - Sincerity—25%

    In the event of a tie, duplicate prizes will be awarded. Decisions of the judges are final.

4. All entries become the property of Torstar Corp. and will not be returned. No responsibility is assumed for lost, late, illegible, incomplete, inaccurate, nondelivered or misdirected mail or misdirected e-mail, for technical, hardware or software failures of any kind, lost or unavailable network connections, or failed, incomplete, garbled or delayed computer transmission or any human error which may occur in the receipt or processing of the entries in this Contest.

5. Contest open only to residents of the U.S. (except Puerto Rico) and Canada, who are 18 years of age or older, and is void wherever prohibited by law; all applicable laws and regulations apply. Any litigation within the Province of Quebec respecting the conduct or organization of a publicity contest may be submitted to the Régie des alcools, des courses et des jeux for a ruling. Any litigation respecting the awarding of a prize may be submitted to the Régie des alcools, des courses et des jeux or for the purpose of helping the parties reach a settlement. Employees and immediate family members of Torstar Corp. and D. L. Blair, Inc., their affiliates, subsidiaries and all other agencies, entities and persons connected with the use, marketing or conduct of this Contest are not eligible to enter. Taxes on prizes are the sole responsibility of winners. Acceptance of any prize offered constitutes permission to use winner's name, photograph or other likeness for the purposes of advertising, trade and promotion on behalf of Torstar Corp., its affiliates and subsidiaries without further compensation to the winner, unless prohibited by law.

6. Winners will be determined no later than November 15, 2001, and will be notified by mail. Winners will be required to sign and return an Affidavit of Eligibility form within 15 days after winner notification. Noncompliance within that time period may result in disqualification and an alternative winner may be selected. Winners of trip must execute a Release of Liability prior to ticketing and must possess required travel documents (e.g. passport, photo ID) where applicable. Trip must be completed by November 2002. No substitution of prize permitted by winner. Torstar Corp. and D. L. Blair, Inc., their parents, affiliates, and subsidiaries are not responsible for errors in printing or electronic presentation of Contest, entries and/or game pieces. In the event of printing or other errors which may result in unintended prize values or duplication of prizes, all affected game pieces or entries shall be null and void. If for any reason the Internet portion of the Contest is not capable of running as planned, including infection by computer virus, bugs, tampering, unauthorized intervention, fraud, technical failures, or any other causes beyond the control of Torstar Corp. which corrupt or affect the administration, secrecy, fairness, integrity or proper conduct of the Contest, Torstar Corp. reserves the right, at its sole discretion, to disqualify any individual who tampers with the entry process and to cancel, terminate, modify or suspend the Contest or the Internet portion thereof. In the event of a dispute regarding an online entry, the entry will be deemed submitted by the authorized holder of the e-mail account submitted at the time of entry. Authorized account holder is defined as the natural person who is assigned to an e-mail address by an Internet access provider, online service provider or other organization that is responsible for arranging e-mail address for the domain associated with the submitted e-mail address. **Purchase or acceptance of a product offer does not improve your chances of winning.**

7. Prizes: (1) Grand Prize—A Harlequin wedding dress (approximate retail value: $3,500) and a 5-night/6-day honeymoon trip to Maui, HI, including round-trip air transportation provided by Maui Visitors Bureau from Los Angeles International Airport (winner is responsible for transportation to and from Los Angeles International Airport) and a Harlequin Romance Package, including hotel accomodations (double occupancy) at the Hyatt Regency Maui Resort and Spa, dinner for (2) two at Swan Court, a sunset sail on Kiele V and a spa treatment for the winner (approximate retail value: $4,000); (5) Five runner-up prizes of a $1000 gift certificate to selected retail outlets to be determined by Sponsor (retail value $1000 ea.). Prizes consist of only those items listed as part of the prize. Limit one prize per person. All prizes are valued in U.S. currency.

8. For a list of winners (available after December 17, 2001) send a self-addressed, stamped envelope to: Harlequin Walk Down the Aisle Contest 1197 Winners, P.O. Box 4200 Blair, NE 68009-4200 or you may access the www.eHarlequin.com Web site through January 15, 2002.

Contest sponsored by Torstar Corp., P.O. Box 9042, Buffalo, NY 14269-9042, U.S.A.

PHWDACONT2